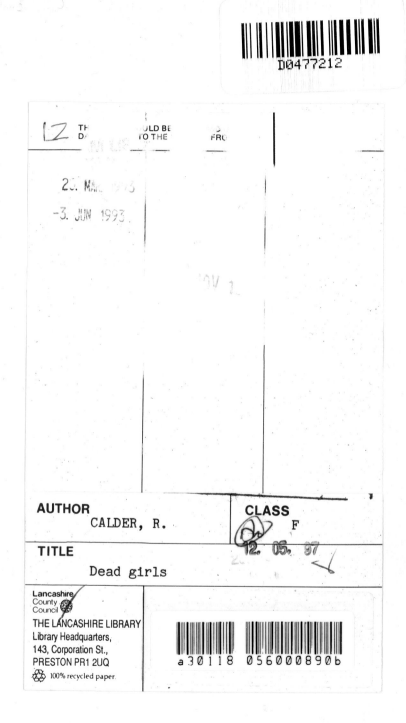

DEAD GIRLS

DEAD GIRLS

Richard Calder

HarperCollins*Publishers*

HarperCollins*Publishers*,
77–85 Fulham Palace Road,
Hammersmith, London W6 8JB

Published by HarperCollins*Publishers* 1992
1 3 5 7 9 8 6 4 2

Copyright © Richard Calder 1992

The Author asserts the moral right to
be identified as the author of this work

A catalogue record for this book is
available from the British Library

ISBN 0 00 224154/4

Set in Times

Printed in Great Britain by
HarperCollinsManufacturing Glasgow

For Gilberte Swann, Dolores Haze
and Wednesday Addams

CHAPTER ONE

Road to Nowhere

They smashed through the door; I vaulted the balcony, running. It was midnight in Nongkhai City and I was lost. The story so far? The Pikadon Twins – notorious henchgirls to Madame K – had pursued me to the banks of the Mekong. But where was the Mekong? Too dark, too quiet – and I used to bright, clamorous Bangkok – this town had me drunk on shadows. Across the Mekong, Laos. From Laos I could escape into China. And from China . . . The roar of Harleys; twin headlights violated the night. There. The lights of a riverside café. And there, there. Glint of moonlight on water. Dogs and chickens scattered in my wake.

The café – The White Russian – opened its arms; I fell into its refuge. *Farang* diners, Thais, all but the gynoids dressed as matrioshkas regarded me curiously. Wiping the sweat from my face, I was trying to still my breath, my hands, trying to assume the disguise of a newly-arrived *farang* celebrating deliverance from Europe. 'I'm like you,' my body language tried to say, 'a roadrunner, a survivor. Genes a little dirty, perhaps, but hey, who's to know?' No police; should I care if they believed me? An ankle had swollen; I sat down. Lights of fishing vessels spangled the unswimmable deep.

From across the river I could make Vientiane in under an hour; but a passing matrioshka (imitation Fabergé, she looked) informed me No sir, sorry sir, no ferry until daybreak. Trapped. End of series. No sequel to my get-away: avoiding airports and the TGV, driving my old Mercedes as far as Hat Yai (as if I were heading for Penang), and then backtracking, taking government buses north, then north-east, towards the Thai-Lao border. That night, arriving in Nongkhai, I'd found a hotel, napped (too long), to be awoken by two half-human battering rams at my door.

Pikadons!

Coolly-cool, those murderesses. Surely they wouldn't make their move here? Not in public, I reasoned. But they were shameless.

'Wodka,' said Bang and Boom, the Pikadon Twins, 'for our friend, Mr Ignatz.' The credits rolled. No reprise of revved motorbikes; like phantom lightsticks, like switchblades keen and spectral, the Pikadons. They pressed down on my shoulders, checking an impulse to flee.

Like their mistress, Madame Kito, mamasan of Nana – that dragon lady with three generals and a cabinet minister in her bed – the Pikadons were the daughters of a Japanese and a gynoid. *Bijouterie*, they called them: hybrid jewels as distinguished from all-precious *joaillerie*.

'Boy run away.'

'Bad boy. Madame miss you.'

'And Primavera. Poor Primavera. She miss you too.'

'Write you love letter, no?'

'Primavera,' I said, 'is a fucking season in hell. I'm not going back. I've had enough killing.'

'But you *like* killing, Mr Ignatz, no?'

Would you like to find out how much? I thought. If I'd had a weapon, even my scalpel, then perhaps . . . but the Twins wore body stockings of artificial spidersilk, a midnight-blue weave grown from *E. Coli* that was as strong and as refractive as the fibres of laser-proof vests.

Why weren't they trying to kill *me*?

'Primavera not work with other boy.'

'Madame try . . .'

'Primavera in love with Mr Ignatz.' The Twins studied the curlicues and flutings of their manicures, eyes cold as crescent moons. 'Every gun need finger on her trigger,

Mr Ignatz. But if you want go, maybe Madame let Primavera go. Home. To England.'

Kito needed Primavera. Primavera was Bangkok's prima donna of assassins. A supervillainess. Hep Cat Shun, dead. Terminal Wipes, dead. Rib-Dot Delay, dead. I was merely her escort; a cover. The Twins were bluffing. Jealous. The cheaper the *femmes*, I thought, the cheaper the *fatales*.

'Little English half-doll.'

'Lilim.'

'Self-replicating cyborg bloodsucker, no?'

'Dead girl.'

'Our kissin' cousin.'

'Land of Hope and Glory *no like* Primavera, *no like* Lilim.'

'If Madame tell police . . .'

'Police Madame friend.'

'If Primavera go back home . . .'

Bang (or Boom) pressed a long fingernail into her abdomen.

'Schstick!'

'Scream, little doll.'

'Scream sexy-sexy!' The Twins began to laugh.

'But you know all about *that*, Mr Ignatz.'

'No?'

I shook my head. I wanted to laugh too; to mock them. I couldn't. My jawbone had locked. Vain, spiteful, faithless Kito: would she really send her little ninja home? There, the Dolls' Hospitals awaited. But why had Primavera refused to work? She no longer loved me. (Had she ever loved me?) She loved only the blood, the killing. Her metamorphosis was complete. My little girl needn't mourn: Kito would find her another beau. An arm to lean on at parties, someone to take her to hotels, to bars. A mask. A human face.

One of the Twins pulled a magazine from her *décolletage*.

'Madame Kito.'

'Her life, her time.'

'Special edition. Page sixty-nine. Message for Mr Ignatz. Look . . .'

Page sixty-nine – the centre spread – was a diorama of a penthouse choking on a miasma of kitsch: Italian marble, jungle-cat prints, fountains, revivalist *art nouveau* and *deco* furniture, corporate art, corporate toys – a backdrop, it seemed, for a soap opera of unusual vulgarity. The Twins smoothed their hands across the photograph. Activated by that biochemical signature pixels crystallized and two figures mounted the paper stage. The figures moved. Photo-mechanicals. Primavera and Madame K.

They sat together, schoolgirl and matron, on a tiger-striped chaise longue. Someone unacquainted with how the bloodlines of hybrids differed in East and West might have assumed that the two women were related, for both had the green eyes, plump lips and kiln-glazed flesh that signalled Cartier workmanship. But whereas Kito's progenitor had been an imitation doll (as were all dolls in Bangkok's Big Weird), Primavera's distaff side could be traced back to the fabulous automata of Europe's *belle époque*. Kito – stroking her ward's bleached hair like the wicked stepmother of a thousand fairy tales – resented *bijouterie* whose claim to the Cartier logo was more genuine than her own. Her snobbery was equal to her viciousness.

'Such little English rose,' squeaked Kito, her voice – in contrast to her usual husky tenor – small, tinny and distorted. 'But what *nasty* place England become.'

'She's going to have me deported, Iggy,' said Primavera. 'Repatriated. She means it. You know all my papers are false. Like yours. She only has to tell her friends. Come back, Iggy. Come back to the Big Weird. I miss you. We can have fun together. Like before.'

Primavera was a melodramatic little doll. Wearing a cropped T-shirt that erroneously declared her *Miss Nana '71*, the third eye of her umbilicus played peek-a-boo with the camera as she shuddered with the effort of restraining bitter tears.

'It would be slab, Mr Ignatz. Spike. *Tzepa*, as you English say. It is good my Pikadon find you. Boy like you have no place to run. England very bad now. English roboto go *crazy*. Doll bite man, man fuck lady, and lady have baby turn into doll. People say have world of doll soon. World of Lilim.'

'Primavera's done everything you've asked,' I mumbled. 'Just because she was human once . . .'

'And I *never* human? That what you mean, Mr Ignatz?' My hand sprang from the page; the magazine ran interactive software. Kito rose and walked to the missing wall of the proscenium, her geisha-white face filling the page. 'Sure,' she said, 'my *mae* roboto. I half machine when born. Bangkok nanoengineer use foetal template – no grow doll atom by atom like in land of *farang*. Sometime, just sometime, Siamese roboto ovulate.' An eyebrow twitched like the beat of a butterfly's wing that threatened to precipitate a storm. 'But Primavera – ' her lip curled; thunder growled in the distance – 'Oi! Twenty-six year ago, I remember, doll-plague begin: not with us Cheap Charlie counterfeit doll; no, it was *farang* roboto, *genuine* Cartier get virus, go crazy, give virus to man. Now when little English girl go pubescent, she go roboto too. You think I want be like Primavera, Mr Ignatz? Walk through wall? Jump over car? Spit death? Fly? Primavera reproduce herself; I sterile, mule. But my software not fucking *crazy* . . .'

The storm passed; Kito's face withdrew, and Primavera, having surrendered to schoolgirl hysterics, was revealed stamping her feet and tearing at her hair.

'Not the *tzepa*. Iggy! Please!'

Primavera always overacted . . .

Beyond the still life of the apartment, through a panoramic window, beneath the stalled course of a ruinous sun, lay Nana Plaza, arrested in time and space, denied forever the night. Night. Ha. Then the capitalists of narcissism would emerge, the warrior merchants who had raped Europe's empire *de luxe* and carried off her ideas, her names, her designs, to sell them in the thieves' market that was Nana. Then street vendors would hawk Europe's vandalized dreams: a magpie's hoard of imitation *objets* and *couture*: psychotropic perfumes from Chanel, off-world jewels from Tiffany, and, dissembling the cut of an Armani or a Lacroix, a de Ville, de Sade or a Sabatier, dermaplastic, the outlawed *farang* textile woven from live tissue culture. Then Kito's gynoids – Cartier and Rolex, Seiko, Gucci and Swatch – would step from their vacuum-sealed boxes promising to fulfil the most baroque desires. This was Nana, Kito's stake in the Big Weird: a pornocracy of copyright ponces and technopimps; an island shimmering with the bootlegged flotsam of Europe's shipwrecked past; an apotheosis of all that was fake.

And was this plea from Primavera – this SOS from a castaway of human shores – was this too a fake? A photomechanical maid had begun to serve drinks.

'You always seem such gentleman,' said Kito. 'I always think every Englishman – '

I slapped the magazine shut, crushing its paperdust CPU, and searched the cover for the date. My language skills, even after three years in Bangkok, were still rudimentary. I struggled to decipher the fiery tongues of the Thai characters; the Pikadons yawned.

'Magazine come out yesterday, Mr Ignatz.'

'Primavera Weirdside, still . . .'

Whether Kito's threats were empty or not they had offered an excuse. ('Shut up!' I told those angels – good?

bad? – who were whispering Trick! Hoax! in my ear.) Maybe that's what I'd been waiting for during those fugitive days: an excuse to return. I was a doll junkie; my limbs ached for the kisses of dead girls. For vampire kisses. For the allure.

Not the tzepa, *Iggy! Please!*

It had been a cry across a war zone of desire. Should I step again into no-man's-land? Outside the coconut trees were swaying, fainting to an alien tide. Primavera was here, even here, her hunger that of a dog picking at the world's remains; her stealth, the scuttling of a cockroach. Escape. Get up; go, before . . . But across the star-filled paddies she reaches out; like a serpent, her torso twists, strikes . . .

Primavera was twelve; her DNA had begun to recombine. She sat in front of me in class, her long blonde hair betraying its first streaks of Cartier black. Primavera Bobinski. One day a classmate similarly progressed in doll metamorphosis had said something to her in a giggly undertone. Primavera shook her head. Throughout that lesson – divinity? history? geography? – scraps of paper appeared on her desk, passed on by that handful of girls who, like her, wore the green star of the recombinant. I grew nervous. Primavera was a girl I had stared at, I suppose, too long; whom I had been observed following down those interminable school corridors, or across the park after last bell; and now the adored one was being goaded to take revenge. At last, piqued by their teasing, eager to show she could take a dare, she waited for our teacher to avert his gaze, then turned contrapposto, put her face close to mine, bared her teeth, and cut open my lip with a swift, expertly aimed glance of one of her newly extended canines. 'Oh?' she said, in pert demotic Londonese, 'did I *hurt* you?' her death mask of a face insolent as the toothy laughter of her peers. I put my hand to my lip; felt blood; flushed.

Did I love her, still?

London, Marseille, Bangkok. From the *Seven Stars* to across the Seven Seas. Three years, now. Escape. We had spent our small lives escaping. But there are watchtowers of the mind, of the senses, machine guns, bloodhounds one can never flee.

'Not so bad for you, Mr Ignatz.'

'A team, you and Primavera.'

'Come from the land of sex and death.'

'To the land of smiles!'

'Stay with Madame.'

'Madame say just one last job, Mr Ignatz.'

'*Jing-jing*, Mr Ignatz, you no want to leave.'

'Skunk hour for Europe now.'

No escape. I was possessed. And from what had I been running? *Bastard*, she whispers, *boy-slime, hypocrite, prig. You made me what I am. You think you're better than them, don't you? The medicine-heads. The Human Front. But I know what you like* . . . I lift my hand to my lip; still, there is blood; still, I flush; still, the throb of desire and hate.

'I'll come,' I told the Pikadons, 'of course I'll come.'

Fatalism, these days, comes easily to an Englishman.

CHAPTER TWO

Wine and Roses

We sat in *The Londoner*, a newly-opened restaurant in the downtown Weird that indulged the morbidity of Bangkok's nighthawks. 'If this is Kito's idea of a joke,' said Primavera, 'then – ' A cry, sharp and girlish, excised her indignant conclusions. There followed a gentle balm of applause.

The tables were arranged about a circular arena. Inside that little O, equidistant, like the spokes of a wheel, three marble slabs presented a pageant of life and death in contemporary England. Upon each slab, prone, naked, wrists chained to an iron ring, a gynoid writhed in a ham display of agony, a glistening needle emerging from the small of her back.

The muted sighs of those *in extremis* mixed with the sounds of polite conversation, the clatter of cutlery, the popping of corks.

'You're saying that you *didn't* refuse to work? That Kito lied when she said she'd have you repatriated? And that you lied too?' Sorry, angels. Next time I'll listen.

Primavera fidgeted, playing with an ice cream sundae as blonde as her bottled hair, her flesh. 'Don't get *upset*. I *like* having you around. It was just a little *white* lie. Anyway, Madame *said* I was to; and what Madame *says* . . .'

I looked about the restaurant. Something festered beneath the nasty theatrics; something real, something nastier; one cut, and the pus would ooze.

I had arrived at Nana that afternoon. Kito hadn't deigned to meet me; instead, I had been briefed by her PA, Mr Jinx. No, Kito wasn't angry; one last hit, he'd said, and we'd be free. Free of all obligation. There followed my reunion with Miss Bloodsucker '71. No words, just the sex-game (sticky plaster covered my chest and groin); and we had walked out, everything right, so right. But now – our intimate dinner disturbed only by those aping the death agonies of England's damned; about to confess my addiction to certain kisses and pledge that I would never despise them again – Primavera had claimed the spoils of her victory: my dignity and pride.

'I know you don't want my love, Primavera, but why do you have to humiliate me?'

'I said don't get *upset*.' She pushed her ice cream to the side of the table. 'I wasn't supposed to *tell* you *actually*. But since you *did* come back . . . Okay. So it was a game. One of Primavera's little games. Madame said you loved me; I said no, it wasn't *like* that. She said she could prove it, that you'd come back if you thought I was in trouble. Wanna bet? I said.' Surprise, hurt, guilt, malice: Primavera could combine the look of a woman betrayed with that of one caught in the act of poisoning her lover. 'Iggy,' she said, with slippery plaintiveness, 'why did you have to run away? Am I really so bad?'

'Kito,' I said. 'I can understand her having me followed; I can understand her wanting me offed – I know too much. But why bring me back to Bangkok? If you'll work without me, she doesn't *need* me.'

Primavera – bored by any script in which she wasn't the leading lady – let her eyes drift from the floor show to the gallery of newspaper clippings that lined the walls: headlines and photographs from the English tabloid press. Beneath dozens of grainy pin-ups of impaled young girls ran captions like: 'Tatyana, 16, from Brixton, says all her girlfriends have had a bellyful of the Human Front, and she was gutted after the HF won the General Election! Now she knows all about bellyaching! Got the point, Tatyana? Another skewered lovely tomorrow . . .' Beneath an air-conditioning vent a tattered Union Jack (monochrome since the kingdom's dissolution) fluttered as if atop an outpost at the world's end.

'Primavera – I'm *talking* to you.'

'It wasn't all fibs, you know,' she said, exasperation counterpointing her skittishness. 'I do like having you around. I don't *love* you; I'm Lilim; we don't *do* that sort of thing. But I can *miss* you.' She shivered. 'You introduce me to such interesting boys.'

'I smell a rat.'

'And I,' she said, leaning over the table, 'smell the blood of an Englishman.' Her bright red tongue ran over ranks of tiny cuspids.

'Sit down,' I muttered, 'and close your mouth. You want someone to see?'

'But you *like* it, Iggy. And you know it only hurts a little.'

How pretty she was. She was always at her best before a kill. Tonight she wore a black dermaplastic cocktail dress that clung to her like the excoriated but still living hide of a Harlem beauty queen. Fifteen years old (the same age as me, though my anaemia made me look older) and milky pale with a sweetness that had sickened of itself, curdled and turned rancid, Primavera was a little dream of feminine evil: hateful because desired; desired because hateful. She was the dream of the age.

At an adjacent table a group of Japanese *salarimen* had summoned a waiter. 'This one – she dead – can have another please?' The waiter, dressed in surgical gown, rubber gloves and mask, saw to it that a fresh gynoid, her programme engaging obligatory signs of fear, replaced her cataleptic sister. On all fours, wrists chained, the steel needle pointing uncompromisingly to that ritual spot midway between pubis and umbilicus, it remained only for the condemned doll to tremble in expectation until the waiter should grasp her ankles and pull . . . The

17

salarimen – eyes screwed in states of voyeuristic satori – clapped and whistled with drunken glee.

'God,' said Einstein, 'does not play dice with the universe'; but Primavera did. Her green eyes grew bigger, more luminous, as they focused on something beyond the restaurant's walls, beyond the Big Weird, beyond the world. Reality, for one moment in which the universe held its breath, existed in those eyes alone, eyes tunnelling into endless possibilities. For Primavera the universe was a fixed table. The dice rolled, loaded with her will.

Beer glasses exploded, showering the Japanese with Singha and broken glass. Waiters mopped anxiously at spattered suits, picked splinters from beer-anointed hair. The fire in Primavera's eyes died to a smoulder. Newton and Einstein shifted in their graves.

'Right through her *clockwork*, Iggy. Right through her *matrix*! They really shouldn't laugh.'

The belly of the doll (say Lilim) is sacred; it is the womb of uncertainty; the well of unreason; the quantum-mechanical seat of consciousness.

'Sometimes,' said Primavera, 'sometimes I don't like boys.'

'I guess tomorrow night they'll settle for Soi Ginza. Now no more games, he's just walked in.' A tall *farang* in a bespoke suit was being ushered to a ringside table.

'Is he the boy I get to kill? I like those sorts of boys.'

'Antoine Sabatier. Parisian fashion slut. Angry with Kito for stealing his designs. Prosecuting her through ASEAN.'

'I do it here?'

'Unless you mind getting blood all over your new frock?'

'My table manners are impeccable. But doesn't a girl get to eat in peace any more?'

'I'll find you a nice takeaway later.'

'But Iggy, you're so *tired* of killing, remember?'

I tapped a spoon against a glass, calling an end to playtime. 'All we have to do is wait for the *maître d'* to . . . There. He's being told he has a telephone call. That he can take it out the back. Just like Mr Jinx said. Come on, c – okay, he's going.'

Primavera, tossing her bleached mane over her shoulders, had already risen. Hurriedly, she took a mirror from her handbag and reapplied her lipstick, then dabbed a little of her favourite perfume, *Virgin Martyr*, behind her ears.

'For you, Titania,' she whispered, 'sweet queen of dolls,' and touched the brooch on her left breast – a pentacle of emeralds; symbol of pride won from shame – that was her most (perhaps only) sentimental possession. I watched her leave, the two vertical seams of her stockinged calves weaving between the tables and chairs like the exotic markings of a rare and deadly reptile. The doors leading to the kitchens and toilets swung shut. *Bon appétit*, little witch, I thought.

A Filipino quartet had begun to sing their cover of 'Oh doctor, doctor, I wish you wouldn't *do* that,' the latest hit for English zygodiddly band *Imps of the Perverse*. The waiters had pulled up their surgical masks and – assuming the roles of mad gynæcologists – performed unspeakable mimes in the aisles. I hid behind the menu – *Fish 'n' Chips, Pie 'n' Eel, Steak 'n' Kidney Pudding* (lead sent the Romans crazy) – and put on the complimentary headphones that hung from my chair. '. . . the beautiful carefree days of the *aube du millénaire* were over: England braced herself for what was to come . . .' Those films they showed us at school: *Hamlet, Richard III, Henry V*; the voice synthesizer was an Olivier. I reselected and then stabbed PLAY.

'Europe, during the days of the *aube du millénaire* – a historical period that some have compared to the *belle époque* preceding the First World War – had absorbed the moribund Soviet empire to become the hub of the world economy. Not seeking to compete with the manufacturing might of the Pacific bloc dominated by Japan and its junior partner, America, Europe became the world's arbiter of elegance, an empire of style, a luxury goods conglomerate dedicated to satisfying the age's narcissistic pursuit of health, beauty and longevity. Its investment was in superminiaturization: the creation of objects that the rootless *nouveaux riches* – the Information Revolution's *arrivistes* – could carry on or in themselves, to define their social value and status. As these objects lost their functionalism and became *objets*, the empire *de luxe* became a magic toyshop, a creator of adult fantasies. And amongst its *bimbeloterie*, nothing was so fabulous, so desired, as the *automata*.

'The Cartier automata designed by the man we know today only as Dr Toxicophilous were of a series called *L'Eve Future*. Built 2034–43, in Paris and London, this series represented an attempt to create a synthesis between the world of classical physics and the submicroscopic quantum world. The human brain, it had long been realized, is unlike any artificial intelligence because it had learned to harness quantum effects. Toxicophilous nanoengineered his machines from smaller and smaller components; he manipulated particles, waves. What Toxicophilous called "fractal programming" – wherein hardware and software is indivisible – resulted, not so much in a human intelligence, but in a mind, a robot consciousness, which acted as a bridge between classical and microphysical worlds, a consciousness that manifested "quantum magic".

' "Tricks," said the inventor of *L'Eve Future*, "that is all they perform. Party-pieces. Entertainments. *Feux d'artifice!*" But even then their programmes bubbled with toil and trouble . . .'

Nothing new. It was what they dumped on you in

school. I nudged the fast forward.

'The life cycle of . . . The doll's imperative is to reproduce itself via a human host . . . Infects the human male through . . .'

A *farang* had sat down in Primavera's chair. 'That's taken,' I said, removing the headphones.

'You'll excuse me.' He was American: confederate drawl; a Nobodaddy somatotype with white hair and beard. 'I've always wanted to meet an Englishman, and the waiter said . . .' I was second-generation Slovak: what Thai would have been able to identify the mid-European distortion of my East London vowels? My accent was as inscrutable as Primavera's Balkanized cockney.

'I'm not English,' I said.

'But the waiter was so sure!'

'I'm from Slovakia.'

'People still live there?' He swallowed his laugh and grimaced in distaste, as if it had been a clot of phlegm. 'I'm sorry, that wasn't funny.'

'My sister will be – '

'Poor kids.' His eyes were on the cabaret. 'I know they're just machines, but what about those little ladies back in England? What do you call them? Yeah, Lilim.' He pointed to a gynoid faking a death orgasm, her performance akin to that of a gymnast, a contortionist, a dancer, rather than that of a girl so cruelly wounded. 'For heaven's sake, she can't be no older than my daughter.' He put his finger to a puddle of beer and drew doodles across the table.

I checked my watch. Primavera had been gone ten minutes. A long time for her. After weeks of abstinence, she would be offing her trick slowly. Playing with him. Sucking the slut dry. I decided to humour my interloper; my jealousy needed a distraction.

'He's economized,' I said.

'I'm sorry?'

'The proprietor: he's economized with his gynoids. These girls are a fleet of second-hand gigolettes from one of the Big Weird's discos. Imitation Seiko, I'd say. They've been customized to look like Lilim, but you can still see the coin slot between their breasts. See?'

'Yeah, I do see.'

'Ten baht a boogie,' I said. 'Happier times.'

'Look, I'm sorry to bother you, Mr – ' I didn't reply. 'Let me get you a drink before I go.' He hailed a waiter. 'Boy, I wish you *were* English. Sure some amazing things going down there. Been five years now since my country restored diplomatic relations. Sometime I hope to get to visit.' Two beers arrived. 'Jack Morgenstern,' he said, extending a hand (and proffering a heavy tip with the other). 'Cheers. Let's hope that sad little country gets a better deal under the Human Front.'

I took a sip of my beer. 'The Human Front,' I said, 'are scum.' Morgenstern's hands fluttered about his glass.

'Believe me,' he said, 'I'm no fan. Anybody who could do *this* . . .' He gestured towards the circus of blood and its *artistes.* 'But you have to admit those fellas have established something like order. God knows, if those Lilim ever got out – and some say they already *have*, that they've been seen in mainland Europe – if *anybody* got out, started spreading that doll-plague around . . .'

'Then it's just as well I'm *not* English.'

'Lord, not everybody's infected. I'm not prejudiced. Only Londoners have the virus, and London's sealed off. Quarantined. It's just a pity the English didn't handle things as well as the French did all those years back when the plague began. Anyway, nobody gets out of London.'

'That so?'

'Sure. But my waiter friend tells me there's lots of *clean* English people in South-East Asia . . .'

Was he being naive or ironic? The English who sheltered in Thailand necessarily held forged papers; despite the assurances of Her Majesty's government, it was an open secret that the plague had broken London's *cordon sanitaire*. From this exclusive club of exiles, Primavera and I had ourselves been exiled. We hadn't had the Deutschmarks to bribe the requisite officials in this most bribable of countries. Besides, club rules barred inhuman refugees. Blackballed their paramours. We had had to rely on the sour charity of Madame K.

'Why are you so interested in the Lilim?' I tried to ask. I wanted the dope on Morgenstern's dopey act of American innocent abroad. But my lips hadn't moved. They were as numb as if I'd snacked on a cocaine popsicle. How many beers had I had? I had a strong head, but the room had begun to spin, and Jack Morgenstern's voice was as faint as if he were calling station to station from Mars.

'So you *could* be English. Theoretically, that is . . .' I wiggled a finger in my ear; an insect was buzzing inside my skull. 'You could be from Madchester. That's what everybody calls the capital now, eh, Madchester?' My skin, filmed with sweat, was as cold as the slick of condensation on my beer glass. 'Sure would be something,' he said, 'if you *were* a Londoner.'

I got up. I was going to be ill. Where was the *suam*? And Primavera, where were you? Where were you when I ever needed you? Tucking me into bed Mum would tell stories about when she was a little girl. The farm outside Bratislava. Summer walks through the Carpathians . . . The floor hit me like one of Primavera's hexes: a dimension unpredicted by unified theory, something that should *not* have been there. Carpet bristles invaded my mouth. My veins were full of ice – like allure, but pleasureless, no fun – and my muscles were frozen. I was a statue that had fallen from its plinth. Tik-tik-atikka, went the drum machine. *She did the hula-hula*. Tik-tik-atikka. *And then*

I had to shoot her. Tik-tik-atikka. *C-cos she'd stolen my computer.*

I beheld the paralysis of my face in a patent leather toecap.

'Sir, sir?'

'It's all right,' said Morgenstern. 'He's a friend. Our car's outside. You'll give me a hand?'

CHAPTER THREE

Beata Beatrix

The stretch limousine turned amphibious at the Ploenchit Road. Conscious but immobile, my eyes like fused glass, I stared, unblinking, through the spray-flecked windscreen at the cleft black water of the *klong*. High-rises, shopping malls, *jeux vérités* arcades rose like giant nenuphars to spill their photoelectric sap into that dead, viscous sea; a sea that had reclaimed the city of angels and made it once more the Venice of the East. From the water protruded *chedi* and *prang* of sunken temples: indices of an obsolete civilization. The traffic – splashing those humbled steeples with their blasphemous slalom – shimmered behind a veil of luminous gas, a gasoline-methane smog lit by the green lasers and floodlights of advertisement hoardings, holographic and photo-mechanical; by the green mercury-vapour glow of underwater road signs; by the green paper lanterns hanging from the shop-houses of adjoining *sois*. Sheet lightning scattered the moonless sky and for an instant the green filter dissolved and the city was delineated in hues of sepia, like a time-damaged print of Fritz Lang's *Metropolis*. This was an *art nouveau* city, a *deco* city, its sinewy, undulating lines and geometric chic copied from the fashions of the *aube du millénaire* and imposed on the slums of its twentieth-century inheritance and the sublimities of its ancient past. Again, the pall of greenness descended, a peasouper, a gangrenous membrane, a steamy decay of tropical night. Monorails, skywalks, with their hoards of winepressed humanity, passed above us; autogyros too, with their fat-cat cargoes, hovering above the city's stagnant pools like steel-hulled dragonflies. Once more, the lightning; and then the rain began, coagulating the green tint of the night so that we seemed to be moving through an ocean's depths. Green was that year's colour; green, the colour of perversity; a green as luminous as a certain pair of eyes.

I could see her in my peripheral vision. She was muzzled, blood dribbling from the side of her mouth; her dress (the dermaplastic palpitating against me) rucked up, with something resembling a chastity belt girdling her waist and hugging her perineum. Below the waist the dress was torn, bleeding a midnight dye; through the tear a glass cable disappeared into her umbilicus. Part of a scanning tunnelling microscope, perhaps? Or an ovipositor spawning a dust-brood of malicious little machines? Whatever it was, it had turned the lock on Primavera's box of tricks. Like me, she sat in the front of the limo like a dummy being delivered for display.

Morgenstern read the question in my wall-eyed stare. 'Took six men to clamp that on,' he said. 'Two of them are on their way to hospital. They had particle weapons too. Pity about Monsieur Sabatier. He was very cooperative. I guess the Paris catwalks will have to do without him next season. Another nail in Europe's coffin. First the crash. Then the plague . . .'

In the back, other voices:

'Jesus, they're just kids.'

'The Neverland – that's what they call London now. No one gets to grow up. It's a city of kids.'

'Lost girls, lost boys.'

'Don't weep over these two. They're animals. The kind that'd slice 'n' dice an old, lame, blind, pregnant woman.'

'That kind, eh? But hell. What we do for democracy.'

'It's building bridges. It's the Special Relationship.'

'It's hearts,' said Morgenstern, 'and minds.' The two goons in the back made huh-huh-huh noises of mock amusement.

Well fuck you, Jack, I thought, as we entered the

grounds of the American Embassy.

They left us in a dark windowless room, with a marine standing guard. The squawk of lizards, the grunting of frogs, carried across the night. The ceiling fan slewed round the shadows . . .

'Oh?' she said. 'Did I *hurt* you?'

The left canine, a speck of blood on its enamel, overlapped her lip with gothic coquettishness. 'Lil-im,' whispered some of our classmates, 'Lil-im, Lil-im.'

'Stop that!' said Mr Spink, our form teacher, his vodka-ruined larynx rasping with the attempt to muster authority. 'I've told you before: I won't have any of this superstitious "Lilim" nonsense in my class.'

A massed raising of hands.

'Sir,' said the girl – a human girl – 'Primavera just bit Ignatz.' The susurration peaked, then died.

'Primavera?'

'I didn't do anything, sir, honest!' A pencil dropped to the floor. My classmates scraped their feet, chewed their lips: a pack of wolf cubs at bay.

'What about you, Zwakh?'

'I'm all right, sir,' I said, my cheeks still flushed. Primavera glanced over her shoulder, her eyes narrowing with contempt.

'Primavera, I think you'd better see Nurse.' And the contempt surrendered to confusion, the green-speckled irises dilating with fear.

It would mean an appointment at the Hospitals, another checkup where she would be probed, examined, observed, an updated prognosis entered in her records. A doll remained an out patient (they said) until the unassuageability of her appetites was thought to threaten public health. Interned – committal papers signed by parents or guardians with sometimes marvellous haste – and disabled with magic dust, her brief mortal term was concluded (they said) in conditions similar to those of an eighteenth-century madhouse, a Bedlam where, racked by visions of ruptured jugulars, of banquets of blood, she died (they said) drowned on her own monstrous salivations. The corpse was used for medical research.

So they said. But could you believe them? The boys in the playground; the grown-ups whispering in corners; the TV, with its coded references to London's fate? On a hot summer's day, with your nostrils filled with the perfume of the prettiest little girl in school, you could believe anything.

Primavera sloped out of class; a backward glance, as she closed the door, sent me and the human race to perdition.

Our teacher had sat down and was staring at the stack of exercise books that, for months, he had never opened, never touched. Quiet desperation, Dad called that despair (its quietness sometimes disturbed by Mr Spink's hacking coughs, his lungs besieged by the mutant bacillus that had been the forerunner of the doll-plague). I gazed out of the window. Sparrows wheeled over the roofs of abandoned houses; dogs prowled empty streets.

You could walk through these depopulated suburbs, Dad said, as far as the M25. That was the line of interdiction. For humans, barbed wire, personnel mines, watchtowers; for dolls, the screen. The Americans had linked elements of their strategic defences (neutral particle beam space platforms) with the interdiction's early warning system. A doll-shaped blip on radar and an NPB would score a neurotronics kill, grounding the escaping doll and leaving her in the throes of a *grand mal*. At night, from the top of the tower block where I lived, I would look out over the Rainham marshes and, seeing the searchlights panning the sky, imagine myself, high above the deserted city, eluding our captors and disappearing into the wild vista of England's other shore. But none crossed the ring road of the M25.

'We'll get her for you, Ig,' whispered a boy to my right. It was Myshkin. Myshkin had the knobbly, dirt-caked aspect of one of Phiz's street urchins. He turned up his lapel to display a tiny steel badge: the winged double helix of the Human Front. 'England for the organic,' he said, taking from his pocket a pair of rubber gloves. Myshkin was a medicine-head.

The bell sounded; it was lunch-time. I gave myself to the current: the subterranean stream of boys and girls that poured through the narrow caverns of our school to spill into eye-splitting sunlight.

The playground – a tarmacked yard half melted in the summer heat – held a microcosm of the Soviet diaspora: the children of those economic migrants who, since the end of the last century, had turned westwards in search of food and jobs. The old nationalist hatreds – which had once set Armenian against Azerbaijani, Transylvanian against Romanian, and just about everybody against dispossessed Russia, had been submerged in a new chauvinism in which speciesism supplanted ethnicity. In the playground, human children who, before the plague, would have segregated into warring tribes, celebrated their inverted cosmopolitanism in the sun, confining the recombinant to the shadows of the bike sheds.

I crouched by a wall; my lunch, a bag of crisps. About me, a grey facade pocked with broken windows and scarred with lichen and desiccated moss drew a stone curtain across the flood-ruined Neverscape. Only a few slummy towers, like the one I lived in (like the ones we all lived in), sanctuaries against the winter's deluge, were visible above the blinding concrete. Why wouldn't the floods come now, and drown my shame? Rise, sea. Fill the Thames. Lap, then overlap the barriers. But the streets were as dry as a dust-filled cistern. I hated June.

I had borrowed *The Adventures of Tom Sawyer* from Dad's small but uncompromising library. ('The Battle of the Books,' he'd say, laughing, as he clubbed to death one of my government-issue primers with the aid of a Hasek, Havel or Seifert.) The book fell open at a passage I had read again and again. Tom had arrived late at school and had been told to sit with the girls. That was okay with him. It meant he could sit next to Becky Thatcher, the new girl in town whom he secretly adored. Becky ignored him. Then he gave her a peach. Drew pictures on his slate.

Now Tom began to scrawl something on the slate, hiding the words from the girl. But she was not backward this time. She begged to see. Tom said:

'*Oh, it ain't anything.*'

'*Yes it is.*'

'*No it ain't; you don't want to see.*'

'*Yes I do, indeed I do. Please let me.*'

'*You'll tell.*'

'*No I won't – deed and deed and double deed I won't.*'

'*You won't tell anybody at all? Ever as long as you live?*'

'*No I won't tell anybody. Now let me.*'

'*Oh* you *don't want to see!*'

'*Now that you treat me so I* will *see, Tom*' – *and she put her small hand on his, and a little scuffle ensued. Tom pretending to resist in earnest, but letting his hand slip by degrees till these words were revealed:* 'I love you.'

'*Oh, you bad thing!' And she hit his hand a smart rap, but reddened and looked pleased nevertheless . . .*

Why wasn't it like that? Why wasn't it *ever* like that? I savoured my self-pity. I would never grow up, but I would never be a child; never know childhood's grace.

Myshkin came to sit beside me. 'Look at them,' he said. Jostled by the scampering figures of two football teams a group of Lilim walked across the playground and took asylum amongst the scooters and amphibious bikes.

They were older girls, fifth formers, their humanity spent, girls no longer, really, but simulacra, dolls. Wrapped in shadows, and wearing black, black sunglasses, they still seemed to wince at the sun. An irritability coursed through their limbs: they mussed their hair, arranged and rearranged their clothes, applied make-up with a tic-like, incipient hysteria. Muzzled, like all dolls achieving metamorphosis, some slurped at raspberry slush ices through straws; one doll, finishing her ice, and seemingly unsatisfied, removed her shades, shielded her eyes, and squinted through the convective air as if seeking life across a bloodless desert.

'*Gopnik*,' said Myshkin. 'Slink-gang. Call themselves the *Nutcracker Sweets*.' He had pulled on his rubber gloves and was tying a surgical mask to his face. 'They'll die soon, of course. Two or three years. They'll burn out. Go mad. They always do. Their bodies can't accommodate all those crazy molecular changes. Two or three years. You can spoil a lot of seed in that time . . .' He drew a dog-eared magazine from his blazer. 'My Dad has a library too,' he said, taking *Tom Sawyer* from my hands. 'He's . . . a *collector*.'

The magazine was called *The National Health*. Inside were photographs of people I had seen on TV, such as Vladimir ('Vlad') Constantinescu, leader of the Human Front. There were also lots of photographs of young girls in straitjackets, padded cells, and on mortuary slabs; of pathologists caught *in flagrante delicto* as they performed hysterectomies on the dead; of kidney dishes full of tissue, polymers and bloodied steel.

'Medical experiments,' said Myshkin, who smirked as if he knew I only dissembled revulsion. 'They have to try and find a cure. Not as if it's *pre*mortems, is it? Anyway, they're not like us. Not self-conscious. They're *robotniks*. Sets of formal rules . . .' His apologia trailed off as, slack-jawed, I flipped through the glossy pages.

31

'They don't move,' I said. 'The pictures don't move.'

Myshkin took back the magazine, disappointed less, I think, by my lack of candour than that I had failed to appreciate the antique beauty of photographic still life. 'Bitches,' he said, surveying the playground, his eyes pausing whenever they encountered a serried group of dolls. 'They're taking over, Ig.' He passed a hand through the stubble of his hair. 'My brother's sixteen. The interdiction began when he was born. People still lived in central London then, not just in the suburbs, like us. Now there's only a quarter million of us left. Every kid you meet these days has a doll for a sister, or a sister who'll most likely turn into a doll.'

'*As a population gets smaller, it gets younger*,' I quoted.

'Neo-Malthusian economics. Yeah. Bloody right. We'll be outnumbered by dolls in five years. In, say, ten, fifteen years, who'll be left? And if the plague gets outside . . .'

'Maybe it is,' I said. 'They say that in Manchester . . .'

'The Human Front – your Dad going to vote for them?'

'What do they care? None of their leaders live in London. My Dad says they're just exploiting us for – '

'Vlad's the man, Ig. It's the only way.'

'*Zut!* You mean all that stuff about his ancestor? That's just *toffee*. Anyway, dolls have Mums and Dads too. You think they'd vote HF?'

'What we vote for don't matter. There's not enough of us. But sure: the Neverland'll vote HF. Like the rest of the country. A doll is a changeling. Mums and Dads want their *real* daughters back.'

'That's superstition! That's – '

'Mums and Dads know that their daughters are returned only after the changeling dies. Returned in spirit! That's what the HF wants: to give parents back their kids. To save souls!'

' "Sanitization". Oh yeah. I call it murder.'

'It's them that's murdering *us*. They're parasites, Ig.

They use us to propagate themselves. For them, we're just *vectors*. If we let them carry on they'll take over the world. And when we're gone, and they can't replicate, they'll die, and that'll be the end. Of everything.'

'They'll find a cure,' I said. 'Some day. They'll find out how it all started, and then – '

'The only cure,' said Myshkin, 'is us. Me and my mates have begun work already. Up West.'

'But it's not allowed.'

'Up West where the rogue dolls are. Runaways. Girls in need of a little radical surgery.'

'You'll be infected. You'll bring the infection home.'

'Don't be wet. Anyway, I'm never going to have sex. All these kids making *babies* all the time. Agh – *le nombril sinistre!*' Myshkin wrung his hands, the gloves emitting rubbery squeaks. 'Sex is for *robotniks* and junkies. Sex is . . . Sex is bad news. You won't catch *me* making Lilim.'

'You've got junkie written all over you. You'll be dead before you're twenty-one.'

'It's a crusade, Ig. You've got to make sacrifices.'

A football bounced into my lap; I returned it to the dirty-faced mêlée. The slink-gang, the mooncalfs, the misbegotten little mommas who were the *Nutcracker Sweets*, had begun to play hopscotch in the asphalt bower of the sheds.

'In class – what you said about Primavera . . .'

'*La salope* – she's pretty.' Myshkin laughed, his voice breaking in mid-pitch. 'Don't worry. My brother's a prefect. We'll take care of her. After school.' He patted the magazine under his blazer. 'We'll play doctors. It'll be Psycho-Zygo. It'll be diddly-woo!'

Corridors. Corridors. Dark highways through childhood's ruins. Corridors threaded with boys and girls who seemed to be picking their way through an attic, vast and musty, foraging for the bric-a-brac of innocence.

Sunbeams intercepted their progress, splintering through the cracks of boarded windows; I slipped into the throng, the throb of mote-lousy air counterpointing my temple's metronome. Beneath eaves, over rafters: no shouts, no screams, only an enervated mumbling as tongues wagged lazily, fattened by the summer heat. A pair of bluebottles, coupled in flight, fell satiated to a mildewy wainscot. A bloody-nosed boy lay blubbering on the floor. Such urban pastoral; it called for surrender, to seek no more in that attic of dreams . . .

All afternoon I sat behind her, heart thudding, unable to escape, so near that I could smell her piebald mane, so intoxicatingly newly washed. Primavera ignored me. I thought to touch her on the shoulder, to say Don't cross the park, or Let me walk you home. But desire took the charity from my heart, and I thought of her in the gulag of the Dolls' Hospitals, and me, in surgical gown and mask; I thought of straitjackets, padded cells, slabs; and the cheap schoolgirl scent of her hair seemed to mix with the smells of chloroform and ether.

Sunlight fell obliquely across the room; I breathed deep, and then deeper again. My sinuses tingled with black romance. I would have to do it. Do the medicine thing. How else did boy meet girl? How else. The alternatives were abstract; you read about them in *Tom Sawyer*, and in history class they taught you of times before love had become indistinguishable from pornography. They meant nothing to you. You were a Never-Never Kid, sent to school only to show the outside world that there was hope, that you didn't deserve to be abandoned, that you were worth the food and materiel dropped from the night skies. Tom and Becky? Forget it. History? God damn it. Love? Abuse it.

Last bell. Home time. The corridors, in their eternal dampness, a counterpart to our sticky adolescent bodies, channelled the four o'clock rout onto the streets. Myshkin passed me a scalpel, and we ran through the milling schoolchildren to rendezvous with his brother in the baked mudflats of the park. A policeman – a joke policeman; one of our heroic citizens' militia – seemed to have an intimation of our purpose, and wandered away.

We lay in wait behind a dying strip of hedgerow, shaded from the sun's mellowing embrace, our school's postmodern gothic (with its Oh so funny references to Victorian warehouse, workhouse and blacking factory) playing incongruous mood music – a lugubrious black mass – against the brilliant and deceptive optimism of the late afternoon sky; it was a mood that had long been my own; it clung to me as the smell of decay, of mildew, clung to my clothes, my flesh; I had grown up to its fetid sway. Ever since I had been little, school – not the visible school, the school of appearances and discipline, but a wraith-school, a school of the umbrageous heart – had inculcated in me, through the violence of the heart, that voluptuous mood, that music of wanton despair. My memories were all of strange angle shots, monstrous close-ups, distortions, blurrings, dialogue broken-tongued and inane: the bullying in the bell tower (the bell was still ringing, carrying over the housing estates, the marshes); the diagrams, stick-figures and exhortations in the boys' toilets; our science master's lectures on posthuman biology, the biology of master and slave; and, of late, that half-metre of yellow-black hair, those bratty ways, that promise of transcendence.

A haze-distorted column of kids began winding between the liverish pools that had resisted evaporation. The Myshkins pulled up their masks and unsheathed their scalpels. No need for a particle weapon, no need for magic dust; Primavera was still half girl, refractory, but weak. As she passed by the Myshkins broke from the bushes; Primavera's dollfriends scattered across the park. By the time she had been bundled into the cricket pavilion, around fifteen, twenty boys and a few girls – human girls – had gate-crashed the party.

The pavilion was hot; its odour, urinous. Half naked (her blouse had been torn open and her brassiere used to tie her hands behind her back), Primavera knelt in the shadows, head bowed, crying.

We taunted her.

'Witch!'

'Baby killer!'

'Vrolok!'

'Dead girl!'

'Changeling!'

'Robotnik!'

'Out Patient!'

'Sangsue!'

Bored with this sadoschlock exercise (a tired borrowing from one of Myshkin's razzle mags), and, despite the cravenness of our law enforcers, fearful of discovery (dolls then still possessing some rights), her tormentors soon departed; all but one. I lingered, hidden behind a locker. Looking about, and seeing that we were alone, I emerged, tremblingly, to stand before her. She studied me from behind sharp metallic eyelashes, her eyes those of a run-to-ground animal, pitiful but calculating. I felt a stinging in my cheeks; I turned away; then, biting my lip with resolve, swung about to face her. 'Witch,' I said, voice hoarse with its confession of love. I aimed a kick into her side. The adored one moaned and keeled over.

I sat on my haunches and put a hand to her cheek. 'I'm sorry,' I said.

'You b-bastard. You fucking *boy-slime.*'

Big tears rolled over my fingers. Cool and inhuman, they were; and her skin – like a compound of PVC and epidermis of milkmaid – plasticky cool, and white, with an impurity that allured and saddened; an impurity to which the blonde hair, scarred with Cartier black, and

36

black eyes, veined with emerald, added their testimony.

Teeth flashed; a rush of pain. With bestial speed her cute kittycat fangs had bitten through my shirt and chest. I raised my fists, but the opiate of her saliva was already in my wounds; I cried *kamerad!* to the invasion of her kisses.

Shells burst behind my eyes; I was her beachhead, first blood in a guerrilla war against humanity. Fifth columnists leaped from her spittle, a microrobotic army dedicated to overthrowing my gametes. They infiltrated in their billions. Ignoring Y, digging in to X, they would wait, wait for me to fill a human womb so that they might stage their *coup* and set up a puppet government.

A blue-white flash . . .

Tombstones. The coach. The fall of night.

Primavera was eating my brain.

I awoke from post-coital sleep on the hard floor of the pavilion, my head rich with traces of midsummer dreams. Primavera slumbered on, fulfilled, it seemed, in her doll-hood, her bosom rising and falling on a tide of ease, her cheek pressed to my own.

Her skirt was in disarray, hoisted to her waist; the umbilicus, that dark well of unreason, rippled to her clockwork pulse.

I disengaged myself, slithered down to her belly, and peered over the umbilical lip. If I had picked up a small stone and dropped it into that well, would I have heard, long seconds later, an echo, a ricochet, a splash? I dismissed the conceit, my hand slipping beneath my waistband to where cold metal ached against my thigh.

Unsheathing my scalpel, I held its blade to the umbilicus; the umbilicus puckered, withdrawing into itself, and the blade trembled like a plumb line above a door to the underworld. I thought of the magazine Myshkin had shown me, the photographs of vivisected flesh; and I moved the blade to the centre of her belly, a hair's-

37

breadth from the taut vinyl skin.

I would not hurt her; I would never hurt her. This was playtime. A game. Pretend. Primavera sighed; I secured the scalpel in my waistband.

Too late: from her umbilicus a light, pale and green, rose like the presage of a genie, diffracting above my head. I panicked, spreading my hands over the bleeding aperture, scared, at any moment, she would awake.

She did not stir.

I screwed my eye to the light source, a Peeping Tom at his lady's chamber.

What was happening in there?

It was a silent picture show; an end-of-the-pier amusement. Men, women, children – figures tinted in shades of green – were flickering into semblances of life. Then came colour. Sound, too: voices of homunculi; the turning of earth; the desolate keening of birds. Primavera was dreaming. And she dreamed of death.

I saw myself standing in the midst of a great cemetery. Mausolea, tombstones, defined the horizon. It was dusk; all was silent beneath a reddening sky. The mourners had departed. Beneath me, an open grave. The stone was carved *Ignatz Zwakh, 2056–68, Remember me, but ah! forget my fate.* Icy fingers entwined about my own.

'It has to be like this. You know that, don't you?' Primavera's cloak was like a designer shroud, the hood – lined with green satin – framing a lifeless face. 'Desire is death. Living death.'

She led me through the necropolis to where a coach-and-four waited. A much-decayed corpse in a surgical mask held the reins.

'Dust to dust. Silicon to silicon. The bullies. The Hospitals. The men in white coats. The dolls.'

We boarded. A crack of a whip. We galloped through the cemetery. Grim reapers, dismembered cherubs and other *mementos mori* gaped in at us as we hurtled past.

Primavera drew close. The opacity of her eyes – dark, with green splinters of mutation – cleared, became mortal. With loneliness. With fear.

'Night is falling.' Her breath was cold against my cheek. 'Stay with me. Share my grave. On and on we can ride. No escape for human, for doll. All is boundless and eternal. Like desire. Like death.'

A hand, small, white and blue-veined, a child's hand, settled between my thighs.

The wheels clattered over rocks and bones.

The light faded; the picture show dissolved. Primavera was waking. I crept into her arms.

'What's the time?' she murmured.

'I don't know. My watch – ' My watch was broken.

As if she had been slapped, Primavera spun her head to one side, gasping with alarm. 'Outside,' she said, 'it's getting dark! Quick, untie me!' I freed her lace-manacled hands. 'I have to go home. I'm late. Mum thinks it's bad enough as it is, having a doll for a daughter. I don't want her to think I'm *delinquent*.'

Shaking, she buttoned her blouse and brushed the dust from her gymslip. 'I couldn't help it,' she said, her eyes moodily fastened on the green pentacle emblazoned over her breast. 'It's the poison.' She put a hand on her belly. 'Here. Inside. Sometimes – sometimes it hurts. I don't want to be Lilim. I don't. I want everything to be like – like *before*.'

In England every girl is human; or was human, once. And Primavera was but a few months into her metamorphosis. Such a girl, like a chrysalis disturbed from sleep, may sometimes scratch at her cocoon, afraid. She knows that she is becoming that other, that vertigo of desire, that dead girl who shares her name.

'You won't tell, will you?' she said. 'If you tell . . .'

'I won't tell,' I said. 'I promise.'

39

She knelt to kiss me. It was a ghost's kiss, light, impalpable. 'You mean that?'

'I'm not like the others.'

'Boy-slime.' She laughed softly.

'I mean it,' I said. 'Listen: it's my birthday next week. I'm having a party. Why don't you come?'

'And whatever will your Mum and Dad say? A doll at their little boy's party?'

'Mum and Dad aren't like that.'

She frowned and cuffed me playfully across the nose. 'Maybe,' she said. 'But human boys have so *many* birthdays. Not like us dolls. I don't know if I *should*.' She stood up. 'I have to go.'

'Primavera,' I said, 'be my girlfriend.'

'*Stupid!*'

'I wouldn't let them hurt you,' I said. 'Not again.'

She walked towards the door, chewing thoughtfully on a strand of dishevelled hair. 'I might come to your party. Your Mum and Dad sound nice. My Mum, well . . . Lilith's your mother now, she says. She wouldn't be seen dead with me. The older girls: they always say it's the human bit left inside that hurts.'

It would be a mercy when she became doll entire . . .

I lay in the darkness, fingering the puncture wounds beneath my shirt, counting (as she had insisted) to six hundred and sixty-six (the shirt would have to be destroyed; it was red with sedition) before following her into the evening's gloom. To be seen together at this hour . . . *People talk so, Iggy, really they do*. The sky was violet, shifting to black, and the ruins bordering the park's savannah echoed to the hush of shadows. Primavera was gone, scurrying to meet her curfew. It was late – too late to be on the streets; with the sundown came the big kids, cocks of the militant boardwalks of the night. I trotted into the desolation of ordinariness that was north-east London's suburbs.

The Rainham Road was littered with tomb-robbers' castoffs: sunburst clocks, prints from Woolworth's, plaster knick-knacks and smashed aquaria – the unwanted booty of forgotten, vulgar lives. I began to sprint (the sounds of distant parties restating the dangers of the dark); out there, amongst the remains of England's beached Leviathan, things prinked, prowled and preyed, boy-things, and girl-things. I crossed the A125, and paused to catch my breath. Beyond a strip of marshland the towers of the Mardyke estate, honeycombed with light, cast an emulsive sheen across the benighted city. (Evidence of other habitation came from far, far away where the lurid glow of Dagenham Hospital rose above the horizon.) There were other communities; one in Upminster, I'd heard. But I had never seen them. I knew only the area bounded by school and the marshes (though Dad had once taken me to see the Thames). Travel was taboo; it spread plague.

I crawled beneath razor-wire, ran, paused, massaged my side, ran again. The dry sedge whistled about my feet. Soon, I had reached the snaggletoothed root of *Solaris Mansions*. I dawdled, bracing myself for the long climb, the inevitable scolding from Dad. Gazing down the street, my eyes settled upon the Bobinski residence; five floors up, it was signposted by a neon intensity that seemed to burn away all competition. Was she already abed, singing herself a vampire lullaby? Did she touch herself as I visited her dreams? My eyelids drooped; the light was chromaticized by the fine denier of my lashes, and rainbows arced across the boondocks of my world, filling it with love's spectrum. The marshland, flat and monotonous, was irradiated: dykes, sluice-gates, windmills; the nauseous replication of looted semis; and beyond the marshes, beyond the lonely conurbations of Essex and Surrey, Middlesex and Kent, beyond the fairy ring of interdiction, England itself was surely radiant, its shires

– where moneymen telecommuted to and from the world – dreaming bright dreams of long ago and a girl named Britannia. A stillness descended, a stillness quite unlike the bleak quiet I was accustomed to, and all dissolved into a tearful, multihued mist. I had become a prism of desire! Primavera and I would transform everything. Where her light could not reach, and where I could not see, even the shadows, I knew, would have lusher gradations, more purposeful depths.

Later, when Mum came to kiss me goodnight, I asked her to tell me a story of when she was little, a story of the forests and of the village where she grew up, a story of the Carpathian mountains.

'Is it true,' I said, after she had finished, 'what they say about dolls: that they're the daughters of Lilith, Adam's first wife? That Lilith steals human children and puts her own in their place?'

'It's just a fairy tale, Ignatz. Like the ones I tell you. Tales of the golem, the wandering Jew, the vampire.'

'But the dolls – they *are* vampires.'

'Not real ones.' She smiled and stroked my hair. 'Dolls are not devils. Such things do not exist. They're just little girls. Little girls who are very ill. You must pity them, Ignatz. The world is cruel.'

Primavera never came to my party, but we often met in secret. Throughout that summer she would come to the roof of my tower block and stay until after dark. 'I don't care about Mum any more,' she'd say. On the roof I had set up a telescope, and we would gaze at the stars, or try to spot an escaping doll caught like a moth in the city perimeter's searchlights. And we would play our game, and afterwards we would both say we were sorry, until the night came when we no longer cared to make apologies, to ourselves, each other, or the world.

CHAPTER FOUR

Black Spring

With four marines to act as my pall bearers (the Mickey still mummifying my joints) I was taken to an elevator, dropped three, four, five floors, and carried, in a mockery of pomp, through the embassy's cable-wormy bowels. My cortège, on entering a gymnasium, came to rest. After leaning me against some wall bars at forty-five degrees (my rigidity uncompromised), the marines solemnly departed. Jack Morgenstern was pumping iron. We were alone.

'How's the voice?' he said. 'I thought we might talk.' The daily exertions of the American *corps diplomatique* had left the gym with a residual stench of humanity; I heaved. 'That's good. That shows the drug's wearing off.' He dropped his weights and moved to a rowing machine. 'But your friend – you'll understand we're going to have to keep *her* secured, even if her girdle *is* killing her.' He began to whistle the chorus of the 'Eton Boating Song'. 'I guess you could call me an Anglophile; it's a fine thing our two countries are enjoying warmer relations.' He paused to wipe his hands and tighten his bandana. 'I'll tell you straight: Her Majesty's government wants you back. Both of you.'

I went to speak, but my mouth seemed filled with marbles.

'What's that?' said Morgenstern, hovering in mid-stroke.

'The Human Front . . .' I managed, before the marbles began to choke me.

He sighed. 'Don't think we're happy about any of this. But the President happens to believe that the Human

Front are the only people who can control the plague. And I'm inclined to agree with him. It's not as if we expect the HF to put the Great back in to Britain, but it's a chance for us to make up lost ground, regain some influence in Europe. The Human Front may be bastards, Zwakh, but they're *our* bastards.'

'The slab,' I spat out, 'Primavera will go to the slab.'

'Didn't you hear? I said we're not *happy*. Not that you two don't deserve the worst.' He passed the finishing line and hung over his oars, his Hash House sweatshirt sodden. The lights went up on his show of temperance. 'You're monsters. Animals. You're . . .' The English language faltered before our seemingly limitless depravity. He rose and walked to a vaulting horse on which lay a manila file. '*Ignatz Zwakh*,' he began to read, '*born 2056* . . .'

'Kito,' I interrupted. 'Why did she betray us?'

'We've been monitoring you and the girl for weeks,' he said, eyes still on the file. 'Ever since the English approached us through their representatives at the Swiss Embassy. Then you suddenly high-tailed it out of here. So we asked Kito if she could get you back. We didn't want any *official* Thai involvement.'

'Money?'

'We have in our arsenal,' he said, 'greater aphrodisiacs. And darker persuasions. Let's just say Kito's a clever lady. Or machine.' He waved his hand through the air. 'Whatever she is, she's an accomplished liar. I can respect that. Lies have a beauty all of their own. Their own life, their own symmetry. Kito sure knew how to do the number on *you*. Now let's see how you rate on self-preservation.' He ran his finger along a line of type. '*Born 2056. In London. To Slovak émigrés.* Tell me, why the hell didn't your family get the hell out of London before the interdiction came into effect?'

'Nobody wanted us.'

44

'We're a nation of immigrants ourselves. It's hard to believe you couldn't – '

'Why are we having this conversation? Why don't you just put us on the spaceplane and have done with it?'

'The *Orient Express* doesn't leave until tomorrow. Besides, my government wants to satisfy itself on a few points. For instance . . .' He put the file down and walked over to me. 'Who, or what, is Titania?'

I felt pain in my lower back; I had begun to sag.

'Limbering up, eh? A boy your age should soon – '

'I don't know anything about Titania.'

'Let me tell you what *we* know.' He drew up a stool and sat down. 'Remember our conversation in the restaurant? *Nobody gets out of London.* That's the HF's official party line. But you and I know different. You're not the only kids to have escaped. Dolls have turned up all over England. Scotland. Wales. Mainland Europe, too. Though I guess you're the only runaways to have got *this* far. Someone, or something, is getting them out. Now we believe the Human Front can stabilize things in London, but not over the country as a whole. They're going to need US help.'

'You call mass murder stabilizing?'

'I told you,' he said, his face haggard with a lifetime of trimming to the times, 'we're not happy about this. Now our intelligence indicates that there's something in London organizing these escapes. Something powerful enough to penetrate the interdiction. We think that something is a Big Sister: one of the original Cartier automatons.'

'They were all destroyed,' I said, too hastily.

'I think not. Tell me how you escaped, Zwakh.'

I rolled my eyes to the ceiling.

'Look,' he said, '*I'm* not going to make you talk, but *they* sure will back in England. You realize that, don't you? It's better we know than them. We can act as

45

intermediaries. We can plea-bargain.'

'No,' I said.

'The girl,' he said. 'We could help her. I guess she didn't *mean* to kill. You know what we can say? We can say she didn't want to spread the doll-plague. So she cleaned up after each meal. Real hygienic. She never really *wanted* to murder anyone. After all, Lilim don't kill; it goes against their programming. We can say it was that bitch Kito who – '

'She enjoys it,' I said. 'You were right the first time: we're monsters. Animals.'

'We'll find out about Titania sooner or later,' he said. 'I thought I might save you a little grief, that's all.' He clapped his hands and sprang to his feet. 'That's it then. For now. *Operation Black Spring* has become something of a hobbyhorse. I just can't let go of it.' He chuckled as my body sagged a few more inches. 'Jesus, boy, you look *uncomfortable*.' He manoeuvred me into a ninety-degree upright. 'You know, when I joined the foreign service I genuinely felt I might be able to do something to make the world a better place. Seems a long time ago now. The *aube du millénaire*. Lord, those were times. My wife and I spent our honeymoon in Europe. When I think of what Europe's going through now . . .'

'Primavera enjoys killing,' I said. 'How about you? You dine at The Londoner often? What do you do when you're not sending little girls to their deaths?'

'I don't need no lecture from a hired assassin, Zwakh. Maybe we'll talk some more later. In fact I'm sure of it. When you've had time to think. And while you're thinking, remember what I said about aphrodisiacs. And persuasions. Remember we have your little friend. Your little *stash*. No one has to die. Wise up. I can help you.'

He called the guard.

I rejoined Primavera in our lovers' tomb. A marine

resumed position by the door, stony-faced as a piece of mortuary furniture.

Escape, escape, I thought. Always that unrelenting need: to make plans, to run, to lie, to cheat. Sometimes you had to fight, too. (I didn't like that; I was no good at it; fighting was Primavera's department.) Why couldn't they give it a rest? I tried to concentrate, but unsolicited images kept interposing themselves between my thoughts. Jack Morgenstern in Kito's penthouse; and Kito, looking untypically flustered, toying nervously with the titanium chain about her neck, her bracelets of spent uranium.

'Kito tricked me,' Primavera announced inside my brain. I cried out.

'Try to get some sleep, sir,' said the marine.

'Did you *hear* that, Iggy? Shit, I didn't know I could *do* that.'

I gripped the sides of the couch; relaxed. I had lived with Primavera too long to be panicked by her quantum magic, however unprecedented its manifestation. 'Primavera?'

'Uh-huh?' Hey. I could mindspeak to her too. Clever, these Cartier dolls.

'They're sending us back to London,' I said in a dead man's whisper. 'Satisfied?' – I twisted the knife – 'You should be. This is where all your little games end.'

'I'm sorry, Iggy.' There were tears in her thoughts.

'Can you move?'

'Can't feel a thing. If I could just get these cast-iron *pants* off, then – '

'I can move a little. Any ideas?'

'You keep still. If I can get into your brain I can get into GI Joe's.'

'And then?'

'Just close your eyes. Pretend to be asleep.'

Primavera, signing off, left my head crackling with an anxious static. After a few minutes I heard the creak of a chair and a surreptitious shuffle of footsteps. Peeping through half-shuttered eyes, I watched the guard kneel before Primavera's couch, take a securicard from his wallet, and enter it into the gleaming zone that swaddled her waist and loins. The contraption released its grip, and the guard laid it circumspectly upon the floor. Breathing heavily, he let a hand slip beneath the wisp of black lace that barely covered her pubis. There was a snapping of teeth; a gasp. The guard pulled back his hand and stared at it, hurt and puzzled. The top of his middle finger was missing. Small pathetic noises gave notice of his scream. Before he could summon it to his lips, Primavera delivered a jack-hammer of a left hook, and he somersaulted across the room in a graceless confusion of arms and legs.

'My first telepathic seduction,' said Primavera, tearing off her muzzle. 'Talk about *allure!*' The marine lay in a corner imitating a trampled insect. I gave him ten out of ten.

Primavera rolled off her couch and stood up unsteadily, slim adolescent legs wobbling like a newly-born colt's. I was staring at the dead marine.

'You know I don't let anyone inside my pants except *you*, Iggy.'

'Just get us out of here.'

'Well, pardon *me*. So *sorry*. I keep forgetting how *sensitive* you are.'

She put her ear to the wall; then, removing an evening glove, glided her hand over the plaster, and . . . Disappointment seized her face; whatever was supposed to have happened – events in the quantum world finding no interface with the classical – hadn't. She kicked the 'chastity belt' across the floor.

'Magic dust. That thing was full of tin microbes; there must be some left inside me.' She gripped her abdomen. 'Yeah, I can feel them: lots of little nanobots. They're fucking up my matrix.' Again, she put her ear to the wall.

48

'I can't use my hocus pocus, Iggy. This is going to wake the babies.'

Etching a small cross into the plaster with her fingernail, she closed her eyes, drew back her head, and furiously butted her target. The building shook, and Primavera disappeared behind a veil of atomized ferroconcrete. '*Shit!*' she yelled. 'My fucking *skull!*' In the corridor: screamed orders, the whine of walkie-talkies, the click-clack of safety catches disengaged. The dust cleared; a man-sized hole gaped in the embassy's masonry.

I got to my feet, my legs stiff and cumbersome.

'Help me out of this,' said Primavera. I unzipped her dress; filleted, it fell wriggling to the floor with the sound of raw steak hitting a gridiron.

'You're hurt,' I said. A purple weal was blossoming on her forehead.

'*Stupid!* I'm a doll. My important bits are all down *there*.' The door began to melt. 'You want to hang around and say goodbye?'

Taking my hand, she jumped.

We fell through the hot night and hit the stagnant water of a *klong*. I kicked my feet, intent on resurfacing; but Primavera, cleaving to me like a wicked mermaid, seemed equally intent that I should not. I opened my eyes; the water stung them; I screwed them shut, retreating into blindness. I had seen only Primavera's face, lit by its two green lanterns; the dim play of torchlight through the depths. I began to struggle; Primavera put her arms about my neck and I felt her lips on my own. She blew, and oxygen filled my lungs. As we touched bottom, Primavera loosed her hold, leading me across a scrapmetal jungle, stopping only to refresh my lungs with kisses that, for so many, had proved *de luxe* and noxious.

When our heads breached the surface we found our-selves in a narrow *soi* leading to the Sukumvit Road. The green light of a million-pixel Coca-Cola sign lit the water;

a taxi floated nearby. Dragging me by the collar, Primavera swam to the little boat's side. It was empty. We pulled ourselves aboard and lay, exhausted, staring up at the dawn-fractured clouds. It still rained, but the storm had passed.

'I think,' said Primavera, 'I think I know why she did it.'

'Kito?' I said. 'Money, of course. No honour amongst dolls.'

Primavera shook her head. 'The Americans have got something on her. At least she thinks they have, but – ' Primavera gave a short scream and doubled over, clutching her belly. 'She's the only person who can help me, Iggy.' She spoke through gritted fangs. 'These nanomachines: they're turning me into a demolition site. They're taking me to bits.' She held her breath, and then released it in a long sigh of pleasure. I put my hand on the pale flesh below the suspender belt.

'It hurts that bad?'

'It's faecal, Iggy. Really faecal.' She lay back. Mascara ran down her cheeks in a delta of black tears. 'Some of the best nanoengineers in Bangkok work for Kito. And she's got all these laboratories, all this *stuff*.'

'You're crazy. She betrayed us.'

'They blackmailed her, Iggy, and I think I know how. It's something I heard. At the embassy. In my mind. Something I dreamed. If I can prove to Kito that she's got nothing to fear . . .'

I leaned over the gunwale and voided what remained of the Mickey. The streets were coming to life. Food stalls were opening for business. A column of monks passed by, collecting alms. I checked my money belt; my electric baht were intact.

'We've got to hide,' I said, 'clean up, get some clothes. Then we'll talk. Sensibly.' I crawled to the stern and lowered the boat's long rotor arm into the water. The outboard had been modified to guzzle synthetic gasoline. (Filthier, said those who remembered, than the real thing, the gas – banned by the West – was another of Bangkok's lucrative black market industries.) I treated the engine to a little mechanical foreplay until, at last, it growled a response. We drew away, trailing black smoke, black foam.

We entered the big waterway of Sukumvit with Nana behind us, her lights winking out with the arrival of the day. The scent of spent passion, the sharp bouquet of sex, lingered in the air, the smells of a thousand bars mixing with those of a thousand cars. The Bangkok rush hour was in its early morning heat. My clothes began to steam; Primavera hid her face from the sun. The city was warming up its daytime stew of smog; simmering, the smog rose past my ankles like some second-rate special effect. As a sop to the European Parliament the Thai government had proscribed environmental nanoware. It was good public relations: it placated some of the West's fears (Europe had outlawed all nanoware at the outbreak of the doll-plague); it only affected the poor (the kingdom's rich lived in high-rise air-filtered condos); and left untouched the huge underground nanoindustry upon which much of Bangkok's wealth was based.

Cowboy, the Triad-controlled pornocracy that was Nana's chief rival – Primavera had offed Terminal Wipes, its Red Cudgel, last year – fell to the black cloud of our exhaust. From a skywalk a banner proclaimed *Welcome to Fun City*. No more wars. Just squabbles, big and small, over the turf of artificial realities. Fun was the world's universal currency. Primavera had killed for it. Who wouldn't? That's life. (That's death.) That's entertainment.

I turned into a *soi*, narrowly avoiding a Toyota Duck, and then into a short-time hotel called the *Lucky*. The attendants, seeing us approach, swept back the curtains that partitioned one of several parking spaces; we entered, and the curtains swung shut. A little quay surrounded us; in one corner, the door to our room. I fed some baht into a nearby teller. A short-time hotel – a house of assignation for adulterers – would, with its concern for discretion and anonymity, provide a temporary bolt hole. We disembarked.

CHAPTER FIVE

Shopping and Fucking

Primavera peeled off her stockings and underwear and skipped into the shower; when she emerged it was to take some baht from my money belt, turn the pages of the TV, and shop. 'I'll order for you,' she said, as I dashed into the bathroom. The stench of the *klong* had become intolerable.

I was still showering when *Daimaru*'s Zen bullet service delivered our goods. Re-entering the bedroom I was confronted by a candy-coloured assortment of boxes, wrappers and parcels, the living contents of which had been slopped onto the floor. Shivering, their raw nerves exposed, the clothes seemed to plead to be worn and so be put out of their misery. I kicked them aside.

'Real girlygirl, no?' said Primavera. 'What do you think?' She was holding a pink top and skirtlet against her nakedness and appraising herself in a mirror.

'I think I'm bankrupt.'

'As if you ever used a bank. As if they'd ever let you. There's life in your card. Just. Human boys *worry* so.'

She let her clothes slip; momentarily, they pawed at her ankles. The room grew cold; again I was drugged. And this time the Mickey was Primavera's. Call it psionics. Doll pheromones. Her allure was in the air, an ultrasonic whistle, and my hormones responded with a *yap*! Irresistible, that siren call.

Was she beautiful? No; like all her kind she possessed, not beauty, but the overripe prettiness that is the saccharine curse of dollhood. Beauty has soul. Beauty has resonance. But a doll is a thing of surface and plane. Clothes, make-up, behavioural characteristics, resolve, for her,

53

into an identity that is all gesture, nuance, signs. She has no psychology, no inner self, no metaphysical depths. She is the glory, the sheen of her exterior, the hard brittle sum of her parts. She is the ghost in the looking glass, the mirage that, reaching out to touch, we find is nothing but rippling air. She is image without substance, a fractal receding into infinity, a reflection without source and without end.

She is her allure.

Primavera's eyes misted. 'I can read your mind, Iggy. Have you really always felt like that? *Always?* But it's the truth: I don't have a soul. I'm Lilim, a daughter of Lilith.' She sat down on the bed, her back to me, and began fumbling with lipstick, blusher and eyeshadow. Long orientalized fingernails clattered like the sword play of miniature samurai as her tiny hands reapplied her mask. Working with a desperate vigour – 'What you see,' she was saying, 'is what you get, is what I *am*' – her face was soon coated with its varnish of inviolable chocolate-box prettiness.

'Look at me,' I said.

Sad clown of desire, she had tried to drown herself beneath a flash flood of artificiality. Her eyes wore aureoles of peppermint green, and the sliced pomegranate of her lips matched the rouged circles that emphasized her round toytown cheekbones. The skin was bleached, her war wound – the purple badge of courage on her brow – powdered with a camouflage that blended with her sickly complexion.

'Primavera, I – '

'Who wants to be human anyway? What's so great about being human? I'm glad I'm a doll. I don't care if I *am* going to die. I believe in everything Titania told us.'

I sat down by her side. 'I'm sorry I ran away,' I said. 'It's because I don't want to be like them. The Human Front. And – and all the others.' I stared at the floor.

'Sometimes I'm ashamed to be human. What we do. What we feel. I want to love you, Primavera. I've always wanted to love you.'

'But the blood gets in the way?' she said. 'I know, Iggy, it's like that for me too. We're the same: we want to love, but we love the blood more. The pain. The humiliations. All the deaths, big and little.'

'I wasn't running away from *you*,' I said. I put my hand on her thigh. 'If you could let me . . .' My throat tightened. 'Don't you remember? In Calais. Don't you remember what you said? What you almost said . . .'

She regarded me with uncharacteristic shyness. 'Fuck off,' she said softly, beseechingly.

'I believe in Titania too. I'm on your side. I don't like humans, I like – '

Primavera put a finger to my lips, her nose wrinkling in an allergy of indecision. 'You're right,' she said, 'humans stink.' She grabbed the towel that I had used as an improvised sarong. 'Sometimes, Iggy, you're so full of shit. I know I can't love: I'm a doll. But you're a doll junkie: you can't love either.' She jerked the towel from my waist. 'You think you like dolls. But I know what you like.' She picked up the remote and shut the endlessly turning pages of the TV.

'Let's play,' she said, standing. Wading through her newly-bought clothes she soon came upon our playhouse's key prop. I secured her hands behind her back; she turned round, pressed herself against me.

'Bastard,' she whispered. 'Boy-slime. Hypocrite. Prig. You think you're better than the others, don't you? Better than the Human Front. The medicine-heads. But I know what you like. Oh yes, Iggy, I *know* . . .'

Her teeth scratched at my ear, and the thick pulse of her clockwork heart beat against my own. Her plasticky flesh warmed, grew tacky, its illusion of soft wantonness betrayed only by the rib-cage, hard as vat-grown steel, adhering to my solar plexus and imprinting its decal of black and blue. Breathless, I ran my hand down her hair, the crenellations of her spine, to settle upon her sacrum, the small trephination of which – its concavity hidden beneath an epidermic seal – I teased with my knuckles. She wriggled with disgust.

'Tell me,' I said, 'tell me what I like.' Her tongue, rough as a cat's, scoured my tympanic membrane.

'You like what all boys like . . .' She was broadcasting directly into my head. 'You like the sound of torn silk. Flesh on cold marble. All the *no sir, please sir, no sirs . . .*'

I pulled her head back and kissed her. She drew my tongue from my mouth as if it were a bloated leech, her teeth piercing it; and then she drew the blood.

Her saliva hit a mainline. The rush brought me to my knees.

'Bitch,' I tried to say; but my mouth had filled. I haemorrhaged onto the floor. Jumping up, I lashed out with my foot. Primavera fell, broke from her bonds, clawed at me with razor-tipped fingers. Taking her by the hair, I dragged her onto the bed.

'Dead girl. Lilim,' I said, each syllable spraying blood. I collapsed and my wounds turned the counterpane scarlet.

'You b-bastard. You fucking *boy-slime!*'

'*Robotnik!*' My words had become little more than gurgles. I sat up. 'I've got to do something about this,' I said with the voice of a half-drowned man. 'Maybe you should get a doctor.'

Between Primavera's depilated thighs her labia opened with the terrible grin of a prehistoric fish. The *vagina dentata* gnashed and snapped.

'But we've not finished *playing* doctors yet,' she said.

Her other lips turned back and the ice picks that were her canines entered my flesh a millimetre above the left nipple. Saliva and blood ran down my chest in a rivulet of sarsaparilla.

Night fell. We were speeding through the graveyard of the world, crashing over rocks and bones. Her kiss was death, of the future and of the past; all dissolved, all promised to cease. But desire carried us beyond the grave. The night was ours.

Lightning . . .

The dead shook their fists; we felled them like skittles, breaking them beneath our wheels. 'Oh?' said Primavera. 'Did I *hurt* you? Did I *hurt* you? Did I . . .'

Thunder boomed; the coach sped on. Into darkness, rain and sleep.

Spreadeagled on the bed, I observed myself in the ceiling mirror as Primavera applied sticky plaster and lint to my wounds. After satisfying her thirst, she had rung room service and ordered – in addition to other pharmaceuticals – a cauterizing agent for my tongue.

I raised myself by my elbows, dropped ice in my Singha, and cooled my mouth's fire. About us were the remnants of our lunch: bowls of noodles, a plate of lightly fried grasshoppers (bite their heads off, suck their juices, Primavera had advised), and a cuttlefish soup spiced with rat-shit chilli that had spread over the thinly carpeted floor. Magazines and comics that Primavera had ordered over the fax sopped up the carnage.

'Don't move,' she said, 'this is the last one.' She smoothed the plaster into place. 'There. All better!'

'That was quite a party.'

'We party too much. Some day it'll all go *too* far.' She lit a cigarette, inhaled a mouthful of smoke, gargled with it, then expectorated a grey-blue plume into the air. 'But if my programme won't allow me to love you, Iggy, at least I can love your blood. It's so delirious. It's so . . .' Above, the mirror held us like malignancies trapped within a specimen slide as Primavera sought a superlative; but a doll's appetites are untranslatable; she sighed, and drew a fingernail across her left breast. 'I lost my brooch. In the restaurant. In the fight.'

'I'll get you another.'

'It was special.' She put the cigarette between my lips. 'Iggy, before they catch us – *if* they catch us – promise: you'll kill me, won't you?'

I studied her in the mirror. What kind of life was she? Dead girls, they called them. Sets of formal rules, without free will. Imitations of life. Souldrained. To destroy such ones was not murder, they said. But if Primavera died, then I knew I would die too. I lived in the nothingness at her heart, my life mortgaged to her allure.

'You could do it,' she said, in her little girl's lisp, 'you know, the way you want. I'd buy you a scalpel. Just like the one you had in England. You could – '

She was inside my mind; she turned to me and frowned. 'Why?'

'I just can't, that's all.'

'Junkie.' She sneered. 'What's the matter – scared? You're not going to live much longer than me anyway.' I replaced the cigarette in her mouth, shutting her up.

'This business,' I said, 'about seeing Kito. Why don't we try to get help from one of the other pornocracies: Cowboy, Patpong or Suriwongse? They all employ nano-engineers.'

'Iggy, sometimes you're like a little child. I've offed people in all those places. We can't risk it.'

'But you're willing to risk walking into Nana? Kito never liked you, Primavera, and she likes you even less now.'

'Kito will help. I know it.'

'How?'

'Easy,' she said, snapping her fingers, 'we tell her about Titania!'

I picked up the remote. 'I don't want to hear any more.' Deselecting the shopping channel, I surfed the phosphor-dot sea from World News (something about an African famine) to the latest Thai ghost movie, *Phi Gaseu* 26; from an interactive game show (win your own dreamscaper) to a francophone channel called *Alliance Française* (the world still Frenchified in its tastes, despite the demise of the world's fashion capital). *Alliance* was running *Trans Europe Express*, a colour-dubbed piece of Old Wave shit. But what was this? Some *louche*-looking guy tying a woman to a bed. I turned up the sound . . .

Primavera snatched the remote and killed the transmission. 'Titania wouldn't mind.'

Primavera, Primavera, Primavera Oh! Did you really think that *I* minded. About your crazy porcelain queen? I cared only that you cared. For that rabid vision. For everything she had said that made you walk tall. To have betrayed Titania would have been to betray you.

'What do you think all this *ordure* has been about?' I said. 'The HF are on to Titania. They want to know how we escaped.' Primavera slammed her fist into the mattress. 'We don't tell anybody about Titania. She saved our lives. If it hadn't been for her you would have gone to the slab.'

'I didn't know,' said Primavera. 'You should have told me. I just wanted to tell Kito that it wasn't *her* that started the doll-plague. That's how the Americans frightened her, don't you see? It's how they blackmailed her. And we know the truth.'

'What's Kito got to do with the doll-plague?'

A sharp intake of breath; Primavera ran to the bathroom. I followed and discovered her kneeling before the *suam* and vomiting blood.

'Don't worry,' she said, 'it's yours. But something's going wrong. Inside.' I helped her to her feet and half carried her back to the bedroom.

'Close your eyes,' I said. 'Sleep.'

'No!' She staggered to the dressing table. 'I have to see Kito. I have to get her help. I won't tell her too much. I won't betray Titania.' She picked up the dismay of my thoughts. 'You stay here. Human boys can be such . . . such *scaredy cats*.'

'Let me get you to a hospital.'

'Don't mention the word 'hospital' to *me*.'

'I just thought – '

'Don't be a pin.'

She took a hypodermic from the dresser and filled it with *Virgin Martyr*. Hypo and scent bottle – the bottle, black and engraved with the image of a crucified girl – trembled in her hands, like the sceptre and orb of an olfactory queen with delirium tremens. She injected, and her eyes revolved, white as two boiled eggs.

'Ahh,' she sighed, 'that smells so good.' The hit subsided and she began to comb her hair. 'If Kito won't cooperate,' she said, 'I'll kill her. It's simple. But it won't come to that.'

'Why . . .' I said; a dying fall. Why had I come back, why was I her slave? I knew the answer. So, it seemed, did the photo-mechanical above the bed. She laughed, mockingly. They were like that, those starlets. A hacker had introduced a bug into their two-dimensional world that was designed to make you feel small. Human melancholy activated it. Some prank. I took the poster from its hook. Wafer thin, it tore easily; the paper dolly ducked. I tore again, and she retreated to the poster's margin.

Ignatz the slave. Ignatz always back returning. Why? Why? Because a junkie always runs away; always comes back. That's the way it is with junkies.

Primavera giggled in triumph. 'Because I'm the *dolliest*. Isn't that right,' she said addressing the mirror, 'aren't I just the dolliest of them all?'

The photo-mechanical, with the aid of a half-torn mechanical octopus that had been her 2-D friend, switched her pose from soft to hardcore, pouting with sexual defiance. I tore her in two; what was left of the poster fibrillated with her scream.

'Leave that poor photo-mechanical alone,' said Primavera. 'Hooligan. You're as bad as Mr Jinx.'

'Then it's true what they say . . . ?' I scrunched up the poster, tossed it in the trashcan, and knelt down to inspect Primavera's purchases. Clothes slithered through my hands, their fibres insinuating themselves into my pores with sartorial flirtatiousness.

'Dermaplastic,' I said, extricating a soggy pair of trousers. 'Why couldn't you get me something normal? Something *ordinary*?'

'If you *are* coming,' she said, 'here . . .' She handed me an aerosol. 'Spray me. I can collect the other stuff when we're through with Madame.'

She moved to the centre of the room and held her arms and legs in a St Andrew's cross. I shook the can. When I had finished, her body, with the exception of the ghost-white face, was coated in a patina of glossy black gelatine.

'How soon will that dry?' I said.

'Almost ready. It's the latest. Oo! There – its nerve endings are coming alive!'

To complete her ensemble she stepped into crippling stilettos and clipped gold rings to her nipples and clitoris. I took longer to dress, queasy at wrapping myself in what felt like someone else's skin.

We pigged out on TV until late evening (Primavera almost won a dreamscaper); then, leaving behind a chaos of half-eaten food, used bandages, broken glass, cigarette butts, syringes, blood-stained sheets and teeth, we slipped out, ready to retake the night.

CHAPTER SIX

Going to A-Go-Go

'Like I said, what's Kito got to do with the doll-plague?'

We were on the skytrain, Nana-bound. I had my panama pulled over my eyes, fearful of recognition (we were only two stops from Kito's lair); but Primavera bathed in the furtive glances of every voyeur aboard.

'Don't you know what they're thinking? Another dermatoid junkie, that's what, another "skinny" addicted to artificial flesh.'

'Of course I know what they're thinking, *stupid*!' Her broadcast jammed my amateur wavelength. 'What do I care? They're all robofuckers anyway. Bipedal phalloi, Madame calls them. And you're a fine one to call me junkie.'

'Yeah, well what if someone in this crowd identifies us?'

As a concession she reached into her shoulder bag and donned a pair of widow-black shades. Then, shaking out her hair (a weekly investment in a bottle of hair dye had, for three years, provided her sole disguise; contact lenses? no, no, not her), she turned her back on the skytrain's throng and gazed out into the night. Her feral teeth worried at a hunk of gum.

'So?' I thought. 'Kito – doll-plague; doll-plague – Kito. What's it all about?'

Below, the Big Weird sparkled like a fathomless black pond infested with a million phosphorescent water lilies: corporations, banks, hotels, condos, that Buddha – in the shape of a million giant holograms – guarded and preserved. The monorail, visible as it snaked round a bend, was almost over Nana.

'Well?'

Primavera's eyes had glazed. She was staring into the distance, where the needle-like tower of the Siamese Space Agency pointed a covetous finger at the sky.

Unreal. A reflection. A shadow cast by nothingness. As if I care. I'm a vanity of vanities. Proud. Monstrous. Without shame. I'm talking to you, Dr B. Where are you now? Still got your head between some little girl's thighs? Still playing the Pied Piper? Blue Mondays at the clinic. Mid-menarche in mid-March. It's cold. Wet. And I'm thirsty. How are we today? Dying, Dr B. Dying into the new. My flesh's like nougat. My brain's like hubbly-bubbly. And I see things, you know? Crazy things. Like corridors. Corridors lined with doors. Endless, endless. Mirrors seething within mirrors. And behind each door, behind each mirror, another world. Another time. Primavera, you know you mustn't open those doors? Yes, doctor. Or break the mirrors? Of course, doctor. And the pills? Every day, doctor. Morning, full moon and night. And the hemline neurosis? Yes, much better, really much better, Dr Bogenbloom . . .

'Well?'

'Sex diseases,' whispered Primavera's mind. 'Madame is a past mistress of sex diseases.'

'She makes them?'

'Not any more. But years ago she fought a lot of trade wars that way. Europe would sabotage her dolls, so she'd cook a virus to sabotage theirs.'

'But that,' I said, a sliver of comprehension jemmying loose my tongue, 'has got nothing to do with the doll-plague.'

'No,' said Primavera, 'that's just the point.'

'*Nana Plaza*,' droned a synthetic voice, '*please alight here for Nana Plaza*.'

'Now be quiet,' said Primavera, 'and follow me.'

Our carriage emptied. We lost ourselves in the crush,

borne along by a scrum of male libertinage (Nana was dick-slobber city; a heterometro): *farangs* mostly, garbed in the tired, emulative threads that the Weird had been producing for more than a hundred years. I picked out accents: American, Australasian, pidgin European . . . A glass escalator – as big and as wide as those staircases in ancient Hollywood musicals – dropped us to the streets. The band struck up, and the streets went into their routine. It was the big number about narcissism, sex and greed: a song Nana knew by heart.

We were in the Plaza, a tiered arena of go-go bars that ascended, circle upon circle, like a neon-lit wedding cake celebrating the marriage of man and doll. The Plaza's upper limits were still developing: steel tanks, seeded with nanoware, were growing next year's bars. From the lowest stratum, conflicting sound systems, in a cacophony of half tones and quarter tones, smeared the brain with white noise. Pungent smell of barbecued squid, open drains, gynoidal pheromones and all-night pharmacies. 'MOLECULAR ROBOTS – HORMONES – GENE SHEARS – CSFs': on-off, on-off, the lights.

They were looking at me. Everybody was looking at me: *farangs*, through steins holding enormous philtres of beer, dolls with gimlet-eyed quid pro quo, holotoys stalking me, hopelessly rubbing themselves against me, that balloon seller trailing his stock of decapitated hydrogen-filled heads. Nana was full of eyes, the eyes of madmen and madwomen. And now the eyes, a market of circles and ellipses, were on fire . . .

Killer visions stormed my ascending nerve tract.

I began to twitch; my right arm was convulsing. My clothes had been seized with a fit.

'Iggy, stop it! This is no time for . . .'

'I can't help it! It's, it's, it's . . .'

Dermaplastic is a somatic textile, a sense amplifier. Microscopic fibres hardwire the material's peripheral nervous system to the wearer's own.

Primavera understood. She reached to the back of my trousers – an area just above the coccyx – and tore away a handful of second skin. The convulsions ceased.

'I got its cortex,' she said, crushing the white plastic until its customized melanin ran through her fingers. 'Bad trip, eh? The electromuscles will relax now. That's the last time I shop by Zen. How do you feel?'

'Like nothing a blood transfusion couldn't cure.'

Nana was bisected by the Sukumvit Road, and we had to take a skywalk to cross the water and reach that farrago of restaurants, tailors, jewellers, surgeries and bars that had been known ever since the *belle époque* as the 'French Quarter'. To this demimonde of cut-price style came the ruined aristocracy of Europe's information elite to pretend to the snobbery they could no longer afford.

'Look,' said Primavera, 'Martian jewels!' She elbowed past two window-shoppers, pressing her nose to the glass. The shop radiated with neo-Lalique confections ostensibly made from the candyfloss rocks of the red planet.

'We don't have time,' I said. 'Besides, you know they're not real.' The man whom Primavera had pushed aside looked at me angrily, then – mumbling something in what sounded like defunct powerhouse German – ushered his female companion away. Their kind were everywhere: Europunks fleeing from reality. Boys and girls looking for their lost toys.

A muggy breeze swept an ankle-deep smog across our path, carbon emissions collecting with methane bubbling from the nearby *klong* (and with other pollutants so novel and so peculiar to the Big Weird that they might have been awarded a conservation order) to form cheapo house of horror atmospherics. A tourist cast a cigarette aside; Primavera and I shied away. A flash; a whoof of combusted air; and the *farang* turned to us, half in apology, half in accusation, his face blackened as if by an exploding cigar.

We headed for the *Grace Hotel*.

In the doorways of *Tin Lizzie*, *Robogirl* and *Kiss and Panic*, mechanettes ran through their repertoires of solicitation. Ridiculous, those creatures (but 'men like their women ridiculous' ran the automaton-nerds' blurb), the phallocentric night tripping their tropismatic switches as they tensed before the scrutiny of the throbbing multitude like bowstrings burdened with arrows of desire. Primavera took my hat and pulled it over her ears, too near, now, to the queen bee to risk identification from her hive of workers. 'It's not the gynoids I worry about,' said Primavera, 'it's the proprietors: all the *farangs* Kito has hanging on her skirts.'

'Like Willy Hofmannsthal?' I said. Hofmannsthal – an old, old man (more android than man), whose body was a patchwork of flesh, steel and plastic riddled with tissue-repairing nanomachines – sat outside his bar, the *Doll Keller*. I steered Primavera to a newspaper stall, bought a magazine (little figures danced across the cover) and employed it as a fan in an attempt at concealment. 'This is too obvious,' I said. 'In here . . .' We entered a *jeux vérités* arcade.

Walking along its length, screams, laughter and other vocal intensities greeted us from each gamester's booth. Maybe they were murdering their mothers, taking over the world, or fucking St Ursula and her 11,000 virgins before wasting them with napalm. Alpha-wave monitors on each door gave notice of those who, in their drugged sleep, had awoken while still in REM to the dreamscaper's martinet urging. Primavera put her hands over her ears. 'Shut up!' she cried. 'Shut up! Shut up!' But the arcade was deaf with reverie.

As we ran out into the streets the *Grace* rose before us, the cosmetic surgery of its *deco*-clad exterior unable to conceal its antique cancers. At its summit, a penthouse: Kito's nest. The eyrie of vanity, spitefulness and deceit.

A small boy with the face of an angel tugged at my leg, looked up at me big-eyed with ingenuousness, and made a little *wai*. 'Please sir, ten baht. Very hungry.'

Primavera's fist crashed into the child's skull. It ran away, circuitry leaking from its left ear. 'Madame really should get rid of those things,' she said.

'So how do we go in?'

'Front door. No heavies. We'll go through the coffee shop.'

'But it'll be packed.'

'So no one will notice.'

Taking me by the arm, Primavera squired me through the portals of Kito's fortress.

'Just like the old days,' she said. I gripped her arm. In fear? To comfort? But what comfort did Primavera need? The vampire had scented blood. It was fear, my fear, that I betrayed. 'Relax,' thought Primavera, 'this is doll business. Go easy. Your job's just to make me seem human.' In embarrassment, I eased my grip.

Smiling at the bellboys, I assumed my role, and escorted my 'sister' (such had been our double act during our sojourn in the Weird) into the coffee shop's *mélange*. A year, two years ago, our act had been so disarming. We'd looked innocent; sweet. But these days – with me like a Photofit of a kid who'd escaped Borstal, and Primavera the image of a teenage parricide – the act was proving thin. Thin indeed.

'I'll take care of you,' I thought, adding over her mental sigh, 'really, I mean it.' She wasn't listening; she was trying to unravel a hundred compacted wavebands that were the babblings of human desire. *Farangs*, dreamy, or dark-faced with self-loathing, were making liaisons mad, bad and egregious with the gynoids crowding the lounge.

We squeezed past dolls nostalgic, zoomorphic, ludic:

67

repros – ball-jointed, porcelain-skinned 'antiques' – proffering brass umbilical keys; a *Felis femella*, whose prehensile tail attempted a tourniquet about my arm; and the cephalopods, zombie dead and see-through Sallies. (For other *jeux d'esprit* the palette of the human body had moved into the realm of abstract expressionism.) There were traditional models of course: clichés of femininity microdressed in doll-couture *tropique*, who, in their Mlle Butterfly sub-tongue, offered standard conveyor-belt sex. But the *Grace*'s clientele had spent too long on that night-shift; jaded, they sought the *frisson* of the new.

'Corpse grinder?' said something that seemed to have fallen from a threshing machine.

'X-ray sex?' asked a translucent Sally.

'Action painting? You want me oil? Gouache? Water-colour?' The doll's flesh began to drip onto the floor.

'Become your trousers?'

'Love suicide?'

'Sunset Boulevard?'

'Do fucky-fucky with knife?'

Several *bijouterie* were in evidence; not the real thing, but converts. For some men, to lie with one whose humanity has been compromised is the mark of the perfect rakehell; and since Thai *bijouterie* were freaks, whose rarity made their favours often impossibly expensive, there was a bull market for village girls for whom mechanization provided the only alternative to poverty. (In Nana there was a bar – *Pretty Girls Are Human Too* – full of such posthuman schismatics.)

'It'll be humans next year,' thought Primavera.

'Yeah?'

'Sure. Everything'll come full circle. Gynoids are going out of fashion. A doll may do the weird on you, but she's got no free will. A trick's got no real power over her. But a human . . . A human you can really humiliate.'

'Is that what it's about?'

'You know it.'

We approached the bar.

A pianist and a singer – doll boys *tutti frutti* to their cybercamp hearts – were performing a cocktail lounge version of 'Oh doctor, doctor, I wish you wouldn't *do* that.'

'That fucking song,' I said.

Primavera's fingers skittered across Formica. 'Hey, Pongpet!' she said, calling the barman. 'Remember me?' She lifted her shades, her eyes flashing as they emerged from eclipse.

'The green death!' The barman stepped back, dropped a Mekong soda, reached out despairingly for a com; but Primavera, her claws hooked into his shirt, had already pulled him flush against the bamboo lintel.

'I don't want to hurt you, Pong,' she said, 'but if I don't get what I want, I'll . . . Well, remember the *last* time you fixed me a Bloody Mary?'

The barman nodded with servile eagerness. I looked around; no other bar staff (no one came here to drink); and the sex talk of machine and man was unabated.

'Madame say you go home, Miss Primavera. For holiday.'

Primavera spat out her gum and secured it to the underlip of the bar. 'Pong, I want you to take us to your kitchens, your stockroom – wherever your dumbwaiter is. And I'm not talking about one of your friends.'

Keeping hold of our press-ganged accomplice, Primavera scissor-jumped the bar; I followed more modestly.

We passed through a beaded curtain and into the coffee shop's kitchen – one of several that the hotel possessed. Primavera had by now stowed her sunglasses in her bag, and the kitchen staff – a boy and girl about our own age – immediately put a table between themselves and the green-eyed fiancée of death. The boy picked up a cleaver.

'*Mai!*' cried his companion. '*Phi see kee-oh! Phi pob!*

69

Phi Angritt! Dtook-gah-dtah Lilim!' Though we shunned the public, preferring to be as shadows amongst shadows, the legend of the green death had become part of the legend of Nana. The boy cast his weapon to the floor.

I bound our captives with a ball of spidersilk that Primavera had produced from her bag, and then gagged them with dishcloths.

'Is that it?' said Primavera, pointing to an aluminium hatchway in the wall.

'Dumbwaiter,' said the barman.

Primavera knocked him cold.

'Get in, Iggy.' She slid back the hatch. 'All these things terminate at the penthouse.'

'We can't both – '

'We can.'

'It's too small.'

'I said we *can*.' Primavera looked down the tiny ski-jump of her nose with minx-like dismissiveness. 'I may be sick,' she said, 'but I can still origami.' Tossing her bag aside, ankles together, legs parallel, knees locked, she fell forward from her waist and curled her arms about her calves, head emerging from between the vice of her thighs. She spasmed, searing the eye with anatomically impossible configurations. In seconds she was rolling across the floor, a black plastic beachball.

I picked her up – staggering at the concentrated mass – and clambered into the dumbwaiter. 'Press the button marked *K*.' Her voice was muffled by the clingwrap of her flesh. 'You'll have to reach outside.' My body, more painfully, if less dramatically contorted than Primavera's, accomplished the feat to a snap, crackle and pop of outraged joints.

The hatch slid shut; in darkness, we ascended.

Broken conversations; the blare of TVs and magazines; and the undertones of passion, bitterness and remorse, slipped by as we passed each floor. Somewhere off that tunnel of lust was the abandoned suite that for three years had sheltered us from retribution. We had never called it home.

'I can feel her,' said Primavera, no longer speaking, but transmitting from deep within her hermitage of flesh. 'She's alone. Unless there are gynoids or androids with her. *Bijouterie* I can read; but machine minds . . .'

With a hiss of air brakes we stopped.

'Are we here?' Her mind rustled with impatience.

I eased back an eye-width of hatch. We were in a kitchen similar to the one in which we had hitched our lift; but here a seven-foot Negro, wearing nothing but the heavy electromusculature of a primitive walking, talking AI, was prissily attending to the evening meal. His fire hose of a member was like a third leg amputated just above the knee.

'Android,' I said subvocally. 'Big one.' I felt Primavera grin inside my head.

'Making dinner?'

'Yeah.'

'That's Mr Bones. He's dangerous. Pull back the door and don't get involved.'

The hatch squealed on its runners; Mr Bones looked up. At once, Primavera dropped into the kitchen and bounced across the floor.

'Lordy,' cried Mr Bones, his nigger-minstrel programme seemingly a leftover from Nana's patriotic S-M revue (pirated from Broadway and premiered before the country's top brass) *The Birth Of A Nation*, 'it de white lady Miss Kito bin tellin' us about!' Primavera, on bouncing off wall, ceiling and work surface, unravelled with a damp whipcrack of limbs in mid-air, to land (tottering a little on her six-inch stilettos) on the table where the giant android had been dicing meat. Mr Bones smoothed a hand across his shaven head.

'De white trash brother too,' he said, as I fell from the

71

dumbwaiter. 'Miss Kito sure gonna be mighty upset!' A huge hand shot out; Primavera hopped to safety.

'Stay back, Iggy,' she said. Kicking off her high heels she sprang upon her opponent. Her feet found purchase on the ledge of his hip bone; her claws made hand-holds in his neck. Hanging as if from some perilous cliff face of obsidian, she bared her teeth and bit. The fangs penetrated his forehead, champing at a red mush of biochips.

Mr Bones danced about the kitchen in a clumsy rendition of a cakewalk, smoke issuing from ears, nostrils and mouth, until, freezing in mid-stride, he collapsed, Primavera riding him to the ground. 'Where,' groaned the android, 'are all de white women . . . ?' The brain box combusted in a flash of sparks.

'He tasted really *faecal*.' Primavera spat onto the floor. I ripped an extinguisher from a wall and gave Mr Bones a dousing.

'Somebody must have heard that,' I said.

'No; Kito's in her bedroom, and if other automata are around they're likely to be gynoids. They're not programmed for security. They might hear, but they won't care.'

'Pikadons?'

'I can't feel them. There are some guards – human guards – in the corridor outside. But I know where all the cameras are; and there'll be no closed circuit in Madame's *boudoir*.'

Primavera led me through the apartment's blind spots. A children's game, it seemed, as we ducked behind sofas, crawled behind curtains, and shuffled beneath tiger skins and Persian rugs. The lights were out; but Primavera's night vision allowed us to negotiate the obstacles with ease.

We stood outside Kito's bedroom. Primavera placed her hand on the doorknob; turned. Darkness. Primavera was past me, leaping into the void, her cat's eyes like green kryptonite streaking to Earth as she described a trajectory calculated to bring her prey to ground.

Lights.

Primavera screamed. She knelt on a heart-shaped bed and in her hands wriggled a python-sized millipede. She threw it across the room. It was *Kuhn Yow*, one of Kito's bioengineered pets. On Sundays, Kito would walk through Lumpini Park, *Kuhn Yow* trailing on a long pink leash, his bejewelled chitin scintillating in the sun.

Kito made a sarcastic *wai*. 'Good evening, children.' Replicas of Mr Bones – five in all – surrounded the bed. Each held a particle weapon. Kito tightened the sash of her peignoir and indicated that I should join Primavera. I was thinking, Well done. Thanks. I *told* you that . . . Primavera silenced me by throwing the mental equivalent of a glass of iced water in my face. Her tongue ran over her fangs; and her eyes – like those of a decadent Byzantine princess – appraised the virility of Kito's mechanical slaves. She was ready to rumble.

'I know what you think, *bijouterie*,' said Kito. 'You down one of my six-pack, only five to go. But move and I scramble your womb.'

'It's scrambled already. Cervix, ovaries, Fallopian tubes. You name it. The works. I'm sick, Madame.'

'This I know long time: so girlygirl, but – ' and Kito raised an eyebrow – 'so sick.'

'I mean *really* sick. Ill. Unwell. I didn't come here to hurt you.'

Kito took *Kuhn Yow* into her arms. She cuffed it; its mandibles were nipping at her breast. 'You come here to give present? Say goodbye? Eat rice?' Cheek pressed to the exoskeleton of her disgusting pet, Kito paced back and forth, taking care to stay behind her phalanx of electric blackamoors. 'Mr Jack tell me you get loose. Why you come here? Crazy. *Pasad!* Kito have many eye: TV, photo-mechanical, human . . .'

'Of course,' I began, 'Madame is a lady of dark influence. A godmother. A *chao mae* who . . .'

'Shut up, stupid boy.'

'Yeah, Iggy. Don't be so creepy.'

'Well?' said Kito. 'Why come here? You want go England so bad?'

'You still make sex diseases, Madame?' said Primavera.

Kito ceased her pacing. 'Tell you before, I stop all that after trade war with Cartier. Forty year ago . . .'

'Madame,' said Primavera, 'I know why you turned us in. I know – '

'You know *nothing*,' said Kito, 'half-doll *Angritt*. You *are* disease!'

'Yeah, well at least my Mum wasn't *roboto*.'

'Don't call *me* roboto, you little tramp!'

The exchange died. In green-eyed perplexity the two women faced off, lips feinting insults that were never thrown.

'Jack Morgenstern,' said Primavera, swallowing her gall, 'he told you that you were responsible for the doll-plague, didn't he?'

Kito blanched, her complexion achieving the pallor of a full moon on a winter's night. *Kuhn Yow* slithered to the floor.

'*Klong fever*,' continued Primavera. 'Didn't he say that's how it all began? Forty years ago Cartier Paris – getting pretty tired with the way people like you were flooding the market with imitation dolls – cooked a virus that could bridge the hardware-wetware divide. A bug that could be transmitted from machine to man. Cartier stole some of your dolls, your imitation Cartier; infected them; then returned them to the Weird. The bug was an STD, but it was also ethnically selective. It was turned on by genes peculiar to oriental DNA. *Klong fever*, the Thais called it. It made men impotent. Sort of long-term genocide *à la beau monde*. Nobody suspected the source of the virus; dolls are supposed to be disease-free. Nobody, that is, except you. You chose to retaliate. You cooked your own virus. Had it taken to Paris to infect *their* dolls. It was supposed to induce priapism, which I suppose you, Madame (you are *so* predictable), thought you could exploit. But according to Jack Morgenstern things didn't quite work out that way . . .'

'How you *know* this?' said Kito.

'About twenty-four hours ago,' said Primavera, 'I became telepathic. It's tasty. When they had me and Iggy in the embassy I dreamed . . . I dreamed of Jack Morgenstern. And I dreamed of you. Morgenstern was saying that there was no place on Earth you could hide if it got known that you started the doll-plague.'

Kito pulled a transcom from her peignoir. 'The sooner they get you back England . . .' She began punching numbers.

'Except you didn't,' said Primavera, looking at her nails.

'*American Embassy*,' piped a voice over the ISDN.

'Let me have the duty officer,' said Kito. She cupped her hand over the mouthpiece. 'What you mean?'

'I know who started the plague, Madame. And it wasn't you.'

'*May I ask what it's in connection with?*'

'Put the com away. They don't have anything on you.' Kito frowned; hesitated. 'I can *prove* it.' The com died; Kito replaced it within the folds of her gown.

'I waiting,' said Kito.

'First,' said Primavera, 'you're going to have to get me cleaned up. I've been dusted.'

'No,' said Kito. 'You forget I in trouble too. With *America*. So tell me about doll-plague. What you know?'

'Madame,' said Primavera, getting to her feet; her software cousin withdrew behind Mr Bones, one through five. 'I'm sick. Really. You've got to help. In fact even now . . .' The black phalanx closed ranks.

'More reason,' said Kito, 'to do as I say. Then – *maybe*. We see.'

Primavera flopped down and lay her head in my lap. 'I'm so tired, Madame. So tired. But I'll try. I have to tell you about Iggy and me. How we got out of London. I have to tell you about Titania . . .'

CHAPTER SEVEN

Westward Ho

In the antechamber several young girls await execution. The girls, seated upon a curvilinear bench that follows the contour of the walls (one can almost feel the bench transfusing its coldness through their thin diaphanous shifts), have their eyes fixed, with dark surmise, upon the man who is walking through the door. Pupils shrink from the superfluity of light into pinpricks; lips quiver; there is a rattling of chains. The man takes a ballpoint pen from his clipboard and, making a cursory tick, assists the night's first victim to her feet . . .

'It's no use,' said Dad. He had just returned from the roof. 'Doesn't matter where I point that dish, all we get is BBC.'

The girl is led down a long corridor littered with wheel-chairs and stretchers. The white light is unbearable . . .

'From A to Z,' said Dad, 'from Z to A. So it will go on. Unending.' Dad put the TV to sleep. My veins clotted with anger; my heart clenched. 'Nothing for a child's eyes.'

'It's late anyway,' said Mum. 'Who'd like some Oval-tine?'

I shook my head. 'I think I'll go upstairs.'

'You haven't done your French yet,' said Dad.

'I've got a headache.'

'It's only for half an hour.'

Mum put her sewing to one side. 'You should really teach him what it means. Ignatz finds it all so boring. All he knows are the bad words the other boys use.' She left the room and went into the kitchen.

'Half an hour,' said Dad. 'Just to get me started.' He

began to lower himself into the dreamscaper. A primitive model, the dreamscaper resembled a large water tank and hogged a sizeable portion of our lounge. It had taken Dad five years to pay for it. He still couldn't afford the software. (His black market creditors were browbeating him; once again, we queued at the co-op.)

Dad sealed himself inside. 'Are you ready?' he said.

I selected the *Pléiade* edition of *À la Recherche du Temps Perdu* from Dad's autodidactic shelves. At first, before Dad had taught me to pronounce written French (no time, he'd said, for grammar or semantics) I had gone through the collected works of Charles Dickens. But Dad said that it was the past that he wanted; the world of Dickens was too much like our own. The English, Dad said, were reverting to type; John Bull growled with atavistic savagery.

What was Dad doing? He was quiet. Desperately quiet. 'You got the catheter fixed?' I said. 'And the autocerebroscope?'

'Give it five minutes, then start reading.'

I waited, scanning the incomprehensible pages. The book was something to do with the *belle époque* (a different one, I learned later, than the one Dad used to talk about); something about regaining lost time. *My time machine*, Dad called his dreamscaper.

'*Longtemps* . . .' I murmured.

'Not yet. I'm not in REM. Keep your eyes on the alphawave monitor.'

Time. The melancholy of memory and lost time. *Have You Seen These Girls?* asked the posters at street corners, Primavera's face amongst the wanted. Night-times, on the roof of the tower block, I had focused my telescope on the streets, on houses, on deserted faraway warehouses and factories, on anything that might have served as a hideaway for a doll. But the distances framed only the drones making their nightly supply drops from across the interdiction.

That summer had been wrought of gold. Her eyes. Her hair. Her lips. Her teeth. The golden ecstasy of her venom. But now summer had come to an end. All was lost, as Primavera was lost: to the world's baseness.

'The dolls who run away,' I said, 'do they ever get far?'

'What?'

'The dolls who run away.'

'Not now, Ignatz.'

Dreams. Maybe they were the only escape. Software dreams you could walk into as you would your own brain (or, in Dad's case, wordware dreams, realtime and analgesic). I checked Dad's alpha waves. Soon, I would begin my recital, downloading what to me might as well have been machine code into a trough for Dad's dream-hungry head. I was hungry too; Primavera had been missing for a week; I was going into withdrawal.

'*Longtemps . . .* '

After thirty minutes I left Dad to his oneironautical explorations and retired to my room.

That night I too seemed to wake in the midst of dreams. Primavera was outside the tower, twenty floors above the street, her nightdress billowing in the midnight breeze, and she was tap-tap-tapping against the window. I somnambulated across the bedroom and let her in.

'Shit, that was some climb – just look at my nails, just look at my cuticles!' She slapped me across the face. 'Wake up, pinhead!' I crossed the dividing line between sleep and consciousness to find that nothing had changed. 'Every day, in every way, I get a little bit dollier.'

I wanted to switch on the light; she caught my wrist. The amoral flippancy that animated her brittle face had drained away; she was again a child, a twelve-year-old whose brittleness was that of human vulnerability rather than that of porcelain.

79

'I'm cold,' she said. I put my arms about her. 'I ran away at night. I don't have any clothes.'

In her white nightdress Primavera seemed the incarnation of those bubble-gum cards we swapped in school: No. 52, *Carmilla*. An underage Carmilla. Carmilla's kid sister, perhaps. I ran my hand down her spine to where the sacrum had been trephinated to allow passage of the *tzepa*.

'Where have you been?'

'The cricket pavilion.'

'The whole week?' I could feel her bones through her flesh; what had she been living on? 'You should have come to me. I can hide you.'

'Hiding's no good. I've got to get away. You'll help me, Iggy, won't you?' I tightened my grip about her waist and went to kiss her; she turned away, transfixing the TV with a cold, serpentine stare. 'On,' she said. The TV woke. 'Tasty trick, eh?' A broken fingernail snagged in my pyjamas. 'But how can they *do* this?'

A great circular chamber; three black marble slabs; and on each slab . . . The pictures flickered across my bedroom walls like the projections of an infernal magic lantern.

'That one there,' said Primavera, as the camera closed in to catch a subtle delineation of pain on a pale adolescent face. 'That's Anna Belushi! My God, I *know* her!' The gentlemen of the English press mobbed the dying girl: stage-door Johnnies fêting the star of death's chorus line.

'*Miss Belushi, what do you think of the HF's success?*'

'*Are your mother and father watching tonight, Miss Belushi?*'

'*Miss Belushi, how about a scream for the viewers at home?*'

Flash bulbs exploded as Anna Belushi obliged.

'She ain't *got* no Dad,' said Primavera. 'Her Mum had

her at fourteen. Her Dad died a few years later, junked up on allure.' I pressed my finger into the small indentation at the base of Primavera's spine. 'Please,' she whispered. 'Don't.' I turned the TV off.

'There's nowhere to run,' I said.

'There has to be.' Her voice was an earnest tremolo. 'Lots of dolls run away. They don't find them all.'

'There's only the city. Central London. We'd be hunted down.'

She slipped the nightdress off her shoulders and let it fall to the floor. She pressed herself against me, her body's chill filtering through my pyjamas and into my muscles and veins. She took my hand and placed it on her abdomen.

'It's yours, Iggy. Prime sirloin. I give it to you.' I felt the precious throb of the abdominal aorta locked safely within its casket of mutating flesh. 'Don't throw it away. It's something to be cherished. A box of magic. A box of tricks. Everything's there. Everything in the universe. Everything that's happening. Everything that *can* happen. Look after it and it'll look after you.' She nuzzled my chest. 'Now,' she said, 'make a wish.'

'Escape,' I said.

'That was easy, wasn't it? And you still have two wishes left.'

'You know I love you.'

'You hate me,' she whispered. I felt the scratch of her fangs. 'You want me to dirty up your genes a little more?'

'Not here,' I said. 'Mum and Dad . . .'

When she had finished I took her to the roof and left her to sleep in an old pigeon coop beneath an eiderdown of canvas and straw. I returned to my room and turned on the TV. The only way to kill vampires, said the HF. Why didn't they run? They were Lilim. Nutcrackers. Why didn't they fight? Death's chorus line moonlighted in pornographic movies, bit-part actresses passively colluding in their own obscene deaths. I noted their performances, the slippery agitation of their thighs, the pelvic frenzy of their transfixed equators. I watched the red puddles swell about the ungirt hips, heard the complaints that death was too long coming. Surely I was becoming a connoisseur, an aficionado, to perceive (though not penetrate) even then, the conspiratorial mystery of those transmissions, a perception boys like Myshkin, I knew, could not share. How could they? Before the broken loveliness that filled our screens they could only bray, spit and pick their noses, reviling and cheapening the ache of their own flesh as much as the agony of their compliant sisters.

Sisters, poor sisters, sisters, why weren't you all like Primavera?

Monday through Friday I had sat behind an empty desk; on the Friday, the day Primavera was later to climb *Solaris Mansions* and petition me for help, a hallucination, conjured up by the hyperaesthesia of withdrawal – an afterimage of flashing eyes and teeth – turned to confront me. 'Just look at him, that Ignatz Zwakh, always *staring*.' The girl, still human, who occupied the desk beyond Primavera's, had herself turned, curious, angry. The ghost dematerialized; I dropped my gaze and tried to refocus my eyes on my textbook.

'I am required,' said Mr Spink, 'to add to your curriculum a period devoted to . . .' He hesitated, coughed, then chalked *Vox Humana* on the blackboard. *Vox* was the BBC's television broadcast for schools, renamed by the HF. 'I must say, boys and girls, I do this . . . I do this under protest.' There was a drumming of feet. 'Stop that.' Stoppered laughter compressed the silence; I could feel the pressure against my ears. They had won, and they knew it, my companions in crime, the tyke vanguard who would be tomorrow's hell-hounds; they had won, and the mockery of peace that pinched the air seemed to unsettle

Mr Spink more than if he had had to endure a barrage of giggles and hoots. 'Ak, ak, ak – all girls registered with the Hospitals may leave.' Zoe, Zika and Zarzuela (most dolls were at home, or interned) traipsed, with the fatalism of the abandoned – the self-abandoned who regard themselves as neither martyrs nor criminals, but as things – into the holding pen of the corridor, their faces quiet as my nights were unquiet, when I lay abed, thinking of Primavera. Zoe, Zika, Zarzuela –Zzz! They walked through dream palaces and dream prisons, through figments of my fragmented life: school, park, streets, towers: a broken jigsaw rearranged into something more intense, more real than its original, a world-picture where corridors stretched to infinity, and blood was always flowing from beneath a locked bedroom door.

'The integrity, the integrity of our emotions . . . affection, abhorrence . . . may be undermined, corrupted . . .' Mr Spink was behind his desk, retreating behind a barricade of piled exercise books. The monitor above the blackboard crackled; organ music swelled; and Vlad Constantinescu – our *Conducator* – looked down on us with the gunmetal eyes of a strict but loving paterfamilias.

'*Last month, when the extermination order passed through the Lords and received royal assent, England – after years of obfuscation and muddleheadedness – at last acknowledged the evil in her midst and submitted herself to be cured. The road to national recovery is a long one, but –*'

But. The afternoon was long. Long and hot. I rested my head against the desk and turned drowsy eyes upon the window. Election leaflets, like tarred, crippled birds, fluttered across the playground, with nothing to do now, nothing to do. *Demonesses*, said Vlad. *Witches. Whores.* And he spoke of his ancestors, the spirit people who gave him his instructions, his power. Outside, small boys – on their way from one lesson to another – had armed themselves with pieces of driftwood and were enjoying a game of war. SSSS! said one. His adversary fell, squirmed, wriggled and was still. DRRRP! said another, appropriating the forgotten glamour of lead. Bodies arched in the slo-mo 'poetry of violence' of a Hollywood bloodfest. *Vampires*, said Vlad. *Sanitization*.

Unquiet nights. Gothic nights. You lay in bed (as Vlad must lie) arranging and rearranging the jigsaw of the Neverland until it sanctioned your darkest desires. But of all the universes to be called into being, why this? This puzzle mean, banal and incomplete? A world-picture that seemed to have been inspired by a zygodiddly video? I turned my head. Myshkin was looking at me, vulpine, suspicious. Wog, I thought. Rainham wog. Sexless, scummy Slav. *Métèque . . . Until London is clean. Until England is clean. Until the planet is clean. Sanity through sanitization!* The frosted glass of the door blurred to a flourish of white knee socks: Primavera's handmaidens were doing handstands against the wall. I closed my eyes. The afternoon was long. Long and hot.

The ringing of a bell, at first quiet, and deep within my skull, grew, quit its muffling, sang along the soundbox of my desk, to be joined by sounds of shrieking chairs, the cruel laughter of children. I sat up. The classroom had emptied. Only Mr Spink remained, in thrall to the hypnotic power of unmarked school books. The monitor hummed. Zoe, Zika and Zarzuela stood hesitantly at the door. 'Can we get our things, sir?' Mr Spink gave a nod of indifference. Avoiding my eyes, the three girls collected their books; Zoe and Zika left, but Zarzuela had her head buried inside her desk, a disaster zone of comics and discarded make-up. With blackbird-sheeny locks, her metamorphosis was more advanced than Primavera's, though her two-tone eyes indicated that it was far from over.

'Ignatz?' she whispered. Mr Spink hadn't moved. I got

up and walked to where she sat, pretending to study the wall display behind her.

'What?'

'Have you seen Primavera?'

'No – should I have?'

'Oh, c'mon. I *know* about you two.'

'I haven't seen her – I haven't seen her all week.'

'I haven't seen her since we all went to the Hospitals to have that operation. *Savez-vous?* Where they take that little piece of bone from the small of your back.'

'I haven't seen her.'

'If you do –' I kept my eyes on the display, a 'Rise and Fall of the Empire *De Luxe*'. Cartoons depicted the creation of the dolls, their glorious lives, their fall. The narrative began with *Europa* at the height of her power, showering *joaillerie*, *objets* and *couture* upon her children. The following panels dealt with the ultimate *de luxe* status symbols, the automata. A doll was shown rising from her vat like a clockwork Venus rising from a chemical sea. The rubric quoted Christian Blanckaert, managing director of the Comité Colbert: 'Luxury is for France what electronics is for Japan . . .' The last cartoons in the sequence concerned Europe's decline: *Europa* swooning, in economic disarray, forsaken by Taste, raped by Third World technobandits, and witnessing the outbreak of the doll-plague, helpless. 'I know they're looking for her . . . I know she must be frightened, but . . .' Zarzuela rose, clutching her books to her chest. 'Tell her to come home. There's no use fighting it. We have to take our medicine. I only hope that when I'm called I . . . Tell her. She was my friend. I don't want to die alone . . .' She turned to leave. 'Nadia was on TV last night. Nadia Polanski? She was – she was lovely.'

I killed the sound; the screaming had grown too loud. Just the bad girls, Vlad had said. The thirsty ones. The teases. The flirts. The *provocateurs*. But they were interning more and more; and all that they interned, they impaled. They would impale them all. Some said it was being done alphabetically, by name; others said that a computer selected victims at random. A kind of lottery. *Form a queue, please. No pushing. Keep it moving there at the back!* So few ran; so many waited. So very English. The dark heart of England belonged to death. A waxen face, polka-dotted with sweat and veiled in lank black hair, rested upon the slab, teeth snared in the links of a chain that passed through the bloodied mouth. *The white light . . .* Across the country, in homes, pubs, on street corners and in railway stations, Anna Belushi's slain innocence fed the nation's sexual rage.

I had the weekend to make arrangements for our departure.

We fled through the disused tube tunnels that led to the West End. Going underground at Stratford (a stolen motorbike had facilitated our overland trip), we travelled the flooded tunnels in a small dinghy – little more than a child's toy – for which I had bartered my telescope. The tunnels were hot and airless. Rats scuttled under the enquiring eye of my torch.

What would my classmates say? The rumours of my friendship with a doll had been enough to earn me contempt; confirmation of these rumours (I would be denounced at morning assembly) would earn me lifelong ostracism. Dollstruck, they'd say. I had become an outcast. Yet if I was caught what had I to fear apart from remand? Sterilization, perhaps. A daily beating from medicine-heads like the Myshkins. But if they caught Primavera . . . No. No. I dug my paddle into the underground stream and thought only of descrying the station names through the brutal intimacy of the dark.

Bond Street. I swept my torch across the platform and

glimpsed a watery tomb of sweet machines, mildewy tube maps and hoardings. One poster – it advertised 'Skin II', dermaplastic's pret-à-porter derivative – displayed the aerosoled symbol of the Human Front. Sinking our inflatable, we waded knee-deep through sludge.

'There's no going back now,' I said.

'Promises, promises,' said Primavera. She clung tightly to my sleeve, the greening of the eyes that is concomitant with night vision still in her incomplete. The torch illuminated a stairwell. Glad to drag our feet from the effluent, we began our ascent.

'Turn the light off,' said Primavera.

'But–'

'There might be something up there, *stupid*!'

I switched off the torch, hooked it through my belt, and drew my scalpel. We climbed through darkness until I lifted a foot to find nothing beneath it but a horizontal steel plane.

'I'll have to switch it on. I can't see a thing.' Panning the torch through one-hundred-and-eighty degrees I saw we stood at the edge of a flood-wrecked concourse off which ran paralysed escalators.

'Now turn it off,' said Primavera. 'Please.'

We groped our way to the surface.

'Smell it?' said Primavera. 'It's wild.'

'It's West,' I said. Wind gusted across my face, wafting an overture of ruin and decay. Beyond mangled steel gates the abandoned star-haunted streets awaited us.

I removed my backpack and handed Primavera a towel and some spare clothes. We both stripped, changing from our school uniforms (Primavera had worn my old junior school outfit) into jeans, sweaters and anoraks. I stowed our old clothes behind a ticket machine.

'Come on,' said Primavera, striding into the night, 'let's find somewhere to sleep.'

I dawdled, looking back into the darkness of the tunnels. Mum and Dad, I thought, what will you say when morning comes? Can you ever forgive me? Will I see you again? I thought of the note I had left, full of crossings-out, verbal squirming and adolescent rhetoric.

'I said, come *on*, Iggy!' I turned to follow, leaving behind my human past. A past I tried to think of as well-lost.

Bond Street was a desert of broken glass and gutted shopfronts, a desecrated memorial to the *belle époque*. Primavera rescued some tattered couture from the gutter. She held it up, gauging its appeal.

'Hey, this is really *nice*. I could do something with this.' She looked about in wonder. 'All these shops. *S Laurent. Gaultier. Ungaro . . .*'

I imagined Bond Street restored: an emporium of delights, a wardrobe in which I might dress my dolly, the fetishistic Miss P. I would dress her up in tutus and trenchcoats, bias-cut leather, mock-croc underwear and la-la hose; I would dress her down in thigh boots, pink mink battletops, chain, pain and neurotic alleycat skirts. A mean lady of means; a mean machine of the streets . . .

I got out the street map. This was the other London, a city of midnight and daytime nocturne; the place they said our shadows came to when they tired of us. 'According to this, Bond Street leads into Piccadilly.'

'Let's stay here,' she said, folding up her Cinderella gown, 'it's sort of . . . *romantic*.'

A splintering of glass.

'What was that?'

'Shh!' I said. All seemed quiet. A dog, I thought. A cat. A rat. 'We'd better get inside.'

We stepped through the blown-out window of *Ungaro* and climbed the charred stairs. Ungaro, Dad said, had been the first couturier to use automata on the catwalks, and the first-floor office contained several dismembered, ravished examples of those early AIs.

'So these are my ancestors,' said Primavera.

'No more than mine are apes.'

She picked up the head of a former male model. 'Not bad,' she said.

'Be careful of battery acid.' She threw the head back amongst the charnel house of spare parts.

'Not much here, is there?' she said. Dermaplastic dresses, yellowing, crinkled, were strewn across the floor like the sloughed-off skins of ancient women; amongst them, faded polaroids (close-ups of bejewelled navels) and a poster advertising *Virgin Martyr* (beneath a crucified Negress a party of dinner-jacketed men rolled dice for a scent bottle; the cross's titulus read *La Reine des Parfums*).

'We'll look for somewhere else in the morning,' I said.

'At least I get to lose the frump-suit.' She pulled off her jeans and sweater. 'It's one of his,' she said, looking at the label of the frock she had recovered from the street. 'Ungaro.' She drew the frock over her head. Black and scarlet, with comic-strip burglar stripes about the top, a strict belted zone, and a split running from hem to waist (by design or by violence?), the frock – cut for a woman's figure – hung loosely from Primavera's budding curves. I had seen this look in some of Mum's old fashion magazines. It was called *apache*.

'It's dead,' said Primavera.

'Never mind. One day I'll buy you some dermaplastic that's really chichi.'

I walked to the curtainless window; the moon was waning, the streets dark. 'My Dad used to work here.'

'Your *Dad*?'

'He was a janitor. Used to look after lots of these shops. Before I was born, that is. During the *aube du millénaire*. Dad said it was a decent world, then. Decent. "You won't know what that means, Ignatz. Not your fault. We've murdered decency as surely as we've murdered our own children. Thank God we only have you." Dad always used to talk about things like that. The death of decency, love, truth and the rest. But the last few years . . . He never talks now. Not unless he can help it. He just dreams and leaves everything to Mum. But when he does talk . . .' I wiped my hand across the window and studied the grime on my palm. 'I never thought they'd win, you know. The Human Front. I can't believe what's happening. But Dad says it was always there: a malign potency, a rottenness, a horror beneath the surface. Even during the *aube du millénaire* Dad says it was there, just waiting to eat us up.'

'You should be thinking about what *we're* going to eat.'

Below, the fabled ruins of Londontown, a bag-of-bones, starved and alone, offered us a dubious sanctuary. Punk-Dickensian, those streets. Their shadows had almost defeated us. But a doll's fledgling magic (Primavera's navigation had been uncanny) had saved us from being marooned as we biked westwards. Nearer now, the sound of breaking glass, and a dull inhuman howl of pain. Somewhere, Never-Never Kids were ransacking the heartland of their prison. Drones hovered above the rooftops. The military observed; it did not intervene. What did they care for a dispossessed people? Proles, Yahoos, Morlocks: outcasts for whom only the anthropocentric jingoism of the Human Front seemed to offer hope? What did they care for our dance of death? Again, that howl.

'Dog?'

'I am *not* going to eat dog.'

'Me?'

'Better.'

'We have to be inventive. Like the Swiss Family Robinson. We have to –'

'Dog's off.'

'But –' Her arms encircled me from behind; I felt her nose, her lips, between my shoulder blades as one feels the conciliations of a chastised pet. 'Right,' I said. 'Dog's off.' She poked her head through my armpit.

'The stars,' she said. 'Alone beneath the stars. Poor Primavera. Poor Iggy.'

'The stars can't help.'

'Once people thought there was life out there. *We are not alone*, they said.'

I laughed. 'The stars are dead.' She slithered between ribs and arm to a popping electrostatic accompaniment – the corpse of her dress, along with her own flesh, sparking like charged nylon – and realigned her body so that we made a one-backed beast, her rump pressed negligently against my groin. I put my hands over the half-rations of her breasts.

'When the world goes porcelain,' she said, 'when every-thing's snuffed, the stars'll still be around. But they won't cry.'

'Everything doesn't *have* to get snuffed. There's contra-ception. Sterilization. Abortion. That's the way they handled things in France. The "Lost Generation" they called it. I never understand why the Neverlanders –'

'They're in love, Iggy. In love with pain and death. Just like you. Only they don't know it.'

'They don't want to know.'

'Yeah. They just want to work in the doll factory. They just want to make *us*. The end of the world – what a lark! What a game!'

'A game of war. Like I used to play with Myshkin and Beria.'

'SSSS! POW!'

'Wars forgotten. Wars fictive.'

'The Gulf. Antarctica. Oroonoko. Mars.'

'Dying –'

'DRRRP!'

'They liked it. We all liked it, those glorious deaths . . .'

'Ah, Iggy, they got me!'

'They got me too – Ugh!'

Primavera bucked, and the dead flesh of her bustier grew gooey. 'Oh Iggy,' she said, 'you nasty, *nasty* boy!' I thought of the last time we had played the sex-game, when I had thought she would swallow my tongue (you ever jog barefoot in Needle Park?); behind my eyes, the faces of Myshkin and Beria were superimposed over Primavera's, faces wide-eyed, shock-stunned, rejoicing beneath the imaginary fusillade from my toy carbine (lasers were scuzzy; nobody used them in those old videos we borrowed from Myshkin's Dad); my friends fell squirming to the ground. Primavera relaxed, drooped, began to slip from my grasp. 'Let's not talk,' she said. 'Please?' She pulled me down onto a soft fleshy bed of couture; not to feed (her appetite had been lost to exhaustion), but to sleep. She crumpled, cheek against my thigh. *Not one little bite? How can you leave me like this?* So restless was I with desire that for a long time Primavera slept alone. I thought of Mum's fairy tales. *The Transylvanian Princess. Bad King Wenceslas. The Cat People of Prague. Martina von Kleinkunst Gets Spayed.* No, no; that wasn't right. Then I must have begun to dream, for I seemed to be at some kind of fashion show with everybody calling me Monsieur, Monsieur! Monsieur Ungaro! Primavera wore her hair in an elaborate coiffure; she modelled a gown of bloodshot red. Red, too, her jewellery (so Martian), her gloves and slippers. The whole affair seemed to have been shot through a lens smeared with blood-red glycerine . . .

'Iggy?' I snapped awake. 'There's someone downstairs.'

'Probably a dog,' I said. 'Go back to sleep.'

'But what if . . . There – did you hear that?'

In those days (before I learned better) I sometimes played the Big Man. 'I'll check it out.' Arming myself with the limb of a quartered automaton, I descended into the darkness. I pulled the torch from my belt; pointed it, my thumb easing back its switch. Then: twanging elastic; horrible pain; someone opening (it seemed) a door for me (thank you); and the darkness became absolute.

The door reopened. The world had turned red. But this was no fashion show. No dream. Before me was a raging bonfire; above the flames, a winged boy with a bow and arrow. Boys – of the mortal variety (and some girls too), their heads shaved, and wearing medicine-head apparel – were dancing about a diddly-blaster and swigging from bottles of beer. I was propped against street railings, my hands tied to the iron bars. I blinked, trying to clear my eyes of blood; but the red ink in which the world had been dipped was indelible.

'So much for your brilliant plans,' said Primavera. I screwed my head in the direction of her voice. 'Down here,' she said. Primavera lay in a basement courtyard. She was also tied; not with rope, like me, but with an escapologist's nightmare of chain. 'You see the bedsteads?'

About the bonfire, familiarly arranged, the twisted frames of improvised death machines stood ready for their nightly ritual, thin metal spikes emerging from the pavement and protruding through their rusted springs.

'It's no good. I'm just a little doll. I can't break these chains.' I think I started to cry. 'Shut up, Iggy, and think of something!'

'Captain!' shouted a medicine-head. 'Captain Valiant! The pride of London! Over here, over here!'

A bicycle-drawn soapbox cart materialized from out of the blood-red cityscape. It would have reminded my future self of a trishaw.

'We got one!' someone yelled above the hoopla. 'We got a *belly*! Come and see!'

The cart halted, and a tall man in hand-me-down surgeon's garb stepped onto the street. His chauffeur, dismounting, proffered a walking cane. The cane clacked against kerbstone. The Captain was blind.

'One?' said Captain Valiant, petulantly, his voice straining against the uproar of the fire. He was older than his confederates; in his mid-twenties, perhaps; an anachronism in a city where fewer and fewer cleared the hurdle between adolescence and maturity. 'London is full of belly and you can only find *one*?'

The medicine-heads studied their feet, kicked at tinder and scrap. 'Jesus, Captain, belly's dangerous. Last week they got Bobbo. And Danny's lost an arm.'

'Where,' said the Captain, dark glasses aflame, so he seemed like a hungover jackal, '*is* the belly?'

A boy stepped forward (a catapult mounted with an infrared sight stuck from out of his belt) and took the Captain's arm, leading him across the street.

'Belly?' enquired the Captain, tapping his cane upon the rails.

'Leave her alone,' I said. 'You've got no right. You're not from the Hospitals. I'll tell –'

'Who is this pathetic boy?'

'He was with her,' said the Captain's eyes. 'Doll junkie. Addict.'

'Ah,' said the Captain. He reached out and, after wrestling with the air, got a grip about my throat. 'You know what you are? A traitor. A stinking traitor to your race. She's inside you. Can't you feel her? Creeping around inside your cells. Filthy, filthy, filthy.'

'If you hurt him I'll take your face off,' Primavera shouted. She swore in Serbo-Croat.

The Captain hissed. 'I can smell it from here. The belly. Corrupt. Malignant. It must be sanitized. Put to the spike. It must have its moment of truth.' He spat through the railings. 'How did you take her?'

'She's young,' said the eyes. 'Still in metamorphosis. Didn't need the magic dust. She's – she's just a kid.'

'Stop,' said the Captain, 'you're making me weep.' He wiped his cane across the railings in an ugly glissando. 'What brave soldiers I have! I've told you before: I want dolls, real dolls. Three green-eyed bitches a night. They must learn to take their medicine. But most of all I want the Big Sister. I want Titania, spiked and at my feet!'

The Captain froze; spun about. His cane fell to the ground. 'My God – look!' He pointed to one of the nearby streets where, half concealed in shadows, a big black car had parked, its engine still running. He put his hands to his face; covered his eyes; uncovered them. 'I can see,' he said. He tore off his glasses and simpered like a village idiot. 'Surrender my loins to a shark-toothed fellatrix – I can see!'

And then Captain Valiant burst into flames.

'Iggy, what's happening?'

The Captain ran into the street, clawed at his gown, dropped to the asphalt, and rolled over, again and again, screaming, 'It's her! Get her! It's her! It's her!' But his impaling party had dispersed, vanishing into the night; and soon he too was gone, his body a smouldering ruin beneath the pyre of the winged boy-god of love.

'Iggy!'

'I don't know – I don't know what's happening!'

The black car. I recognized its make. It was an antique. A Bentley. A girl, dressed in leathers and a peaked cap, stepped from the driver's seat and approached us. Her eyes burned green, and the opalescence of her flesh, like a highly polished mirror, reflected the tower of flames, so she seemed a translucent cast brimming with molten bronze. She stood over me, sneering. A snap of fingers; the sound of chain falling to the ground.

Cat-like, Primavera scaled her prison's walls and hauled herself onto the pavement. She busied herself with untying my bonds, one eye on our rescuer.

'Who is this human trash?' said the newcomer.

'This is Iggy. My boyfriend. You're not to talk about him like that.'

The doll yawned. 'Oh dear. You *are* a baby, aren't you. Your friend can find his own way home. It's you our mistress wants to see.' The doll turned and walked back to the car.

'We both come,' said Primavera, 'or not at all.'

'Mmm. I suppose part of you still thinks it's human. I almost remember being like that myself. Okay, baby. Bring him along. For the time being that is. She might be amused.'

'And who's *she*?' I said.

'The queen, of course,' said our saviour. 'The Queen of Dolls.'

As we approached the car a door opened. In the corner of the back seat a girl in her early teens – our chaperone, presumably – huddled beneath a wrap of grey fox fur. A box of chocolates was on her lap.

'Hi,' she said. 'I'm Josephine. Call me Jo.' Primavera and I climbed in beside her. 'Don't worry,' said Jo, 'you're safe with us.' The car stalled, performed a series of kanga-roo leaps, and then lurched into the night.

'Where are we going?' I asked.

'To the East End,' said Jo. 'To the palace of the dolls. Please . . .' She offered Primavera a chocolate. Primavera bit down; a dark red juice flowed over her hands, between her fingers, and down her wrists.

'Blood?' whispered Primavera.

'The real thing,' said Jo. 'Where we're going everybody lives happily ever after.' Jo looked at me askance, dabbing at her lips with a tissue. 'Well, nearly everybody.'

Primavera licked her fingers and wound down the window. 'This is the Strand,' said Jo, 'and soon we'll be in the City. See those fires over there?' She pointed down a side street. 'More paramedical scum. Every night Tit-ania sends one of us out on patrol to see if we can pick up any runaways before they do.'

'Did *you* set that man alight?' said Primavera.

'Sure. You'll be able to do things like that soon.'

'All I can do now,' said Primavera, 'is turn on TVs. I say *On*.'

'When your hair turns black and your eyes go green you'll be able to do *anything*.'

'Only Titania,' said our driver, 'can do anything. The rest of us have to be content with working a few tricks.'

Jo seemed a little abashed at her *lèse-majesté*. 'That's what I meant,' she said. 'You'll be able to do *tricks*. Of course only Titania can do *anything*.'

We sped through the silent streets of the City; silent too, my back-seat companions, consumed by the task of devouring their sweets.

'Titania,' I said, after their bloody feast was through. 'Is she a doll?'

'Of course she's a doll,' said Jo. 'But not like us. She wasn't born; she was made. She's an original Cartier automaton. The last of the Big Sisters. She's –'

'She's my mother,' interrupted Primavera, startled but infinitely satisfied by this sudden insight. 'My real mother.'

'Only Lilith,' said Jo, 'is that.'

We drove through an empty concrete wilderness that might have been twinned with Troy, Carthage or Pompeii; all about us were the lineaments of greatness soiled by sudden defeat.

'Whitechapel,' informed our driver. 'Brick Lane.'

Whitechapel. That was where Mum and Dad lived when they first came to England. Jumping the kerb to avoid a burned-out car, the Bentley swung into a warehouse.

We got out, Jo leading us across an oil-stained expanse littered with automobilia – the sort of place grease monkeys dream of going to when they die – to where a rusted samovar stood. There, bending over, she grasped an iron ring set in the floor, and pulled. A trap opened.

Beneath our feet, a spiral staircase unwound into infinity; a plume of green light rose from the depths, casting a halo upon the warehouse's roof.

'Down we go,' said our escort.

CHAPTER EIGHT

A Fairy Queen

Primavera screamed, curling up into a foetal ball.

'What is it?' said Kito.

'She told you before.' I put an arm about Primavera's waist, easing her into a sitting position. 'She's sick. There's a batch of nanomachines inside her, and they're tearing her matrix to pieces.'

Kito wriggled through the pillars of her bodyguards. 'This Titania,' she said, 'she know about doll-plague?' She raised a hand as if to demonstrate to her Schéhérazade the consequence of not resuming her tale; but before Kito could strike, Primavera fell forward, her body limp.

'She's passed out,' I said. 'We have to get one of your engineers to look at her. Now!'

Kito ran her hand over her matronly hips. 'Maybe this all big bluff, *Mr* Ignatz?'

'Listen,' I said, 'if she doesn't get help soon you'll never know the truth. The Americans are going to jerk you around from now until fucking nirvana. And for you that'll be a long time.' I gathered Primavera into my arms. 'Can't you see – she's sick. Really sick.'

Kito looked sick. A *chao mae* is unused to taking orders. But Kito was too clever to be ruled by pride now that her situation had become so desperate.

'Mr Bones number two,' said Kito, 'take friend to private elevator.'

Slinging Primavera over my shoulder, I followed the android through the still darkened apartment; Kito was behind me, arms folded across her small, nonfunctional breasts.

99

'Don't worry,' she said – I was looking at a camera – 'I see no one disturb.'

The elevator took us to the roof.

'New R and D man live here,' said Kito.

We were in a hydroponic garden, the scent of night blooms counterpointing the malodour of the streets.

'Spalanzani,' called Kito, 'where are you, you old fool?'

'Madame?' An elderly man emerged from behind a gazebo, a spray of opium poppies in his hand.

'I have *bijouterie* here I want you to look at.'

The nanoengineer chose a buttonhole, fixed it to his lapel, and walked over to us. 'Is there some dysfunction?' Walking behind me, he took Primavera by the hair and lifted her head for inspection. 'Lilim! *Oh sogno d'or!*' Relenting of his caddishness he cradled her head in his hands. 'Forgive! Forgive! *Mia belta funesta!* I have never seen one such as she before.'

'She's taken a dose of magic dust,' I said. 'She needs cleaning.'

He sighed, pulled out a pair of pince-nez (a common affectation amongst automaton makers) and began probing Primavera's face.

'Take your hands off her,' I said. He stepped back; Primavera again hung limply from my shoulder.

'Please. I want to help. Lilim! I cannot believe. Oh, such marvellous toy! From series *L'Eve Future*. Yes. Let me help her. Let me take a little peep inside!' In the centre of the garden stood a black dome. 'My workshop,' he said. 'Come, come!' He ran before us, stripping off his gardening overalls as a segment of the dome opened obediently at his approach.

Inside, the dome combined the elements of operating theatre, chemical plant and mortuary. Beneath its apex was a rectangular marble slab, about which were arrayed computers, a scanning tunnelling microscope, lasers and a stainless-steel cabinet crammed with surgical tools. Vats lined the dome's perimeter, each one containing a proto-doll; above, in a series of racked drawers, several of which were open, the decanted, successes and failures, slept their undead sleep. In contrast with the dome's exterior, everything within – with the exception of the black marble slab – gleamed with clinical whiteness. Mr Bones squatted on all fours, providing his mistress with a seat.

'Put her down,' said Spalanzani. I carefully laid Primavera out on the slab. 'And help me get this dermaplastic off.' He handed me a pair of surgical scissors. Soon Primavera was naked, her pallid lines thrown into relief by the cold stone bed.

Spalanzani picked up a jeweller's loupe and applied his eye to Primavera's umbilicus.

'The navel of the world,' he said, 'the centre of everything. And of nothing. The wormhole of lunacy! Ah yes, descended from *L'Eve Future*, but what mutations. What exotica!'

He stepped to one side to allow a bar of light to run over his patient from head to toes; a hologram materialized in mid-air. Fleshless, a glittering schema of veins, bones and plastic, the hologram turned, revolving on its axis, displaying itself like a see-through Sally before the eyes of a prurient clientele.

'Most fascinating,' he said. 'Living tissue has adopted the structure of polymers and resins, metals and fibres. It is difficult to perceive in what sense she is actually alive.'

'Dead girls,' I said. 'They call them dead girls. Primavera's DNA has recombined.'

'I don't think we'd find DNA in *this*,' he said, his finger jabbing the hologram's thigh. 'Recombined? The entire body chemistry has been altered, reorganized at the atomic level. Mechanized, you might say. By every definition I can think of she *is* dead.' His finger moved to the hologram's belly. 'This, I suppose, is what gives her life. Animation, at least. The sub-atomic matrix. I read about it in *Scientific American*.' He poked at a ball of green fire that swirled with op-art geometries; chaoses that teased with intimations of order; finitudes that knew no bounds. 'The matrix,' he said, picking up a syringe, 'is where our trouble lies.'

I put my hand on his wrist. 'What's in that?'

'I want – with your permission – to inject a remote.'

'You don't need his permission,' said Kito.

'Please,' he said, 'I must see what is happening in there.' I released my hand.

The needle pricked the taut flesh, emptying a clear solution into Primavera's belly. 'Good girl,' he said, his hand lingering a little too long, I thought, on his patient's abdominal wall. 'That didn't hurt, did it?' He sat down at a keyboard; a monitor lit up, and fractals, in vortices of green, loomed from the screen's vanishing point, like abstract representations of unresolved crescendos, the music of unrequited desire. I tottered forward, those shifting geometries threatening to suck me into some terrible fastness of space and time.

Freezeframe; the germination ceased, and I was pitched forward by my vertigo's inertia.

'The dust,' he said. 'It is carrying an anti-fractal programme that is infecting the matrix with Euclidean imperatives.'

He turned from the monitor, wiped his pince-nez on his sleeve, and sighed. 'At the heart of the matrix lies her source of being. Space-time foam. Ylem. The nanomachines will replicate smaller and smaller until that singularity is breached. And then she will fall victim to the laws of the classical universe. She will . . . He was genius, that Toxicophilous. My own toys . . .' He nodded towards the gestation vats. 'I still work from the periodic table and aborted foetuses. Cheaper, of course. That's all they care about out here.' A printer hummed; he tore off the print-out and scanned it.

'As far as I've ever been able to understand, *L'Eve Future*, and their descendants, the Lilim, retain in themselves a model of the quantum field, a model of creation, a bridge, if you like, between this world and the mind of God. And now it seems that bridge is burning.'

'And if it falls?' I said.

'She'll lose her power. In England, of course, it is what they do to automata before . . .' His face reddened. 'Forgive. I forget, I forget. Barbarous. Barbarous! I want to help. Believe, please! Now tell: has the young lady been able to work . . . *magic*?'

'She's been getting weaker ever since she was dusted. Except – except she can read minds. She couldn't do that before.'

'A temporary side effect, I would think. Compensation, like the aural acuteness of the blind.'

'But you can clean her up?'

'The dust is not of a type I have previously encountered.' He slapped me on the back. 'But yes, yes, I dare say, I *will* say. We cannot have the marvellous toy suffer!' he signed off from his workstation; the hologram vanished. 'Poof!' he said. 'Just like we make the little robots in the matrix do.'

'Before you make Poof!' said Kito, who was lounging across her Nubian slave like a torch singer across a Steinway, 'I want Mr Ignatz tell me about doll-plague.'

'After,' I said. 'There might not be much time.'

'It is true,' said Spalanzani. 'The dust makes weak, but then comes serious dysfunction. Her body will run only fractal software. And that software is being corrupted.'

Kito dug her nails into ebony electromuscle. 'Shut up, toymaker, you want make sex machine for me or you want go back Europe?' Spalanzani's mouth curled into a nervous, placatory smile. 'And you,' she continued, 'little English brat addicted to vampire kisses – you do as I say or Miss Primavera go way of all silicon. I must know. I

103

must know what start doll-plague. I must have America off my back!'

The monitor still seemed to glow with a spectral after-image: snowflakes, green snowflakes, patterns within patterns, geometries enfolding mind and matter, space and time, in a model of reality's infinite permutations.

It was the fount of all allure.

The *Seven Stars* was an embodiment of that allure. The Daedalean corridors, dizzy stairwells and impossible perspectives imitated the topography of a recombinant mind; a mind that is catastrophic, illusory, false. A celebration of surface and plane, of the paradoxes of line, the *Stars* might have been the result of an architectural collaboration between Piranesi, Escher and a fairground tycoon who dreamed of combining a crooked house with a hall of mirrors and a maze. It was an underground palace, a bejewelled goblin city, stocked with the abandoned luxuries of London's *beau monde*. In its catacombs slept a thousand dead girls.

'Titania built the *Stars* in six months,' said Jo, her outsized fox fur dragging across the chequerboard tiles. 'Before my time, of course. But they say the dolls in those days would wake up each morning to discover another room, a hallway, a stairwell where there had been none before.'

The passageways were suffused with a sourceless green light. At the beginning of our journey the walls had been plain, but now, as we progressed (I do not know how far; the labyrinth twisted, fell, doubled back, fell again), we passed frescoes mirroring the barrenness of our path, a parallel world, pointless and sterile, which absented us and refused to echo our tread. And then the light, deepening as if diffused by rainforest, filled a long corridor lined with doors, some two-dimensional, painted, some, it seemed, real. (I saw one open, and, fractionally ajar, betray a green eye framed by a slit of darkness.)

Deepening, darkening; we tumbled down stairwells, the greenness matching our descent exponentially, until that light presented the illusion of obscuring more than it revealed – an unknown face, rearing from the gross illumination, appeared to flicker once, twice, then vanish, to leave only a trace of perfume, electric and sharp. We were in some sub-sub-sub-basement, the crypt of the world, when the walls began to curve, making my eyes itch for resolution. Doors. More doors. One was off its jambs; beyond it, a stark bedroom, empty but for a vanity table and a wrought-iron bed (beneath the bed lay a slipper, its long, slim heel broken and hanging off), a room that called silently, insistently for the overthrow of small pleasures. A hairpin bend, and the passageway, like a green rainbow, ended at a portal of beaten gold: doors that might have guarded Belshazzar's banqueting hall. That face again, rearing out of the corner of my eye, then vanishing, the words 'Oh party time!' left in the air along with the memory of that electric scent. Jo the Psychopomp was putting her shoulder to the doors, and they were opening, moaning; other faces, sister faces, leered through the crack, and music, tough-cookie music, was making the air dance like a mist of febrile green midges.

'Primavera, I don't like this. I feel sick. I want, I want to – '

'Shut up, Iggy. You're not sick. Open your eyes. It's happening, don't you know? At last. It's real. It's true. It's what I've always dreamed of.'

The ballroom was a dragon's lair of shop-soiled furnishings and moth-eaten tapestries and drapes, chiefly in the *nouveau* and *deco* styles popular during the *aube du millénaire*. A group of revellers – dolls in flea-market masquerade costumes (looted from London's uptown wrack) – were performing a courtly dance to the unlikely accompaniment of saxophone and blue-note piano. Where was the music coming from? From the air, it seemed: a sort of jazz of the spheres.

Arranged in a five-pointed star, holding each other at arm's length, the dolls marched clockwise, then, completing a revolution, anti-clockwise, their satin-shod feet shuffling across the boards like superfine sandpaper. Other masked dolls, similarly attired in raggedy ballgowns, leaned against walls or reclined in alcoves, idly fanning themselves with spread lunettes of paper and ivory, overwound, it seemed, with a tensility that at any moment might snap. Beyond the wallflowers, beyond the dancers, was a dais on which sat, enthroned, a girl who seemed little older than Primavera. She was crowned with seven stars, and at her side sat a thin pale-faced man. The girl flicked open a fan and waved to us.

'Come,' said Jo, 'Titania has granted you an audience.' We threaded our way through the revolving pentacle of masquers until we stood before the dais. Jo curtsied. 'Your majesty, we have two guests. Miss Primavera Bobinski and . . . a boy.'

The child queen leaned forward in a rustle of flounces, bows and panniers, and addressed us from behind a sequinned mask.

'The boy has a name?' Her voice was like the flutings of a mechanical bird.

'Ignatz,' said Primavera, flashing an uncertain smile, 'your majesty,' and added, with a vulgar enthusiasm which must have flouted court etiquette, 'Are you really a Big Sister? An original Cartier doll? I though they were all destroyed. And can you do anything – I mean really *anything*?'

Jo coughed apologetically. 'She's still metamorphosing, your majesty.'

'Yes,' said Titania, 'I understand.' She rose from her throne and descended the dais, her gown a conspiracy of whispers. Titania was unlike any Lilim I had seen. Her hair, a smouldering charcoal black, and the cat-like eyes

(Cartier nanoengineers had revived Jeanne Toussaint's panther jewellery designs of the 1930s) were typical of the subspecies; but I had never encountered any doll who so embodied the spirit of artificiality, so qualified as Nature's foe. She stood before us, and her gown, red as a lascivious wound, fell silent. She smiled (her teeth seemed oddly blunt), and raised a taloned hand to Primavera's cheek. 'Don't worry,' she said, 'you'll soon lose those mongrel looks. Now come to my study. There's something I want you to hear. Something all my guests hear before I ask them whether they wish to swear allegiance. And if you do so wish, then I shall tell you the secret. The greatest secret of all . . .'

The two girls walked across the dance floor, Titania a little stiffly, I thought, a clumsy schoolgirl slightly ridiculous in the extravagance of her Madame Pompadour gown. 'You can come too, human boy,' said Titania, adding to her charge, 'Boys have their uses, of course.'

A wallflower, one leg hooked over the arm of her chair, called out, 'Nice dress.'

'Thank you,' said Primavera. 'It's Ungaro.'

A girl (fifteen? sixteen? with mad fairies drowning in the absinthe of her eyes) blocked my path. The upper part of her ensemble – a meat-red corselet woven from 'Skin II' – resembled the flayed torso of a Sadeian heroine. 'Dance with me,' she said. Saliva dribbled from the side of her mouth, onto her chin, and then, her breasts.

'I don't know how,' I said. Piqued, she sidled away.

'Sexual delinquent,' said Jo. 'Crazy automaton! Titania tries to invest her life with meaning, and what does she do? Dance, dance, dance! I tell you that doll's burning out . . .'

The man who had shared the dais with Titania gazed down at the pentacle of masquers as he had done throughout our brief audience with his queen, bored, stupefied, unseeing. 'Who is he?' I whispered to Jo.

'That's Peter. He's brain dead. Titania's sucked him dry. You'll be like that' – she gave no hint of mockery – 'in ten years. If you're not dead before. Still, plenty of time to make *babies*. Babies that'll turn into dolls. And that's all that matters, mmm?'

A crowd gathered, a crowd of wax faces stained green by the palace's hermetically generated light; muslin, silk, taffeta, lace swept past; I felt myself pushed, pinched, tickled; the crowd swelled, then withdrew, giggling; Jo was carried away by its riptide.

Titania and Primavera were leaving the ballroom; I ran after them, skidding across the polished wooden floor.

The adjoining hallway (we left by a route different from that by which we had entered) was lined with mirrors and *trompe l'oeil*, and I found myself lied to by false columns and perspectives. Swaying from wall to wall as if I were in the corridor of an ocean liner buffeted by storm, I soon lost sight of my quarry and wandered lost through rooms and salons silent and identical. I was about to cry for help when a hand took me by the arm and pushed me through a door. I winced, expecting to collide with concrete or glass, but the door gave way to three dimensions.

Titania and Primavera were sitting by an open fire (the palace was mint-cool; the fire, oppressive), half consumed by vast leather armchairs. Along the panelled walls were books and paintings; a heavy oak table scattered with maps and charts, an astrolabe and a globe, suggested the machinations of a general; a ticker tape chattered in a corner. I was in Titania's *chambre ardente*.

'Ah, Peter,' said Titania, 'I see you've found our guest.'

'He's my boyfriend,' said Primavera. 'My first.'

'Peter was my first, weren't you, Peter? But that was another time, another country. Your first is always special. Nothing ever tastes quite the same.'

'I wouldn't know,' said Primavera, blushing.

Peter drew up two chairs, his expression as deadpan as it had been in the ballroom.

I settled myself between the girls. A *buffet froid* of ice cream, chocolates, cream buns and sherbet was arranged by their side. Primavera helped herself to the chocolates. 'How old are you, your majesty?' I said.

Primavera frowned. 'Iggy, that's not – '

'Thirteen,' said Titania. 'I've been thirteen for twenty-eight years. I was made just after Peter was born. Peter and I' – and a bird-like laugh tripped off her lips – 'well, you might say we're related.'

'But you're not human!' said Primavera. 'I mean, you were *born* clockwork. You won't die, like us.'

'Every dawn,' said Titania, 'we die. Isn't that right, Peter?' A poker floated into the air and began to stoke the fire; the flames crackled over Titania's giggles; sweat trickled down my neck. 'But I haven't brought you here to speak of death. I want to teach you how to live. I want to teach all dolls how to live.' Her eyes harried Primavera's. 'Your generation has evolved. So much more noxious than the first born. Those Lilim . . .' Titania slipped to the floor, crawled over to Peter, and lay her head in his lap. 'Those Lilim were *milksops*. Isn't that right, Peter dear?' Her hand caressed her consort's thigh. 'Look into the fire. Do you see the future? Consumed. Us. The world. Everything. Look: the Neverland, in whose doorways and alleys the recombinant feed on those they have beguiled. Look: the Neverland dies, its denizens reduced to starving packs of girls whose teenage mortality will soon leave London's *cordon sanitaire* a dry husk. Look: see those who have escaped, the Lilim who claim other cities, the Lilim who claim the world, instructing their sisters in a religion whose longed-for apocalypse is a world usurped, a world of gilded automata. Look: with no human DNA to pirate, that parasitic race, thirst-crazed, hysterical, dies in an ecstatic *liebestod*, burning

109

on the same pyre as forgotten Man. It is right that it be so. It is our destiny. But look: the past is there too. Tell them of the past, Peter . . .'

Peter closed his eyes. His voice was soft as ashes. '*Peter Gunn* had reached its climax. I shuddered. Titania was robbing me of my human future. But she gave, too. In her saliva, ten billion microrobots – her software clones – coursed into my blood and lymph like a school of mermaids. Ten billion little Titanias swam through me, passing through my urethra, seminal ducts, and into my seminiferous tubules, where they melded themselves with my reproductive ware, corrupting my chromosomes with blueprints for dead girls. I would carry her with me all my life, my Columbine, my sweet *soubrette*; my Titania, queen of the fay; my children would be her children. I too would be a builder of dolls; like my father, I too would be a great engineer! I would complete his work. I would build a world for the chimera, the vampire, the sphinx; a world of childhood perversity; a world of dolls . . .'

'Ah, yes,' said Titania. 'Quite so. But from the beginning, Peter. Tell them our tale . . .'

CHAPTER NINE

The Lilim

*

It was Nursie who told me of the Lilim. 'They shall inherit
the Earth,' she said, the night-light silhouetting her profile
against the wall, where it joined the shadowplay of my
toys. Winding them, she would let the boys cavort about
the dresser, so that the beating of tiny drums and cymbals,
the clatter of tinplate limbs, has always accompanied, in
my mind, the memory of her words. 'Such pretty automatons. Pantalone, Harlequin, Pierrot . . . How your father
spoils you! But beware of *her*, Peter.' And she would pick
up thrashing Columbine, image of my inamorata. 'Beware
of dead girls. Their too-red lips. Their hearts of ice.'

Then stooping, her cheeks hot with shame, she would
mutter, 'Oh dear, oh dear, this really is a man's job,' and
initiate me into the ways of the Lilim. Like most boys I
had, of course, already learned much from the smutty
jokes of my schoolmates. But Nursie spoke not to edify;
she spoke to warn. 'The chambermaid,' said Nursie, con-
cluding her biology lesson. 'You see too much of her.
Unclean, vicious girl! Your father doesn't understand.
Don't think of her!' But how could I not think of her, of
Titania, my living Columbine? And I asked myself then:
Would Nursie tell? (But what was there to tell?) That
thin, high-cheekboned profile haunting the wall, those
flinty, folk-dark words, that smell of lavender water as
she kissed me goodnight: Nursie chastened my dreams.

Each morning that summer the sun effervesced into my
room like a champagne of lemonades. The school holidays
were at the meridian, the world mine and Titania's, and
Nursie's words like last year's snow. Pulling the curtains,
I would look down upon Grosvenor Square, environed

by its big pseudo-Georgian buildings. The ruins of the old American mission stood opposite, half hidden by full-leafed elms; the scented air was murmurous with bees. That summer, my flesh stirred; my voice broke; my heart bloomed. I did not know, then, that my childhood was to end surrendered to the altar of the Lilim.

One morning it began. Titania was in the kitchen. Her uniform, which my father had designed, was inspired by Tenniel's drawings for *Alice*: pinafore dress, not in the usual blue, but pink, swirling about the knees; starched apron; candy-striped stockings; and pink satin pumps. ('And how,' father would say, greeting her, 'is life in Wonderland today?') Cornflakes and a pitcher of milk awaited.

'The land of the *Seven Stars* – we should go there again. Today, perhaps?' I asked my pretty friend. 'There's lots of work to do.'

'I don't think we should, Peter,' she chirruped, her bird-like coloratura ('My nightingale,' Father would say) in contrast to the autistic face. I chewed my cornflakes wretchedly.

'You've got a licence. You shouldn't worry about Nursie.'

'Mrs Krepelkova doesn't like dead girls. You know that. Sometimes . . . sometimes I get scared.' Turning to the sink she began to wash the pots and pans, scouring them with a cold agitation. Suddenly she froze, clutching at her stomach.

'Can't Father fix that for you?' I had seen these signs before.

'Scared,' she said. 'It's happening. I feel it inside.'

I stirred my cereal into a soggy mess. My appetite had gone. The morning darkened.

'Father says Nursie's just a silly, superstitious old woman.'

'The world has become a superstitious place.'

'*Please*, Titania.' My wheedling voice cut through her massive self-absorption.

'I'm going shopping later.' The words bled out luxuriantly. 'If your father says you can come . . .'

It was always the same, that face: expressionless eyes, green and supernuminous, and the mouth, locked in its pout; the blood-drained cheeks; the elfin chin and pointy ears; the cutesy nose of the Disney princess. And the same too (for she had doll blood, and such are dolls) her meekness, so infinitely accommodating.

Everything, everything was to change.

My father's bedroom was a twilight world of pulled drapes, old books and camphor. The books were everywhere: tomes on engineering and art history; vellum-bound editions of 'Second Decadence' writers of the 1990s; chapbooks on toymaking from seventeenth-century Nuremberg; and rarities such as Bishop Wilkins' *Mechanical Magick*. There were paintings, too: amongst them originals by twentieth-century artists such as Hans Bellmer, Balthus and Leonor Fini. (My favourite picture was by the British artist Barry Burman. It was called *Judith* and depicted a pubescent girl holding, from a leather-gloved hand, the severed head of Holofernes.) But dominating the room – apart from the great bed that ridiculed my father's consumptive body – were the automata. They hid in the shadows, their kinetic latency like that of coiled, predatory beasts. Here were masterworks from the Age of Reason: *The Writer* and *The Musician* by Pierre Jaquet-Droz, purchased from the bankrupt vaults of the *Musée d'Art et d'Histoire* in Neufchâtel; singing birds by Jean Frederic Leschot; and a magician, a trapeze artist, monkeys, clowns and acrobats by the Maillardets. From a later era my father had collected a bisque-headed *Autoperipatetikos* by Enoch Rice Morrison; the elegantly dressed girls of Gaston Decamps; a Gustav Vichy musical automaton doll; and (creature of night!) a Steiner doll, with its mouthful of shark-like teeth – which earned it the nickname 'The Vampire Doll' – intact.

'Titania's going shopping. Can I go too?' Father reached for his spectacles and blinked at me.

'Mrs Krepelkova is worried about you and Titania.' I swallowed and dug my hands deep into my pockets. He chuckled hoarsely. 'She thinks I am too *liberal*.' Silence. The invalid tray was burdened with buttered muffins; the curtains swayed gently in the summer breeze. 'Peter, what do you want to be when you grow up?'

'An engineer, like you. A famous engineer.'

'No. You mustn't say that. Not any more. The days of the toymakers are over. Mrs Krepelkova: she's the spirit of these times.' At the periphery of my hearing a Mayday sounded. The grown world was hijacking my life.

'But Titania's not Lilim,' I said. My father seemed quietly shocked.

'What stories has Mrs Krepelkova been telling you? Stories of witches and succubi and golems? I swear that woman's brain is full of nonsense. The nonsense of cheap newspapers and cheaper politicians! There are no Lilim, Peter. You're an intelligent boy: you mustn't believe all you hear.' He wheezed like a punctured concertina. 'Mrs Krepelkova is a good woman. At heart. But we must be careful. Next time you come home from the country bring someone with you. I know you like Titania, but you must make other friends too. For her sake.'

'When I was little we had lots of dolls. It never seemed to matter then.'

'Life was different *then*,' said my father. Unbidden, the memories came: our home filled with the rich patrons of my father's skills; the marvellous automata that waited on our table; my mother, laughing at some after-dinner joke, her cheek even then hectic with the mutant tubercle bacillus that was to savage the Europe of that *belle époque.* 'The invisible worm,' he sighed, taking off his glasses, his head sinking into linen and down. 'It is best to think of happier times: like the day I was discovered by the Comité Colbert . . .' His eyelids fluttered, straining at wakefulness. 'I had just graduated from the Fashion Institute of Technology. They liked my English *hauteur*; the dandyism I had adopted ever since reading the nineties' writers as a boy. France then was the *de luxe* market-place of the world. It's like yesterday . . .' His eyelids closed; his voice became a whisper. 'In Paris I freelanced for Hermès, Louis Vuitton, Dior and Chanel. Later I worked for Boucheron and Schiaparelli. By the time I had met your mother and moved back to London I was the finest quantum engineer in Europe. Automata! They were the most coveted of luxury goods. And Europe monopolized the luxury market with its *L'Art de Vivre*. But quantum electronics has many problems . . .' His eyes snapped open. 'The chief of which is . . . ?' He pulled himself upright. 'Really, Peter, I've told you enough times!'

'Quantum indeterminacy,' I said, rote fashion. 'The imprecise behaviour of sub-atomic particles.'

'Tachyons, leptons, hadrons, gluons, quarks – Mavericks! Hooligans! They were my ruin.'

'The crash,' I said. 'I thought it was the crash that ruined you.'

'Our troubles came after Black Monday. The crash was just the beginning. To compete with the Pacific Rim we delved deep, deep into the structure of matter to make more wonderful, more extraordinary toys.' He passed his hand across his face. 'The invisible worm! It was right that we fell. Ours was an *esthétique du mal*. We shaped life to satisfy our vanities; life has called us to book. When you engineer at the quantum level, Peter, at the level of essence, *style* blurs into *soul*. And God will not be shaped . . .'

There was a knock at the door. Nursie entered, in her hands a steaming bowl of camphor. 'Time for your inhalant, sir.' She set the bowl down. 'Tsk! Has that girl not taken away your breakfast things yet?' And she picked at the bedspread, holding up to the light a wispy thread of lace. 'Pink lace, pink ribbons, pink stockings. A pink girl. Pink! Pink! Pink to her praline heart!' She went to remove the muffins and teapot, but Father brushed away her hands.

'That will be all, Mrs Krepelkova, thank you.' Hurt, she turned to leave.

'Do you want me to wind your automatons, sir?'

'Peter will do it, Nursie. Later. Thank you.' She smiled, shyly, her disappointment tempered by having been addressed by her sobriquet. As she left, she mussed my hair.

I drew away; she had defamed Titania.

'She says they eat men,' I said, after Nursie had gone, wanting her discredited; banished. 'That they're poison. That they kill children and put their own in their place.' Father laughed, but not altogether dismissively; he was too aware of what underlay those penny-dreadful tales used to explain the ascendancy of the dolls.

'Reality,' he said. 'They say it is hard to bear. You mustn't be too hard on her. She's frightened.'

'And frightened people,' I said, completing the cliché, 'say foolish things.'

He sighed, ignoring my sarcasm. 'But why shouldn't she be frightened? We have all been seduced, and the world sickens, gravid with our half-mechanical heirs. No more talk of nanoengineering, Peter. Everyone blames us now, the toymakers. I wouldn't have them blame you too.' He leaned over the bed to where Nursie had placed her aromatic offering and breathed deep.

'Titania will be leaving soon. Can I go with her? Please?'

'When I made her I was at the height of my powers. She was my *best*.' Red-eyed and perspiring, he reviewed his automata. 'Wind them for me, Peter.' My hands dipped into wet, freshly lubricated motors, tightening their sprung lives. 'Titania's a good girl. She would never harm you. Never.'

'Then I can go?'

The automata were waking: a monkey costumed like an eighteenth-century fop took a pinch of snuff; a conjuror sawed at a naked girl; the Steiner doll fell to the floor and wriggled and squirmed and squealed; someone – *something* – played the *Marseillaise*; and birds broke into song. Soon, that cast of feckless playthings was rioting about my father's bed like a mob before palace gates.

'Their day has come,' said Father. 'Yes, you can go. This time.'

The Bentley shouldered its way through the backstreets of Mayfair. Titania drove. Peeking over the wheel, and with immortal abandon, she swung the car into Bond Street. At thirteen (Titania had always been thirteen) her motor-neuron skills often seemed no more accomplished than those of a child; and though in that ghost town vehicular manslaughter was an unlikely prospect, I checked the rear-view mirror for cadavers and the unlikelier police. The street was empty (during the day the streets were always empty), the receding images of boarded-up windows – Cartier and Tiffany, Ebel and Rolex – a glittering slipstream of demise. Now those showrooms displayed only the spray-canned symbol of the Human Front, and graffiti that shouted, 'England for the organic,' 'Proud to be human' and 'Hospitalization now!'

At Fortnum's we bought some corned beef and cabbage (the store was run by an old Ukrainian couple, condemned, like my father, to remain in town), and then set off on the classified leg of our tour, our antique motorcar thundering down Shaftesbury Avenue, Holborn, Cheapside, deep into the City. At St Paul's we noticed a few technicians lowering themselves into manholes to massage the trapped nerve of some pampered AI. They noticed us, too; or rather, they noticed Titania, for they suddenly began gesticulating, scurrying into the depths.

'What are they frightened of?' I said. 'Dolls only come out at night.' Titania, gay as a bird, laughed without irony.

On reaching Whitechapel we pulled into Brick Lane, parking beneath a Cyrillic logo reading LADA. The logo belonged to a warehouse, which – like the derelict 'Borsch 'n' Vodka' fast-food outlets nearby – was a legacy from the years when a Bengali enclave had been ceded to Soviet and East European migrant workers. Lured by hard currency to buttress the West's declining birth-rate – the fashion then being to consort with the artificial – 'Slav' had, for a time, replaced 'Paki' as the taunt of England's bigots. Until, that is, men learned to say 'Lilim'.

We entered the warehouse by a side door. Light filtered through the corrugated roof, falling aslant over exhausts, engine parts and a samovar. In one corner, where rust had eaten away the trap once used for deliveries to the *Seven Stars*, the light tripped, fell and was engulfed. We descended the staircase, Titania's cat's-eyes burning green as, sure-footed, she led me into the cellar's swarthy midst. Though blind, I knew a multitude of candles, like stalagmites in an enchanted grotto, rose from the surrounding debris. I heard the sweep of Titania's hand; the candles burst alight, scattering our shadows; and the familiar beer barrels and wine racks, the pool table and slot machines, were revealed to us like the treasures of an Egyptian tomb.

The old pub sign, which we had repainted, hung from

a wall. A woman dressed in scarlet, clothed with the sun, with the moon under her feet and on her head a crown of seven stars, gazed down upon us, green-eyed and beautiful.

'Our flag,' I said, saluting her.

'Our planet,' said Titania. 'I always feel safe here. At least, I feel safe with you.' She brushed a cobweb from Our Lady's feet. 'What did your father say to you this morning?'

'Nothing,' I said, and picked up a can of paint, eager to change the subject. 'Let's get started. This is going to be our world.' But Titania sat down upon a legless pinball machine, despondent.

'This is just a holiday, Peter. This can never be my world. To them, I'll always be the Thing from Outer Space.' She drew a long red fingernail across the wall, setting my teeth on edge, and incising into the plaster the outline of a heart. 'They're right. I'm a dead girl. You really shouldn't be seeing me . . .' A trace of coyness had infiltrated her musical-box tones. On one side of the heart she drew a T, on the other, a P; then, momentarily wrinkling her nose, scored the heart with a Cupid's arrow. The ensuing smile, dislocated from the rest of her imperturbable face, twisted at my entrails. 'But you're my only friend. What would I do without you? A dead girl needs a friend.'

Only recently, after I had returned from the north, had I realized how pretty she was. So delicate, so pale. Our little chambermaid, for years a mere playmate, had had me tossing sleepless in my bed through all the long hot nights of that summer.

'I like . . .' I said, my mouth and throat suddenly dry. 'I like dead girls.' Her smile rippled across her face like irrepressible laughter at a funeral. 'Don't worry about Father. He says the Lilim don't exist.'

'No,' she said, giggling joylessly. 'We dolls believe in

nothing. Have nothing. Do nothing. We don't *exist*. I wish – ' As if hearing a barked command, her face assumed its customary autism. 'Light,' she said curtly, 'more light.' The candles blazed, their light turning green, so we seemed in an undersea cave, immersed beneath a canopy of seaweed. 'A doll needs something to believe in. Just the same as people like Mrs Krepelkova. We need . . . an *explanation*.' A tear dribbled down her glassy cheek. I had not known a dead girl could cry. 'People say that I am Lilim. Why shouldn't I be Lilim? Why not? They seem to want it so much.'

I knelt before her, burying my head in her lap. 'Don't talk like that. Don't take any notice of people like Mrs Krepelkova.' Her hand, white and inhumanly cool, touched my brow, razorblade nails pricking my flesh.

'I would never hurt you. You do *know* that, don't you, Peter?' She stroked my hair. 'Do you remember, years ago, when your father decanted me and brought me home? How beautiful your mother was. I so liked her. If only life could be like that again.'

'We'll make it so. We will. Believe me. We'll find some way.' I held her hands and looked up into that tear-stained face and the inhuman taint of her perfection. I felt the coolness of her thighs beneath the thin cotton frock, the articulation of her ball-jointed knees.

'I shouldn't mind,' I whispered, 'if you were Lilim.' The candles guttered in a sudden draught, and the room darkened. 'We could – you could – ' A spume of saliva hung from her lovely plump lips. 'Make the dolls come back – like before – a world of dolls . . .' The draught became a wind. Her lips parted and she grew saucer-eyed. Spittle dripped onto her chin. The wind blew through me, a divine mistral, turning me to stone. Still kneeling, I clutched white-knuckled at her skirts, petrified by her cold beauty. Her hair, black and opulent, lashed about her face, now like a malefic cherub's; and her eyes shone like green ice. The wind howled, and the ice was in me.

'No!' she shouted, 'I won't, I won't!' The wind died, sighing with exasperation. Her tongue, darting lizard-like across her lips, licked away a lather of white froth.

I moaned.

'Don't ask me again. Don't tempt me!' She was clutching at her stomach. 'I feel it there. In my clockwork. The poison.' She pulled from her pocket a large brass key. 'Here,' she said. 'Like this. This is better. I can take you back. Back to how things used to be.' The key was about six inches long with a butterfly handle and a tip of uncut emerald. Again, the wind gusted, threatening storm and stress.

'That's Father's key.'

'He doesn't use it any more. He's too ill. He doesn't miss it.'

'I'm not supposed to touch it.'

Titania placed the key in my hand.

'Don't be frightened,' she said, and hoisted her frock above her waist, displaying her white belly. The umbilicus, dimpling the satin hemisphere, dark and deep, exerted its allure. Titania closed her eyes, waiting. 'Please, Peter,' she said, 'make the poison go away.'

I inserted the key.

'Careful.' She flinched. Fumbling, I pressed the key home and felt it engage. She drew her breath in sharply. I began to turn. 'Slowly,' she said, 'slowly.' Deep within her, a hiss and spit: mathematical monsters stirred. In abandonment, she leaned back across the pinball machine, her midnight tresses trailing in the dust. The key tightened; my fingers hurt. I hesitated, fearful something might break. 'A little more,' she said, 'just a little more.' Using both hands I forced the key a final one-hundred-and-eighty degrees. She screamed in an impossible soprano. The pinball machine lit up; bottles smashed against the walls; the candles exploded like magnesium flares.

The wind that had been waiting impatiently off-stage hurricanoed through the cellar. It whirled about me, a private storm, ignoring all else. I joined its dance. Lifted off my feet, and clinging to the key like an anchored kite, I spun in its centrifuge. The cellar was a blur of streaked candle flame; below, her belly, a white expanse, a salt-seared tundra, drew me to its mine shaft of night. The umbilicus had grown huge, a black hole sucking me into another universe. I fell into its velvet maw.

Through a dark tunnel dimly lit with blood-red alphanu-merics I tumbled in free fall. The tunnel stretched to an infinite perspective; and as I fell a jungle rhythm shud-dered through its walls. I was buffeted by waves of turbu-lence; but I felt no terror; my heart raced benignly with the *frisson* of a rollercoaster ride. Blood mixed with crys-tal, crystal with vermeil, amber, glazing into a salmon pink. The tunnel had become a pink glassy membrane. The jungle pulse receded; the membrane ruptured. I smelt grass; felt sunlight on my face; heard the chatter of voices. I opened my eyes.

I was in Grosvenor Square, playing with Mama. About us, the Beautiful People – movie stars, couturiers, artists – scowled at the encircling paparazzi. I was eating an ice cream; father was talking with friends. Our automata, Treacle, Tinsel and the newly-created Titania, danced quadrilles with some of our guests. Doll boys, in the shapes of Harlequin and Pierrot, Gilles, Scapino, Cassan-dre and Mezzotinto, poured wine and served cakes. Half awake, half asleep, I rested on Mama's breast and watched the dancers weave elaborate, stately patterns to the courtly music of some *gamme d'amour*. It was one of father's 'Watteau afternoons': a midsummer day's mime of pleasure, a pastoral from a Meissen porcelain granted a little time and space.

Titania danced by. Was I in love, even then, albeit unknowingly? She was Columbine the *soubrette*, dressed in the sweet satins and rocaille folds of the infant eighteenth century. She waves to me with her painted fan. There is a clinking of glasses, a buzzing of bees. Time lies sleeping.

'My work now' (my father's voice drifts by) 'is to unveil the spiritual physiognomy of matter.' And the conversation turns to nanorobots, the latest molecular machines. 'Reduced to the size of a molecule, a component will become delinquent; but I am learning to exploit quantum effects, to manipulate Chaos. [A flash bulb ignites.] Indeed, I have now developed assemblers that can manipulate not just atoms, but sub-atomic particles. These automata you see today, commissioned by the House of Cartier, have been brought forth from a microphysical realm where mind and matter, dream and reality, co-exist. They are quite *marvellous* toys.' And he extends his arms towards Titania and her clan. 'Gentlemen, I give you *L'Eve Future.*'

Above the applause, a clap of thunder. It begins to rain.

I do not remember this.

It is raining milk.

And Treacle, Tinsel and Titania – fashion accessories we did not credit with life – bedraggled hair pearly with raindrops, dresses wet and sticky, are standing with their mouths agape like newly-hatched chicks; standing like totems of ecstasy.

Titania?

The guests run for cover as the storm bursts overhead; but the white glutinous rain is drowning London. The flood carries me from Mama's arms, bears me forward on an implacable tide, towards Titania and those red, red lips that are like a giant neon-splashed motorway hoarding advertising the bloodiest of lipsticks.

'No!' Titania cries. 'Not you, not you!'

I woke, sweating. The cellar was becalmed. Titania was rearranging her clothes.

'It wasn't like that,' I said.

'I know,' she said. 'I pollute even the past.'

'No,' I said. 'It's all right. Really.'

She pressed her hand to her stomach. 'It's there. You saw it. The malignancy.'

I got up, chewing my lip, embarrassed. 'I said it's all right. It doesn't matter. In fact – '

Titania doubled over, her chalk-white features rearranging themselves into a mask of pain.

'Please leave me,' she said. 'I'll be better in a while. I need to be alone.' I hesitated. '*Leave* me, Peter.'

With misgiving, I returned to the street, took the fold-up bike from the boot of the Bentley, and cycled home; but not before eliciting a promise that she would follow in the car later when she had composed herself.

I always respected her wishes.

But of course, she did not return.

'The Lilim,' said Nursie, winding my toys, 'are every-where.' She pecked me on the cheek, sharp as a macaw.

That evening Nursie had stamped about the house muttering, 'Where is that girl? Where is that *robotnik*?' My father sulked, alone, in his room. Now, at my bedside, my smug nursemaid was saying: 'I told you. I told your father. But would anyone listen? No. Krepelkova is just a silly *babushka*.' She held a well-thumbed paperback in her lap: *The Doll Problem – Lilith And Her Daughters*. It was the bible of the Human Front.

'Lilith was Adam's first love. But she was proud and vain and adulterous . . .' She opened the book, removing a photograph from its leaves. 'Lilith is Satan's consort, Peter. She is Queen of the Succubi. She comes to men at night so that she may corrupt their children . . .' She held the photograph before me. It was a portrait of a young girl, a blonde *manqué* with liquorice roots, in whose pixie-ish face I recognized the traits of the recombinant: green, hysterical eyes and a sickly white complexion that suggested a diet of junket and sweets. 'At first I blamed my son-in-law,' said Nursie. 'He never told me how it happened. But I don't think he meant to be unfaithful. Dolls have their *ways*.' She studied the snapshot carefully. 'You can still see the human part of her. If you look closely. When she was born she was such a lovely child. We had no idea. It's when they're about twelve or thirteen that it happens. The eyes turn green. Luminous green. And the face: it isn't a human face any more. It becomes . . .' She paused, her brow creasing. 'Pretty. So very pretty. But it is a prettiness that is horrible in a child.' The book slipped from her lap onto the floor. 'Poor Katia, she was a daughter of Lilith, and they made her wear the green star of the Lilim. Then the lactomania began. And they took her away. To the Hospitals. My baby's baby . . .'

I went to sleep, clasping, with anxious hands, Titania's key beneath my pillow.

The next day I cycled back to Brick Lane. The Bentley was still parked outside the warehouse. 'Titania!' I called. But the warehouse was empty. I descended into the world of the *Seven Stars*, my pocket-torch flushing out the shadows.

She had gone. I breathed a deep lungful of fetid air and went to mount the stairs. A gobbet of water broke at my feet; I jumped, swinging the torch around. Hanging from the ceiling in what seemed a sac of viscous bronze was the foetal-crouched shape of a woman. She was flesh-less; what remained was a raw, quivering jelly suffused with plastics, metals and jewels. I retched, dropped the torch and ran.

And then I was gunning the Bentley towards Mayfair;

towards the particle weapons and security cameras that surrounded our house; towards the human world.

'Where is she?' asked Father. I told him. 'There's nothing we can do,' he said. 'Nothing.' He fidgeted with the bed-sheets. 'I never thought it would happen. Not to her. Not to Titania.'

'Will she die?' I barely dared utter the words.

'The philistines called them dead. Dead girls. A nexus of formal rules. Non-reflective. No, she won't die. Now she makes her claim on life.' He threw back the sheets and swung his legs onto the floor. 'I must go to her.' A fit of coughing took him and he collapsed in a tangle of flannelette. 'Those Cartier dolls,' he said, gaining his breath. 'I thought I was making elegant, eighteenth-century ladies, spirits of gentleness and grace.' He pointed to the foothills of books surrounding his bed. 'The Deca-dents! Writers and artists who filled my boyhood dreams with chimeras, vampires and sphinxes. Ah, the perversity of childhood . . . I tried, Peter. I tried to deny that dark-ness, programming my atomic machines to pluck angels from pandemonium. But atomic objects can be under-stood only in terms of their interaction with the observer. When we speak of the subquantum world, we speak of ourselves.'

Something terrible snarled in the undergrowth of my mind and readied itself to pounce. I dared it.

'Did *you* put the poison in Titania?'

'I always blamed others,' he spluttered, the words rush-ing out. 'I said it was some bug introduced into their programmes by our competitors in the Far East. But the virus was mine. Between the lines of Titania's pro-gramme, within its infinitely complex, fractal text, lurk my dark childhood dreams. Now that sub-text emerges, the poison seeps . . .' He began to cough.

'I'll go. I'll bring her back.'

'No.' He drew himself up. 'I'll go in the morning. It's getting dark.' The sun, red and bloated, was sinking over Grosvenor Square. The jewelled eyes of my father's automata glistened. He placed his hand on my shoulder. 'She can't come home, Peter. Understand that. Her power . . . It is enormous. I grew her from the quantum field, the essence of all forms. In her, space and time, mind and matter, are enfolded by . . . by what? A reality *I* cannot grasp. She is unconstrained by physical laws, at one with the essential nature of things. She is Creation.' He looked out of the window, his face flushing in the rays of the dying sun. 'But I have poisoned Creation. I gave her life, Peter; I must take it. Tomorrow, before she is reborn.' He sighed. 'Can anyone explain this need to create beauty?'

CHAPTER TEN

Unreal City

'You want me believe – '
  'Quantum indeterminacy – '
  'This bullshit?'
  'At the sub-atomic level – '
  'Why no one say – '
  'His own consciousness, his subconscious – '
  'Before?'
  'The imprecise behaviour of – '
  'Mr Ignatz – '
  'Inventor becomes inventee – '
  '*Mr* Ignatz!' Kito slid off her mechancial stud and pulled out her transcom.

  'Wait,' I said. 'Spalanzani, tell her it's true.'

  'True? But how can I say? Possible, I suppose. Toxico-philous would first have engineered nanomachines on the molecular scale, programmed with the rules of a cellular-automaton universe. The nanomachines would replicate, each time making a smaller model of themselves, until tiny, so tiny, hardware became software, machine became information, mimicking the quantum effects involved in the firing of neurons in the human brain. But how Toxico-philous's subconscious might have affected that process . . . Who can guess? Consciousness physics is not my forte, and fractal programmming is a lost art.'

  'Toxicophilous,' I said, 'is the source of the doll-plague. *L'Eve Future* was a projection of his psyche, just as he himself was a projection of his own age. The Lilim are observer-created.'

  Spalanzani pursed his lips. 'It has always been my opinion that Toxicophilous was used as a scapegoat. But though people have cursed him for building *L'Eve Future*, nobody has gone so far as to accuse him of being the *source* of the plague. Your story, my friend, is mystical. And I am a scientist. Myself, I have long favoured the supposition that a virus from the Far East was responsible for – '

'Shut up,' said Kito, 'quack nanoengineer.' She began encoding her transcom. 'Spalanzani scientist; I cynic, Mr Ignatz. I want evidence, not fucking crazy story.'

'Titania exists,' I said. 'Ask Jack Morgenstern.'

'Ask him yourself,' said Kito, 'when he come take you back England.'

'*American Embassy*,' said the com.

'Forget duty officer, get me Jack Morgenstern, Cultural Affairs Attaché. Say it's K. At home? Then put me through his TV, his android, his fax, his bathtub, I no care!'

'That won't be necessary, Madame,' said Jack Morgenstern, who had just entered the dome along with the Pikadons and Mr Jinx.

'She on slab, Uncle Jack,' said Bang (or Boom).

Morgenstern pointed a lightstick. 'Okay, Zwakh, and you too,' he said, looking at Spalanzani, 'get over there with Kito.'

'Mr Bones,' said Kito.

One of the Pikadons drew a particle weapon from her Sam Browne and fired. The android spasmed, pawed at the air, then fell onto its face in epileptic ruin.

'Kito, don't disappoint,' said Morgenstern, 'I'm no longer interested in you.' Coughing theatrically, as if about to provide an aside during an after-dinner speech, he added, 'In fact, *nobody's* interested in you.' The Pikadons tittered.

'Jinx,' said Kito, stepping over the massive frame of her plastic bodyguard, 'what this about?'

Jinx raised his hand as if summoning the elements to

his aid. 'Stop!' He was a small Rumpelstiltskin of a man from some undefined principality west of the Urals; so astonished was Kito at his display of imperiousness that she leaped backwards, tripped over the still twitching Mr Bones, and fell in an immodest sprawl of limbs. The little man grinned as if he had just revealed himself the master of a long unsuspected black art.

'Jinx?' said Kito.

'Let me present the new chairwomen of the board,' said Jinx, making a *wai* towards the Pikadons (two effete cadets from a notorious military academy, dressed in the kind of style that brings out the sodomite in a man).

'Nana friend with America now,' said a Twin. 'Friend of Uncle Jack.'

'They do the weird on you, Morgenstern?' I said.

'Please,' said Jinx. '*Language*.' He turned to Kito. 'A simple boardroom *Putsch* is what this is about. Madame, you have been mamasan of Nana for over forty years. Life has moved on. We no longer live in a Eurocentric world; a resurgent America is reclaiming its old spheres of influence. Madame is part of the defunct "Empire of Style." But Nana has no time for nostalgia. Time is money. Deutschmarks. Yen. *Dollars . . .*'

'We bought you out,' said Morgenstern. 'Seems US dollars still call some cards. I knew I couldn't trust you.'

Kito picked herself up. 'I was about to ring – '

'We know,' said Jinx. 'Your rooms are bugged. This place too. We've been listening in on you for some time.'

'Interesting story, Zwakh,' said Morgenstern. 'Pity you had to hear it, Madame.'

'What story, Uncle Jack?' said a Twin.

'Never you mind, sweet thing.' Morgenstern smiled at me. 'We'll have to talk some more.'

'Mr Bones – *get up!*' Kito kicked the android's tonsured head; yelped with pain. 'Jinx, Pikadons – they use you. You no see? You become yankee *stooge*, you – '

I put my hand on Kito's arm; she glanced at me and sheathed the claw of her anger that its sharpness might not be dulled for later use.

'Let me get this right,' I said. 'The US government bought enough stock to allow the Pikadons – the *Pikadons*, for Christ's sake – to take over Nana. All to get one runaway Lilim and me? What are you talking about?'

'I told you,' said Morgenstern, 'I'm an Anglophile.' The doors bisected at his approach. 'Let's get rolling,' he called. A golf cart manned by two of Morgenstern's goons purred into the dome. 'Put the girl on that, handcuff the boy, and take them both to the autogyro.' He turned to the Pikadons. 'I'll leave the *boss* for you.' The Twins cracked their knuckles in anticipation.

The goons took hold of Primavera's arms and legs; dropped them; stepped back from the slab. A green shaft of light, like a column of ectoplasm, had risen from her umbilicus.

'Jesus, Jack, what the hell is it?'

'Don't worry,' said Morgenstern, 'she's been dusted some twenty-four hours. She ain't jumping through any more walls, I can tell you.' A breeze stirred a heap of print-out; there was an electrostatic crackle in the air. 'Let's get this thing on the road.'

The two men again took hold of Primavera. The breeze became a wind, and there was a squeal of castors as a metal trolley trundled across the room.

'Monsoon,' said Morgenstern. 'It's that time of year.'

'That's no monsoon,' I said. 'Tell them to put her down.' I moved towards the eye of the storm; the well of unreason would have to be plugged or . . . Morgenstern fired a warning shot; a vat broke open, sluicing its miscarriage over the tiles.

'Stay where you are, *Gastarbeiter*.'

'Tell them to leave her alone,' I said. 'Don't you realize what's – '

The wind screamed into my mouth and lungs. I was pedalling air. Then I was falling, falling through the funnel of a green maelstrom, into patterns within patterns, falling towards something infinitely small, infinitely big, falling helter-skelter, falling into the belly of the doll.

I opened my eyes; the white cupola of Spalanzani's workshop was above me. My enemies were rubbing their heads and getting to their feet. The dome was undisturbed, as if the cyclone, abashed at its carousing, had tidied up before it had left.

'You guys okay?' said Morgenstern. The two men who had precipitated near disaster mumbled a series of goon-speak yeah, guess so, sure, Jack, replies. One of them had vomit-spattered shoes. 'Let's try it again,' said Morgenstern. 'Gently.'

The umbilical light had died; Primavera was lifted onto the golf cart and driven outside without incident.

'Move back where you were, Zwakh. Over there, with Kito.' Hands above my head, I edged across the room.

A cry, EEEE! A slasher, splatter cry . . .

Morgenstern ran outside and I followed, my humanity insulating me from a trigger-happy burst from one of the Pikadons' doll-scramblers. 'Primavera?' I called. She was still on the golf cart, eyes closed, breath shallow. Morgenstern had grasped my arm. His face was bloodless, and his eyes jerked into grotesque attitudes as he strove to assimilate the horizon.

Rising from Lumpini Park, and floodlit, St Paul's cathedral shone majestically above the rooftops of Bangkok. Big Ben leaned over us from the next street, surrounded by *chedi* and *prang*, and the searchlights of the interdiction described their familiar arcs from across the

Chao Phaya river. The Big Weird had suddenly got bigger. Weirder.

'What's happening?' said Morgenstern. I eased his hand off of my arm.

'We never came out,' I said. Jinx, Kito and the Pikadons formed a huddle against the dome wall. 'We're inside Primavera. She's taken us into her matrix. We're inside her dreams.'

'You said she was dusted!' said a goon. 'You said she couldn't hurt us!'

Morgenstern put his hands to his head. 'I got to *think*.' He stamped on the ground. His eyes continued to wander dizzily in their sockets. 'Inside her dreams, eh? Then we got to wake her. *Wake* her. We got to, to – '

'Wake her. Yeah. And how do we do that? This isn't Primavera,' I said, pointing to the sleeping girl on the golf cart. 'This is . . .' But I didn't know who it was.

'A simulation, possibly,' said Spalanzani. He had emerged from the dome and was squinting through his pince-nez at the deranged cityscape.

'Jesus,' said the goons' spokesman, 'is that what we are, Jack – fucking *sims*?'

Everybody looked at Spalanzani. 'It is if,' said Spalanzani, 'we are inside a dreamscaper, with the young lady's software acting as a *jeu vérité*.'

'Some *jeu vérité*,' said Morgenstern. 'We can't control anything. In a lucid dream you can *control* things.'

'We're intruders,' said Spalanzani. 'The game is the young lady's.'

'Wake her up, Jack. Give her a shot of something. Just get us out of here.'

'Pull yourselves together,' said Morgenstern. 'If we're sims, nothing can hurt us.'

'Possibly,' said Spalanzani. 'But if we're *not* discorporate, waking the young lady – even if it is only a simulation of herself – might be dangerous. The dreamer may assume control of her dreams.'

Dangerous. That seemed a good enough reason to wake her. It might be the last card Primavera and I had to play . . .

'I could try,' I said. Morgenstern looked at me suspiciously. 'How else are we going to get out of here?'

'No,' said Morgenstern. 'Spalanzani, you try. Shoot her up with stimulants. Let's take the risk.'

'The risk of her lucidity is but one factor. Say the stimulants work – either as pure symbolism, as therapeutic symbolism, or as a physical correlative – what effect will they have on the young lady in the real world? She is very sick. Dying, perhaps . . .'

Morgenstern stroked his beard. 'Yeah, I guess if she dies while we're in here things could get *really* tough.'

'I planned to operate,' said Spalanzani. 'But I can't. Not now. Even supposing there *is* a correlation, symbolic or physical, between this young lady and the one outside, I would need special tools, customized nanoware. One such as her . . . I never met before. Never.'

'Then let me see what *I* can do,' I said.

Morgenstern nodded. 'Looks like our options are limited. But nothing funny, okay?'

'Yes, my friend,' said Spalanzani, 'maybe our bodies are in the real world, dreaming all of this; and then again, maybe not. For the young lady – for all Lilim – thought is denser, more material, than for you and I. *Her* dreams have substance. Be careful.'

'Not so fast,' said Kito. She began folding and twisting her transcom. After three or four manipulations it resembled a ladies' beam weapon, lethal and dainty. 'I want to know why you ruin me, Mr Jack.'

'Madame,' said Jinx, 'this is not the time for – ' Jinx pirouetted to the minimalist fanfare of Kito's gun, staggered, took a photograph from his jacket, tore it to shreds (it emitted a tiny squeal), and fell noiselessly over the balustrade to the streets below, to resolve, for himself at least, the question of whether or not we were simulations.

'It *was* true then,' I said. 'Mr Jinx really did love a photo-mechanical.'

'Not love,' said Kito, 'an infatuation.' The Pikadons brought their particle weapons to bear on their fellow *bijouterie*, intent on scrambling the symbiotic electronics that riddled her hypothalamus (little doohickeys that had cried sex, sex, sex these five score years). 'A cruel infatuation.' The weapons discharged, ejecting joke-shop flags, one Bang! the other Boom! Kito's lightstick had turned into a steely dan.

'Seems the goddess of this place doesn't like guns,' I said.

'Guess she didn't like Jinx either,' said Morgenstern. He holstered his lightstick.

'Spalanzani,' I said, climbing into the golf cart, 'you think you could get me a scalpel?' Spalanzani disappeared into the dome and re-emerged with a handful of surgical instruments.

'You saw what she did just then,' said Spalanzani. 'Perhaps we shouldn't – '

'Get on with it,' said Morgenstern. 'If she can do that in her sleep none of us are safe.'

'Can no get worse, Uncle Jack,' said a Pikadon.

I selected a blade and applied it to my arm. Spalanzani tut-tutted. 'Keep her jaw open,' I said to him, opening a vein and letting the blood drip into Primavera's mouth. Her throat contracted in a covetous gulp. I squeezed the vein; no question, really, of force-feeding her; she yawned, blood spattering her face and hair. I was gambling that her haemodipsia was stronger than the bonds of her unconsciousness.

The goons were muttering:

'Jesus, these English.'

'De-pravity.'

'A green and perverted land for sure.'

'Wait'll I tell Alice about . . .'

Primavera knocked away Spalanzani's hands, clawed at my arm, brought the slit vein to her mouth, and sucked, like a baby on its bottle. *Ohh – tombstonesown-moaninight* . . . In the land of death and desire our coach awaited us. We shook and shivered. *The car. The girl. The river . . .*

What –

'It's enough,' said Morgenstern, pulling me off.

Primavera drew a hand across her mouth. 'Shit, Iggy, what happened to my clothes?' I took off my jacket and handed it to her.

'We're at the *Grace*,' I said. 'Remember? We were in Kito's bedroom when – '

'And what's this slut doing here?' said Primavera, glaring at Jack Morgenstern. She frowned. 'It's gone. It's *gone*. I can't see inside his mind.'

'We're still here,' said Morgenstern, looking around. 'She's gone lucid, and we're still here. Tell her to pinch herself, Zwakh.'

I took Primavera's hand and led her to the edge of the roof. 'Fuck,' she said, her eyes distending to accommodate the fused skyline of East and West.

'You're dreaming, Primavera,' I said, 'and we're inside your dreams.'

'*Stupid!* If I were dreaming I'd be able to – ' The garden vanished and was replaced by our suite at the *Grace*. 'Anything.' Primavera was curled up on the sofa, her green silk kimono spilling onto my lap. 'You're right,' she said, 'I *am* dreaming.' She was eating popcorn; the lights were turned down; and all five of our TVs were tuned in to the Jack Morgenstern show.

'Very clever,' I said. 'As if I haven't seen enough of your dumb tricks.'

136

Morgenstern, clad in sacrificial white, was being frog-marched down a long corridor. His captors – masked, but betraying long manes of bleached blonde hair – kicked a wheelchair from his path . . .

'I'm going to teach that slut a lesson,' said Primavera, filling her mouth with junk.

The corridor opened onto a big rotunda, at the centre of which two marble slabs displayed the skewered bodies of the Morgenstern goon squad. The third slab, unoccupied, was evidently reserved for Morgenstern himself.

'Just stop the melodramatics, Primavera. We don't have time for this.'

'Sure. I mean he's such a nice guy. I want to have his fucking babies.'

Morgenstern, his gown stripped away, hirsute and horrible, was on all fours upon the slab. A pair of rubber-gloved hands took hold of his ankles.

Primavera picked up the remote and froze all five pictures. 'Hey, Morgenstern,' she called, 'you can hear me?'

The TVs remained frozen, but Morgenstern's disembodied voice was panting over the speakers. 'You murderous little bitch. My boys – '

'Just do it,' I said. 'Get rid of him and start thinking of a way to get us out of here.'

'I want to play,' she said, sulkily.

'Games. Always games. Don't you realize what's happened?'

'It's just a dream, Iggy. Why do you always have to be so *serious*.'

'*Just* a dream? We're inside you. *You've taken us all into* – '

'There's no need to *shout!*'

'Into your matrix.'

Her mouth, pausing in its task of grinding popcorn to pap, hung open; a long red fingernail picked at her fangs. 'There was a guy with an Italian accent. I was lying on something cold. Then the American comes in, yeah . . .' The pulp mill of her teeth resumed work. 'Then you're real?'

'I feel real, though Spalanzani says that maybe – ' Jack Morgenstern had begun to scream.

'Shall we do it?' said Primavera.

'Get it over with. He knows about Titania. About the *Seven Stars*.'

'Naughty, naughty, *naughty*!' Primavera took hold of the remote.

'Wait!' said Morgenstern. Primavera's finger hovered above the freezeframe. 'We were never going to send you back to England. I said that just to scare you. To make you talk!'

'Yeah, yeah, sure,' I said. I looked past Morgenstern into the shadows of the execution chamber. 'It's so dark,' I said. 'Back home it was always so light. So white. So – '

'Clean?' said Primavera.

'All those candles. And masks. And that thing in the centre – like some kind of gibbet.'

'Medicine-heads,' said Primavera, 'have the aesthetic sense of retarded oysters. This is better. More gothic.'

'Yeah,' I said.

'Can't you hear me?' screamed Morgenstern.

'Try to think of yourself as a sim,' I said. 'Maybe Spalanzani's right.'

'We wanted information on Titania. The girls – *they* don't talk. We thought you'd be *different*.'

'If I'd known you were listening . . .'

'We had to know where she hides, what kind of organization she's got.'

'Yeah, so you can zap her from space.'

'No. You don't understand.' He panted and moaned, as if he were about to sell his soul to the moment, and would soon be defrocked, deflowered, disgraced. 'We're *working* with her.'

138

'Slut,' said Primavera.

I walked over to a TV and spread my palm across the close-up. 'Jack. Be brave. Let's hear no more. It's beneath your dignity. Abdominal impalement's not so bad.'

'More like messy,' said Primavera. 'He hasn't been trephinated.'

I tapped Morgenstern's glass forehead. 'Think of something nice. Green fields. The moon on the seashore. Your favourite cake. Mother.' I turned to Primavera. 'Ready?'

'Don't you dare get high and mighty about killing people ever again. Do you understand me, Ignatz Zwakh?'

'But I know the secret,' said Morgenstern, 'the secret of the matrix!'

'Big deal,' said Primavera. 'So do I. We all do. Every one of Titania's dolls.'

'You'll never find him,' he said. 'Not alone. Not without me.'

'Find who?' I said.

'He means Dr Toxicophilous. He's in here too. Sometimes I get a little peep of him just before I go to sleep.'

'Toxicophilous has the key to the matrix,' said Morgenstern. 'He can wake you up. He can let us out!'

'So after we kill you we'll go find him. I'll dream us to Grosvenor Square.' Primavera put down her popcorn and, propping chin in hand, adopted Thinker's pose. 'But you know, Iggy, he's sort of got a point. Where do we start looking? I can't dream us to a place I've never seen. I just can't *imagine* it.'

'But out there,' I said, 'there's lots of things you haven't seen. Half of London.'

'Picture books. Lessons at school. I don't know what. But I've *seen* them.'

I slapped my hand on top of the TV. The picture wobbled. 'How does he know about this *matrix* business?'

'It's obvious, Iggy. He's wrung it out of some doll. S'pose I'm not the first he's captured.'

'Titania told me,' said Morgenstern. 'Titania's people. Voluntarily.'

Sure she did,' I said. 'How come Titania never told me?'

'Titania,' said Morgenstern, 'has told me many things.'

'*Salaud*.'

'Yeah,' said Primavera, 'my queen wouldn't be involved with the likes of *you*.'

'I know Grosvenor Square,' he said. 'I was posted there years back. I can take you . . .'

Primavera blew out her cheeks and exhaled noisily. She got up, knocking over a pile of *manga*, and circulated amongst the debris of our three-year holiday in the Weird: broken chairs, broken fax, ripped, blood-crusted Y-fronts (trophies of the 'interesting boys' she had met), all covered in an undisturbed dust, the ash from the little volcanoes of our lives, and all lit by the phosphor-dot luminescence of the TVs, each one of which beamed Jack Morgenstern's face, surmounted by a tiara of beer cans. A dying ad-sign outside the window filled the room with hiccups of light. Green, black, green, black. Bangkok-London, in all its *noir* packaging, its cheap glitz flashing across the sky, was ever near. Too near. Primavera snapped her fingers. 'Guess I'll have to kill you later,' she muttered. With slick editing, the hydroponic garden reappeared. Primavera had dressed the three of us in –

'Combat fatigues?'

'I'm feeling mean,' she said. She took Morgenstern by his lapels. 'Maybe you're flesh and blood, maybe you're a bunch of pixels. But you know what I can do, so don't fuck with me.' A small audience of three half-humans and one nanoengineer peered about the door of the dome. 'That goes for you too.' Primavera took me to one side.

'Is Toxicophilous really here?' I said.

140

'He's in every Lilim. That's what Titania told me. But it's a secret. The "secret of the matrix". Only dolls are supposed to know.'

'Oh,' I said.

'Some girl's blabbed. Morgenstern must really have used the thumbscrews. I'll get him. You'll see. He's going to know what it's *like*.'

'Toxicophilous can help us?'

'My ROM is all messed up, but Toxicophilous represents the programme that controls my files, my instincts. He's my operating system. Perhaps he can sort things out.' She looked out over the unreal city. 'He's out there somewhere; somewhere where the universe according to Primavera Bobinski becomes the Lilim ur-universe.' Morgenstern was summoned to heel. 'So take me to Grosvenor Square, slut.'

Morgenstern, comprehending, I think, that life and death depended on the morbid fancy of his erstwhile prisoner, composed himself and waved a deprecating hand over the rooftops. 'This place is a g-goddamn mess. I might be able to spot it from the air. Trouble is, you just *spiked* my autogyro pilot.'

'I can be *really* delinquent if you like,' said Primavera. To me she added: 'Seems I can do big-time magic again. In my dreams at least. I'll fly the three of us over town until *slutty* here gets a fix on where this *Grosvenor* place is.'

'What about me?' said Kito. 'What if you no come back?'

'Don't worry, Madame,' said Primavera, 'if there is an exit you can be sure I'll flush *you* out.'

'Where you go to, Uncle Jack?' said a Pikadon.

'You vanish, come back, go again,' said the other. 'Take us with you!'

'Shut up,' said Primavera, 'we're going to see a man who can re-boot me.'

'Be careful,' called Spalanzani, 'be careful when you dream. The city is part of your memory, but we are realtime. So fragile! So soft!'

'I'm not going to dream,' said Primavera, 'I'm going to fly.' She put an arm about my waist.

'Please,' I said, 'you know I don't like flying.'

'Don't be a pin,' she said, 'this isn't Marseille. We're not on the run. Nobody's going to shoot at us.' She took hold of Morgenstern and flexed her knees. 'Hold on, boys.' With a little jump she was airborne; Morgenstern's bulk immediately tipped her to her left. 'Weee!' Morgenstern began windmilling his free arm like an incompetent funambulist. Compensating (Morgenstern was twice my size), Primavera pitched, yawed, then regained her attitude. Where was the sick-bag? I closed my eyes to the dreamscape below.

Morgenstern must have followed my lead. 'Start looking, slut!' said Primavera. 'We haven't brought you along just so you can wimp out.' His breath came fast and heavy. Primavera, her lips to my ear, said, 'This guy got *asthma* or something?' She began to shake Morgenstern up and down. 'A little turbulence ahead, ladies and gentlemen.' Our fatigues billowed as Primavera initiated a lazy dive; car horns, shouts, the rumpus of the streets, carried over the whistle of our descent.

'Okay,' shouted Morgenstern, 'I'm looking, I'm looking! There's Selfridges, so this must be Oxford Street. No. It's a *klong*. But over there – that's Nelson's column. Piccadilly Circus. That monorail shouldn't be there, and those temples . . . Wait. To your right. No. Straight on . . .'

'This is hopeless,' said Primavera, after Morgenstern had treated us to half an hour of manic directions. She brought us down in a thoroughfare that was half road, half *klong*, opposite an electronic café. 'Let's try the Net,' she said, and swung through the café doors; the doors swung back, returning Primavera to the street.

'No good?' I said.

'Best hamburger in town,' she said, and walked away licking ketchup from her fingers.

Primavera put her head through the doors. 'What's keeping you two?' Inside the café her face was everywhere: customers, cashiers, bag-ladies, mechanical beggar kids . . . A seated row of Primaveras looked at us askance, then, with a synchronized flick of hair, returned their attention to their milk shakes.

'Seems I'm the only person who lives in this city,' said their original. 'Except for the good doctor, that is.'

We walked up to a bank of transcoms. A Primavera clone in a two-piece business suit asked, 'Person to person, station to station, or machine to machine?'

'Poison to poison,' said Primavera.

'Yeah,' I said, 'Dr – ' Well, surrender my loins to . . . I didn't know the guy's real name. Nobody did. Over the years we'd grown superstitious about pronouncing it, regarding it as some kind of Tetragrammaton. 'Toxicophilous,' I said.

'And if you can't raise him,' said Primavera, 'try one of his household appliances.'

'Just a moment please.'

The computer listed no such name.

Primavera gave Morgenstern a tired but sanguinary stare. 'Listen, slut, you're going to have to do better or – '

'Darling!' A clone ran across the café and kissed Primavera on the cheek. 'I haven't seen you since school!'

'S'pose not.'

'Toxicophilous,' said Morgenstern (eager, I think, to escape another dose of Primavera's in-flight antics), 'you heard of him?'

'Oh, *him*,' said the clone.

'We need to talk,' I said.

143

'You newspaper people? I thought you knew all about – '

'No,' I said.

'We're oneironauts,' said Primavera. 'Aliens. Take us to your leader. Take us to Dr Toxicophilous.'

'It's a strange world,' said the clone.

Slap! said Primavera's hand. 'Wake up!'

Impassive (though blood beaded her razored face), the clone said, 'Try Soho. Try *Frenchie's*.'

Morgenstern was through the doors.

'Sure,' I said to the clone, 'thanks.'

'Look out for the rippers!'

Outside, a *tuk-tuk* awaited us, a photocopy Primavera ready to take our fare. 'Rippers?' I said.

Primavera jumped aboard. 'My brain cells say the craziest things.'

The three-wheeler buzzed through the crossbred streets, the intersection of a 'cities of the world' theme park where images of London half remembered from school books interwove with the symbols of our exile in Siam. From cabs, buses, water taxis and temples, from pubs, massage parlours, food stalls and theatres, night owls returned our stares, a thousand green eyes that held ours but a moment before refocusing on business, pleasure or the void.

Water was lapping at our feet. 'Where we're going,' I asked the driver, 'are there canals?'

'Scared about getting your feet wet?' she said. The water began to rise; black spray jetted through the *tuk-tuk*'s open body; we were penetrating the city's aquapolitan heart. Upstairs, where the money lived, high above the smog in air-filtered splendour, the lights of penthouse condos shone like the gold bar of heaven. How many rich bitch Primaveras leaned out? We had come to save them. Where were the streamers, the fireworks, the cheers?

Stench of *klongs*; small-hour exhaustion; decay. This

was dollspace. Machine consciousness. Impure, like all thought, but more massive than the consciousness of mankind, its constituents were psychons of iron, glass and steel, a neon-bright vortex of complex simplicity from which rose the aleatory music that so bewitched the world. Music that was solid, dimensional; music that was sinew, muscle, *physique*.

'New to town?' said the driver.

'Yeah,' I said. 'Business trip.'

'You should take in a show. All work and no play – '

I glanced at Morgenstern. 'He's incurable.'

'Over there,' said Primavera. 'Stop!'

We pulled in to the kerb. 'Astoria?' said the driver. 'They do Shakespeare and all that stuff. You should try a musical . . .' Outside the theatre a billboard proclaimed *Salomé – A New Play By Dr Toxicophilous*. 'Anyway, it's a first-night performance. You'll never get a seat.'

'First night? Iggy, he's bound to be there.'

'We're supposed to be going to Soho,' said Morgenstern.

'But it's his *first night*. We can wait until the end and then shout "Author! Author!" '

'That's crazy,' I said.

'It's crazy,' said Morgenstern.

'So who asked you, slut?' Primavera stepped onto the pavement. A passing car sent a sheet of water across her path, leaving her rat-tailed and bemired. 'This is a crazy world,' she said, wiping her eyes. 'Come on. Let's go. Let's go *ape shit*.'

The amalgamation of West End millennial swank with the cut-and-run fabric of the Weird had resulted in a theatreland of High Art, Hucksterism and Hullabaloo. Primavera shoved through clones in snooty evening dress, flower girls and saffron-robed monkettes: Primavera squared, Primavera to the power of 3, 4, 5, Primavera to the power of 100.

'Hey you – kid with the enamel eyes – you wanna buy – ' Primavera felled the tout with the *Muay Thai* kick known as 'The alligator swings its tail' and used her own face as a stepping stone. I tracked her through a crush of curious witnesses, and entered the theatre's foyer.

'First night, huh?' said Primavera. The foyer was empty.

'First-night nerves?' I said. We proceeded into the stalls.

'Iggy, the whole *place* is empty.' We sat in the back row, Morgenstern placing an aisle between himself and his tormentor. The auditorium was a fleapit. A vast network of cobwebs hung from a surrounding frieze that was a burlesque of Phidian art; bat droppings littered the floor; seats were slashed, the stage curtain ragged; and all was illuminated by a sallow light. The light dimmed; the curtain rose.

SCENE

The Palace of Herod. A boudoir – a doll's boudoir – high above the streets of New Jerusalem. Salomé is discovered at her toilette, attended by her maid.

MAID (*aside*): 'Salomé, not Salome,' says the Princess of Judaea, 'Salome sounds like salami and I'm French, *savez-vous*? One more Salome and salami's what you get, salami and tar-water till the end of your days . . .' So call me Electrolux, ma'am, not Electra. I'm English, dooby-doo? I don't say it, of course. You want Greek slave? I do Greek slave. Do it very well.

SALOMÉ: So who is this Jokanaan?

MAID: A prophet, ma'am. With a vision of Christ as Shiva.

SALOMÉ: I've heard he's pretty. Pretty as the Archangel Gabriel. Pretty as the Angel of Death. And famously cruel. Almost as cruel as me.

MAID (*aside*): Well, maybe a bad girl like her *needs* a bad boy like him. Ever since her mother, Herodias, came over from Paris and got hitched to the Big Jew, Herod himself,

146

she's been scratching at the wound of her boredom like a sex-rat gnawing at its own bowels . . . (*To Salomé*) He's a rebel, ma'am. Talks revolution. The decline and fall of the empire *de luxe*. Talks of one who'll come 'after him' and reprogram the race, a bodysnatcher who'll change us all . . .

SALOMÉ: Hosannah in the highest. Maybe I'll go see him. I like guys who're a little sicko. It'll make a change from playing *mahjong* with Mummy's friends.

MAID: So here's your raiment, excessively dermatoid; and here's your shoes, perilously heeled. Now the war paint: lipstick made from marinated foreskins, mascara made from blackened bones . . .

Primavera threw her legs over the seat in front. 'Bor*ing*,' she said. I put my arm about her shoulders. It occurred to me that this was something I had never done: take my girlfriend to a show, or to the movies. It seemed it was something only ordinary people did. (Sure, I'd escorted her to the premiere of *The Birth Of A Nation*. Great SFX, that show. I remember the *Phi Gaseu* – disembodied heads trailing long tails of intestine – that feasted on the unborn of Siam. They were meant to symbolize the Negroid and Slavic decadence of the West so nobly resisted by the Siamese people. Sure. Great. But that had been work . . .) Morgenstern's head fell forward; he began to snore. 'You want me to vampire-fuck you?'

'Kiss me,' I said. 'Pretend that – '

'Get out of it. Snogging in the back row's for kids.'

'Maybe we could – '

'Yeah, and maybe you could get me a good dentist.' She shrugged off my arm. 'Boring. Bor*ing*.'

The play continued, empurpled, street-precious, very 'nineties'. Salomé meets Jokanaan (Primavera in a beard); Jokanaan rants. Seems he wants to turn Salomé into a little Watteau goddess. Seems Christ the great programmer, the black Christ, the Christ of guilt and pain, is coming with sword in hand to harry the world of fashion. And Salomé smiles. Pleased.

'Cut his head off,' said Primavera, 'get on with it. Can't you see that's what he wants?'

But first there has to be the soft-shoe shuffle. Herod (Primavera in another beard) watches from behind half-lidded eyes bruised with sleeplessness. And Salomé, in a derma-riot of second skin, trips across the boards, neck between thighs, or ankle about neck, an invertebrate contortionist with angry, Medusa-like hair. Then the salver, bloodily replete. And the last line, the line the world has been waiting for:

HEROD: Kill the woman!

Primavera sprang up. 'Author! Author!' she screamed, clapping wildly. I added to the applause. Morgenstern blinked, stood, and offered his own hands. The curtain fell; the auditorium again revealed its jaundiced visage. Morgenstern was the first to fall quiet; then I too let my hands hang from my side. 'Author! Author!' Primavera cried, until, forlorn, her applause became the sound of one hand clapping: a realization that the doctor would not appear.

'We've lost valuable time,' Morgenstern sighed. 'We should have – ' Primavera treated him to one of those stares to which he always reacted as if he'd had lime juice thrown in his eyes.

'Soho,' I said.

'Bozo,' said Primavera, and leaped over the rows of seats as if competing for a one-hundred-metre hurdle.

Our *tuk-tuk* had waited, and soon we were again speeding through canyons of concrete and steel. The night sky was veined like marble, like a membrane split open, ruined, useless. It began to rain: it was a fizz-pop kind of rain, mock-atomic. On either side of the waterway wealth gave way to squalor. Inhuman flotsam sat huddled about scrapheap fires in the shells of gutted buildings; figures slunk in tenement doorways, *apache* skirts revealing stilettos tucked between stocking tops and thighs; lines of washing, like the bunting of a carnival of sordidness, were strewn between *sois*; child facsimiles of the screaming Miss P dive-bombed us, jumping from the upper stories of slums into the chemical stew of the *klong*; the rain eased into drizzle.

'*Frenchie's*,' said our driver. On iron stilts that possessed the undulating elegance of a Paris *Metro* entrance, *Frenchie's* rose from its island of silt, its garish vitality contrasting with the boarded tenements, empty restaurants and gloomy merchandisers of Anglo-Saxon smut that lay on either side.

'Stay here,' I told the driver. We crossed a gangplank, and a doorgirl ushered us up the stairs into Big Weird a-go-go shadows.

Morgenstern walked to the bar. 'Screwdriver.' His hands were shaking.

'Must still be getting over the flight,' I said to Primavera.

'Where you come from, handsome man?' Wrong Primavera. This one wore a G-string and spoke Big Weird barspeak.

'Primavera?' I looked around. She was talking to one of her doubles.

Glass exploded against the wall beside me. 'It's *blood*,' said Morgenstern.

'Probably mine,' I said. 'This town must be well-stocked.' I went to sit down. There was something on my stool. A mechanical mammary gland. I tried to brush it away. Stupid. The breast was insubstantial, and my hand passed from guillotined ligament to teat. The place was filled with holoshit.

'Drink?'

'You got anything that's not red?' The bar girl pointed

to a bottle of some off-white *crème*. 'I'll pass,' I said, and turned my eyes upon the handful of dancers (programmed to look bored for human similitude) that were shimmying to . . . The music stopped; restarted. *Oh doctor, doctor, I wish you wouldn't do that.* Talk of the streets, the town, the world. Beat of the galactic arm. Damn them. The *Imps* had a number one.

Number one. That was the name of the lookalike who had chosen to dismount the stage, kneel down on the bar, and perform, a few centimetres from my face, a routine that would have left a human girl dislocated and raw. Raw as salami. Or Salome. I looked through her legs, to where the other dancers paraded about a glass vat centre stage. In the vat's bubbling, aerated liquid, a half-formed gynoid stared back at me with the mindless eyes of mindless creation. No superscience attended her nativity. Above her, a neural network programmed with pirated software instructed the vat's microrobots to duplicate a doll, Cartier, Seiko, Rolex, whatever, not by engineering base elements, but by reorganizing the atomic structure of a human foetus, aborted (so ran the rumours) by force. Illegal, of course. Like synthetic gasoline was illegal. Like prostitution, dermaplastic and psychotropic scent. But this dream bar belonged to the Weird, and the Weird was moneytown, its forbidden technologies commanding huge amounts of foreign exchange. A gynoid was cheap; it turned a quick profit; and a profit made you a patriot.

Primavera joined me. 'Number thirteen says Dr T's been and gone. We've missed him, Iggy. And *nobody* knows where this *Grosvenor* place is.' My dancer was rejoicing in a display of abdominal contractions, the violence of which seemed ready to disembowel her. 'Little tart,' said Primavera. 'Never thought I'd end up looking like that. Look at her: the Bobinski's trashed. Nothing *belle époque* there. All that's left is gynoid.' Primavera leaned across the bar, took the dancer by the hair, and struck her. Hard. 'Am I the only one around here who's awake?' She struck again. Harder. But the mirror image didn't crack.

'Hey,' said Morgenstern. He was standing by the door, filling his lungs. 'There's something happening out here.'

From the door it was possible to see into a nearby alley where a dark cloaked figure was struggling with a whimpering girl.

'Doll ripper,' said a bar girl.

Primavera swept back her hair. 'Nanobot?' The bar girl nodded. Pushing us aside, Primavera jumped to the half-flooded streets.

It's always the same: the fire escapes and mullioned windows, the girl in the party dress you push against the alley wall, the snicker-snack! snicker-snack! of steel against cuspids, the gasp and clichéd expression of 'surprise and pain' . . .

'Come on,' I said to Morgenstern.

'Wait a minute. That thing out there – '

I pulled him after me. We clambered into the *tuk-tuk*. 'Follow her,' I said to the driver as Primavera splashed through the shallows and attained the alley's shore. Ahead of us – cloak spread behind like a comic-book villain – the anthropomorphic virus sprinted into the anonymity of the night. Primavera took to the air.

'We should be giving this thing a wide berth,' said Morgenstern.

'Tell that to Primavera,' I said.

Morgenstern swung his head about. 'Jesus.' I looked behind. Draped over a dustbin was the clone we had seen from our vantage point at *Frenchie's*. The hilt of a knife protruded lewdly from between her thighs; teeth ground on metal, with the sound of fingernails clawing at slate. *It's always the same: the expression of innocence betrayed and of crime discovered . . .* 'Martina, Martina,' I said. 'Martina von Kleinkunst.'

The *tuk-tuk* pulled up; caught in its headlights, the blood-stained nanobot was pinning Primavera against a doorway. 'Iggy! My magic doesn't work on him . . .' She gurgled as the nanobot's fingers tightened about her throat. The figure, throwing back its cloak, turned its face to us, a face as black and featureless as polished onyx. I scrambled out.

'I'm Euclidean!' The thing's laughter was emotionless, canned. 'You can't hurt me! You're algorithmic, you're recursive, you're – '

I rushed it; caught it with a flying tackle; it sank beneath me, yielding like dough. 'Yeah, well, I'm Euclidean too. From out there. And to me you're just another tin microbe.'

Warily, Morgenstern approached us. 'Think this thing can help?' He gave the nanobot an idle kick.

I stared into the opaque face, and into my own black reflection (felt, for a moment, a girl's body struggling against my own, fluttering like a bird clenched in a fist). 'Dr Toxicophilous,' I said. 'We want to find Dr Toxicophilous.'

'So,' said the nanobot (in the preppy voice of an Ivy League closet queen), 'who do you think *us* guys have been looking for the last couple of days? Killing a few biomorphs here and there is all well and fine, but we want to get this job *over* with. It's a matter of professional pride. But the old man – he's not here. Sure, he makes visits. He can go where he *likes*. But as to where he lives . . . The rest of the guys have gone off to try and find him.'

'He has to be here,' said Morgenstern. 'He's supposed to be inside all Lilim.'

'So he is. But the matrix models an infinite number of universes. We think he lives at the crossroads.'

'And where's that?' I said.

'Everywhere,' said the nanobot, 'and nowhere.' Morgenstern kicked the thing in the head. Its immaculate physiognomy fractured. 'Ow! Rough stuff, eh? If this town isn't the *pits*. All these *girls*. Like *ants*, I tell you. Little *reflex* machines. A billion ganglia. Ugh! And now you start to – ' Morgenstern kicked the thing again. 'Listen: we're talking about a singularity of information. A black hole of consciousness.' His head lolled to one side. 'Your consciousness, Primavera Bobinski.'

'Let's kill this doll-ripping bastard and get moving,' said Primavera, massaging her throat. 'He's given me an idea.'

I twisted the nanobot's head, hoping to break its neck; the top of the brain box came off in my hands. Oily globules dripped from the meninges, rolled mercurially across the alley with autonomous life.

'Mirrors,' said Primavera, 'within mirrors. That's no way in. Got to see the back of my own head. Confront the I.' She opened her combat jacket. 'Send the *tuk-tuk* away, Iggy. We don't want her sucked in.' Our driver didn't linger.

'Primavera, don't go screwy on me.'

She sat down, crossed her legs guru-fashion, and stared into the black abyss of her navel. At the first glimmer of green I took a step backwards; Morgenstern copied. 'Time to Ouroboros,' she said. As through the smashed porthole of a depressurizing plane, her hair, and then her head, were sucked into her abdomen. Plop! Shoulders, arms, legs followed, until, self-consumed, she remained only a black disk, small and impenetrably dark, surrounded by a luminous green halo. I regurgitated fried grasshopper. 'Come *on*,' she called, voice faint but edged with exasperation.

'One thing's for sure,' said Morgenstern, 'I'm not staying alone in *this* place.'

We walked into Primavera's event horizon.

CHAPTER ELEVEN

Psychic Surgery

The necropolis seemed (as it always did) limitless, extending out of eyeshot, beyond hope, beyond the world; a singularity of death where the curvature of space-time was infinite. Eternal. Where was our coach? Our horses? It was cold; colder than at any time I could recall; a ground mist slunk at our heels, crept beneath our fatigues. No pleasure trip, this.

'Primavera?' I called. I helped Morgenstern to his feet. Superimposed upon the familiar desolation, like a surreal photomontage, marooned amongst the stone termini of life, a slice of London real estate rose broodingly from the plain. Primavera headed towards it.

'Grosvenor Square,' said Morgenstern, as we picked our way through the tombstones, struggling to match Primavera's fleetfootedness. As we caught up with her, and passed that boundary between necropolis and square marked by chopped outcroppings of macadam, the mist lifted, and we found ourselves wading through a sea of grass, about us pseudo-Georgian terraces and the ruins of the American Embassy. Encircled by night, the square's one lit window shone like a beacon in a lonely tower. The sexton of this world of death was at home.

The door was open.

'Doctor?' called Primavera. All was in shadows, the furniture shrouded in white sheets; piano music percolated through the ceiling. After climbing two flights of stairs we noticed a splinter of light beneath a door. Primavera rapped her knuckles against the wood. 'Doctor? Dr Toxicophilous? It's me, Primavera.' The music stopped.

'Enter.' It was the voice of an old man breathless with

disease and second childhood. We found him sitting before an open fire. Wrapped in a paisley dressing gown, and leaning against a four-poster bed, he held, in his lap, a clockwork toy which, undistracted by our presence, he had set to winding, quietly and methodically. He set the toy before him – a model of a young woman seated at a piano – and the music recommenced. 'Greensleeves. My Lady Greensleeves. I always thought it should be our national anthem. Gentle. Verdant. English. God Save the Queen? Ah, there'll be a new queen soon. And it will be us that needs saving, God damn *her*.'

Automata carpeted the floor. Primavera cleared a space and sat down beside Dr Toxicophilous, surrounded by her nineteenth- and eighteenth-century predecessors. I breathed through my mouth; the smell of camphor was overpowering.

'Phalibois made her,' said Toxicophilous, stroking the horse-hair locks of the little musician. 'Made her during that golden age before the First World War. The golden age of automata. And all these' – he passed his hand over the half-a-dozen toys at his feet – 'from the Marais district of Paris. I worked in Paris once . . .'

'Doctor,' said Primavera, 'I need your help.' Toxicophilous rubbed his chest and wheezed.

'Poor doll. Your clockwork is broken. I know; I felt it break. It broke like . . .' His eyes became rheumy. 'Like this old man's heart.' Primavera's own eyes were raised; her grin, lopsided. 'First the crash. Ah, it ruined so many. Those imitation dolls. People preferred them. They were cheap. Vulgar. But they offered *sex*. Then the plague. Such nightmares.'

'Yeah, well I'm sick of dreams, doctor,' said Primavera, 'I want to wake up. I want to live in the real world again.'

'We want out,' said Morgenstern, who hadn't moved beyond the door. 'Understand? A Lilim has trapped us inside her programme.'

155

'Tick-tock, tick-tock.' Toxicophilous put his hand on Primavera's belly. 'We nanoengineers are much like clocksmiths. Semiconductor technology relied on electronics, but we use physical moving parts. Gears whose teeth are atoms; bearings that are bonds between atoms . . . Yes, you are inside her programme. But you are also inside a physical world. A clockwork world.'

'I *know* that,' said Primavera.

'Yeah,' I said. 'That's just a fancy way of saying that her neuroelectrical activity is more powerful than a human's; that for her reality isn't consensual.'

'I said I *know* that, Iggy.' She sighed. 'It didn't stop me getting scrambled, did it? So doctor: you going to help? Or are you going to wait for the nanobots to arrive?'

The loose folds of Toxicophilous's face tightened with self-reproach. 'You must hate me.'

'Well you did turn me into a fucking *robot*.' Primavera stood up, peevishly kicking over a few of the antique toys that were offering a sardonic comment on her life. 'Trouble is, you're part of me. And I'm pretty sick of hating myself. Titania says – '

'Titania,' said Toxicophilous, 'was never human. But you . . . I know what I've done. I've taken away your childhood. I've taken away your girlhood, your womanhood. I've taken away your humanity.'

'So who wants to be human?' said Primavera.

'Few of us, it seems. But it was my purpose to give a human-like consciousness to my automata. That is why I built the matrix. I wanted to find that fractal vanishing point, that point of complex simplicity from which life would spontaneously emerge. Dead girls, they said. Just because they weren't built around the nucleic acids. Ha! Their consciousness was made up of sub-atomic particles, like ours. Yes, I wanted to give them humanity.'

'You did,' I said. 'Your own. Didn't turn out to be such a good thing, did it?'

156

'If I infected others,' said Toxicophilous, 'I myself was infected. Those first *émigrés* who came to Britain after the dissolution of the Pax Sovietica were intellectuals, former dissidents, underground writers, poets without a cause. They sought new themes, a new purpose. The worst of them glorified the old demons that were again racking their homelands: nationalism, populism, the paranoia of the non-existent foe: madnesses they embodied in a revival of folk tales and images. "The Second Decadence" the critics called their movement. I was a boy and their stories of witches and golems, vampires and the eternal Jew riddled my mind.'

'Those stories have invaded reality,' I said.

'Not that that's such a *bad* thing,' said Primavera, arching an eyebrow as sleek and black as the roots of her hair.

'Ah,' said Toxicophilous, 'but the story of the witch always ends with a burning; the vampire is always impaled. I brought the Lilim into the world, but I brought death too . . .' A tear hung from the tip of his nose, fell and broke over the toy piano.

'Jesus,' said Primavera, 'to think I carry this guy around inside me.' She placed her hands on her hips. 'Stop it! You've been dead for years. Everybody's forgotten about you! We don't even know your real name . . .' She brought her foot down on both piano and miniature pianist, destroying them in an orgy of chromaticism. 'They can't impale us all. We're going to take over the world, just like Titania says. Right, Iggy?'

'Right.'

'The world,' said Toxicophilous, 'will be a little boy's fantasy. The dream of a morbid child.'

'Call it what you like,' said Primavera, 'it'll be my world. The world of the Lilim. Maybe I play by your rules. I don't care. I'm still *me*.'

'Your world. You mean that other place? The place you

call real?' Toxicophilous glanced towards the windows. 'I like it here. It's quiet. Peaceful. Here, at the heart of the matrix. It is this clockwork world, this neuroelectrical world, this world between zero and one, that is the real world for you, Primavera. This world that is unpredictable, uncertain . . . This world of magic. Of death.'

Morgenstern left his position by the door and strode into the centre of the room. 'If this is her world she's welcome to it, but it's not mine. Can you get us out of here or not?'

'You'll get out of here when Primavera wakes up.'

'Great,' said Morgenstern, 'give the man a cigar. Can *you* wake her?'

'She needs a kiss from Prince Charming. Charmless, in your case. The answer lies with you, Mr Morgenstern.'

'Me? What the hell can I do?'

'Tell her the truth. The truth will wake her.'

'What are you talking about?' said Primavera. 'What's this slut know about truth?'

Toxicophilous closed his eyes. 'It concerns my beloved Titania. The queen I love to hate. My dear, she has deceived you . . .'

'Don't you call *my* queen a liar.'

'So many lies. Isn't that right, Mr Morgenstern?'

'You can't expect me to – ' Morgenstern sat down on the edge of the bed. 'It's classified.'

'Then stay,' said Toxicophilous.

'I can't stay, I've got to . . . Hey, how come you're wise to all this?'

'I know Titania. And I've come to understand that part of myself that poisoned her, made her change . . . God help me, I *am* Titania.'

'Something's up,' I said to Primavera, 'something weird. I know it. Make them talk.'

'Weird,' said Primavera. 'I don't like it, Iggy.'

'Weird,' said Morgenstern. 'Weird policy for a weird world. It's weird all right.'

'We're waiting,' said Toxicophilous.

'If it's going to get us out of here, then . . .' Morgenstern spat on his hands, slicked back his hair and beard, and eased open the door of his confessional. '*Operation Black Spring* was all about you, boy. Dolls are tough. We've tried to get the truth out of them before. Without success. So we thought we'd try a junkie. Then you go and spill the beans without us so much as breathing heavy on your fix . . .'

'You've breathed heavy enough,' I said.

'Yeah,' said Primavera, 'maybe I should remove his lungs.'

'Okay, okay,' said Morgenstern. 'Here it is. To start with, what I said a while back's true: we didn't have any intention of sending you to England. I was just trying to scare you, to get you to talk. No; you were on your way to the States. You think we'd share intelligence with the Human Front? Lord, the HF have our token support, but only as a cover for the support we give Titania.

'Just after the HF came to power, Titania had a few of her runaways contact our people in the field. At first we thought it was some kind of hoax. But then something happened. Some people say the President had a vision. Others say it was the President's wife. Whoever it was, the State Department was empowered to set up an exploratory dialogue. There were secret talks in Berlin. Titania's delegation made DC realize that the HF's plans to exterminate the Lilim weren't going to work. The plague had become a pandemic. But the more those girls talked the more we understood that things could work to our advantage, that the Lilim could provide us with the means of reasserting ourselves on the world stage.

'They were stellar, those girls. They were offering nothing less than to become an instrument of US foreign policy. What they proposed was this: Titania would send her runaways to countries of geopolitical significance to us. When the plague began to undermine those countries' economies, Titania would unleash what she called "the secret of the matrix". Only America would be privy to that secret, would recognize it, would know how to exploit it. Every government on Earth would be beholden to us for controlling the plague's spread . . .'

'Shut up!' shouted Primavera. 'It's all lies!'

'The secret of the matrix?' I said. 'You mean the fact that our friend here' – I gestured towards Toxicophilous – 'lives inside every Lilim?'

'Oh it's more than that,' said Toxicophilous, 'much more.'

'Screw you and your *secrets*,' said Primavera. 'Why were you going to take us to America?'

'Things here in Thailand weren't going by the numbers. You, Primavera, the first doll to be sent out east, weren't *infecting* the locals, you were damn well *killing* them. We'd kept track of you, of course, ever since you'd arrived. Jinx had been on our payroll for years . . .'

'It was my *job*,' said Primavera, 'I *had* to kill them.'

'Sure. We could live with that. But what about your spare time? It wasn't good enough. We would have been content with another Lilim, a replacement, but Titania wanted you out of the way.'

'And what did you have planned for us?' I said.

'Debriefing. Titania's been pretty secretive. We don't wholly trust her, and her file's incomplete. We'd do anything to get more information, and anything to protect that information. When Jinx called me and told me what you were downloading on Kito I had my staff buy enough shares on the overnight exchange to make sure I had the muscle to silence any witnesses. Well, maybe Jinx is gone, maybe not. I'll have the Pikadons deal with him after they've offed Kito and that Italian. The bottom line is only the US government can know where Titania lives.' He pulled a CD from his breast pocket. Kissed it. 'And thanks to you, Zwakh, we *do* know. Some day we really *might* want to zap her.'

'Debriefing?' Toxicophilous laughed. 'Are you sure that's all? Are you sure there aren't certain people at the Pentagon and DARPA who are curious to find out what makes a Lilim tick?'

'Hospitals,' said Primavera. The words hobbled out, her mouth lame with despair. 'Titania wanted to send me to the Hospitals.'

'Yeah,' said Morgenstern, 'well, that's not my department. I just wanted to talk. Get the full story . . .'

'But why?' I said. 'Why would Titania conspire against her own kind?'

'She is fulfilling her programme,' said Toxicophilous. 'A doll's purpose is to die. Titania leads her daughters into darkness . . . Her inheritance is the fears, prejudices and secret lusts of *La Décadence*. Like all Lilim, she embodies Europe's death wish. Don't you know how much you want to die, Primavera? How much all Lilim want to die? That is the secret. The one and only secret of the matrix. How you and I long for annihilation!'

Primavera bit her knuckles.

'A Cartier automaton like Titania has the power to unlock that death wish,' said Morgenstern. 'In fact she's done it already. In the suburbs of the Neverland. We asked her to. We wanted proof.'

'Like sheep,' I said. 'They went to their deaths like sheep.'

'She can make it happen anytime she likes,' said Morgenstern. 'Anywhere. But for her next performance Titania will make sure the Lilim die for Uncle Sam. And for Uncle Sam alone. It's going to give us one *hell* of a bargaining chip. Of course some dolls don't surrender so easily, Primavera being a case in point. I understand

Titania's being calling *her* for years . . .' Morgenstern stood up. 'I'm not happy. I'm really not *happy* about all of this. But how do you expect America to protect its national interests? Nobody goes to war any more. History's finished: democracy and capitalism won. We got to do things different ways. We got to find new ways to fight, to goddamn well *survive* . . .'

'Forgive me, little doll,' said Toxicophilous, 'I wish I could have given you life. But something in me cried out for a victim.'

Primavera walked unsteadily towards a window. 'Oh, Iggy. It's too much, too much . . .' Outside, night was falling. I followed her, placed my hands on her shoulders. She focused upon our reflections in the glass. 'It's over, isn't it? That's all I am now. A reflection. Without substance. Without meaning.' I kneaded her flesh; felt the steel girders of her bones. 'You were right, Iggy. A doll is a thing of surface and plane. I've always known it was true. But Titania gave me something. Not a soul. Just something that made life bearable. An identity. A purpose. A kind of substitute soul. And now it's gone. She's killed it with her lies. Why did she do it? Why did my queen betray me? Can you tell me that?'

'Titania's very practical,' mumbled Morgenstern. 'She's got an instinctive grasp of politics.'

'Quiet,' I said, turning around. 'Just keep quiet, okay? Do you know what you've done? Both of you?' I swept my foot across the floor, scattering automata. 'It's not worth it. I'd rather stay here. Titania was all she had . . .'

'We get out now?' said Morgenstern.

I walked up to him and grabbed him by the beard. It came away in my hand. 'All she had,' I said. 'Titania was something to believe in. She made them proud. She turned the tables on prejudice.'

'Lies,' said Toxicophilous. 'All lies.'

'Yeah,' I said. I let the beard fall to the floor. Another trick.

'I never knew my Dad, you know,' said Primavera. 'He was Polish. Married Mum in Belgrade. Came to England. Died when I was six months old. Mum said the Lilim killed him. And for twelve years I'm a good little Serb. Then I get this other Dad. Dr Toxicophilous. What a deal. What a life . . .'

Toxicophilous reached into his gown and held up a glittering rod of brazen metal. He threw it across the room. 'It'll work now,' he said. 'Try it.'

'Primavera?'

'Mmm? Is it time to go home? And where is home? Where do I go now Titania has betrayed me?' She smiled, her lips tremulous.

I picked up the key. 'I don't know. Primavera, please . . .'

She turned her back on her reflection and put her arms about my neck. 'Let's do it,' she said. Her smile had frayed. 'What's the matter – scared?' The butterfly grip grew warm and sticky; her jacket was open, umbilicus peeping above the waistband of her fatigues. She reached for my hand, guided the key towards its ward. 'Don't move.' Her fingernails dug into my neck. 'Don't breathe. Don't even think.' She arched her body, thrusting herself onto the brass shaft in a violent spasm of flesh and will. Her scream splintered over my face.

The windows exploded. A green mist poured into the room. A wind howled across the plain of death.

Morgenstern shouted an exultant curse.

'Primavera – ' A thin trail of blood leaked from where the key had imperfectly cauterized the door beyond which dream and reality were as one. Her eyes rolled back; her bones had become powder, her flesh, liquid. I scooped her into my arms.

'Don't worry, Iggy,' she moaned, 'it's not the real

me . . .' She was turning to vapour, coalescing with the swirling mist.

'Goodbye, little doll,' called Dr Toxicophilous.

Jackknifed, head to the waxing gale, Morgenstern pulled himself to my side. A screw of dense green air rose from the sea of grass outside, opening into the cone of a tornado. The cone advanced towards us, and as the wall of the maelstrom skimmed the wall of the terrace, we were sucked into an emerald gyre and tossed like leaves into the sky.

I opened my eyes; I was inside Spalanzani's workshop, a naked Primavera by my side. I looked at my hand; only the impression of the key remained.

'Welcome back to the real world,' said Jack Morgenstern, subjecting us to his lightstick's one-eyed scrutiny.

'You owe your life to her,' I said.

'Tell it to my boys. Spalanzani was wrong. We were flesh and blood in there.'

'Uk!' said Primavera. 'I need an enema.'

'You think it's funny?'

'Does it matter? I'm just a sick little doll. I left what power I had back there. I can't even read your nasty slutty mind.'

'You've got the information you want,' I said. 'You can tell Titania we're dead. You owe us.'

'Titania?' said Kito, picking her way through the wreckage. 'More crazy story, Mr Ignatz?'

'If you like,' said Primavera. 'The magic's gone. Finished. Nothing matters now.'

'What matters is I get you Stateside,' said Morgenstern, 'according to plan. Now let's get moving.'

The Pikadons were guarding the door, their particle weapons drawn. 'So you got back?' I said. 'Pity.'

'Get back long time,' said a Twin.

'Mr Ignatz sleep *mark-mark*.'

'Now do what Uncle Jack say.'

Primavera and I walked hand in hand. As we approached the door, the Pikadons moved aside, and then closed ranks behind us.

'Not you, Madame.'

'You stay behind.'

'Bang – '

'And Boom – '

'Want to talk.'

Kito drew her peignoir tightly about her and pressed her forehead against the wall. 'Why you *do* this, Mr Jack,' she wailed. 'I not start doll-plague. You must believe – '

'Of course you didn't,' said Morgenstern. 'You think we're stupid? You think we care? But Titania's real enough – '

'Titania?'

'Yeah, Titania. And even if she means – '

'Crazy story true?'

'And even if she means nothing to your greedy peasant mind – '

'No!'

'That makes you a security risk.'

'Who Titania, Uncle Jack?' said a Twin.

'Never mind, sweet thing. But after you've finished with Madame, get looking for that Italian.'

'And Mr Jinx?'

'I don't think Jinx will be bothering us.' Morgenstern prodded me with his lightstick. 'Great girls,' he said. 'Beautiful, deadly . . .' We stepped into the garden; the door closed. 'And stupid. But don't *tell* on me, mind.'

Primavera squeezed my hand. 'I've got to try it, Iggy.' Swinging about, she caught Morgenstern cleanly on the jaw. There was a tiny detonation; Morgenstern stepped back, his eyes crossing, uncrossing; Primavera moaned and put her hand to her mouth. Undissuaded, she extended the same hand as if to administer a hex in a last stand against reality. Morgenstern, his eyes refocused by fear, aimed his weapon.

'No! Not the marvellous toy!' Spalanzani dashed from an arbour of bougainvillaea and frangipani and placed his body before Primavera's. The air exploded; Spalanzani's head snapped back, and he dropped to the gravel, his pince-nez welded to his flesh as if by a thermic lance. Primavera staggered, then regained her balance. A pink smoking hole had appeared between her eyes, its edges bubbling like molten plastic. She looked at me with the insouciance of a wasted loony toon, and then she began to laugh.

The dome opened. The Pikadons ran to Morgenstern's side. 'Don't get *upset*,' said Primavera. 'I'll go quietly . . .' Shrugging her shoulders, she again took my hand. 'He needn't have done that, you know. The poor dweeb.' Her wound was bloodless, though I could see it furrowed deep into her brow. Tentatively, she explored the burn-hole with her fingers. 'Looks as if I'll have to go heavy on the make-up.'

Turning our backs to our captors (Primavera gave a flick of her hair, a little wiggle of her rump), we resumed our gallows walk.

'Wait!' cried Kito. I looked over my shoulder and saw that she was manipulating the dome's entryphone. Like her transcom, it folded into a lightstick. 'This time no become steely dan.'

'This time,' said a Twin, displaying her own gun, 'no fire joke-shop flag.'

The three half-humans faced each other, good, bad and *bijou*, like protagonists in a psycho-zygo western.

'Golden flower trash,' said Kito. Her lips were puffy and she sported a bloody nose. 'You think you take Nana so easy? I mamasan of *roboto okuku* before they cut you from plastic womb. From orphanage to beauty queen – Miss Cashew Nut, Miss Watermelon – all time circuit in brain making fucking *crazy* till come Bangkok work bar, buy bar, buy *soi*, buy Nana: you think can slap me on head? And you,' she said to Morgenstern, 'you number one bullshit man. I such fool . . .'

'I'm too old to be frightened by an entryphone, Madame.' Coherent light, in a microsecond of invisible, but noisy, drama, vaporized a small portion of Jack Morgenstern's thigh. His own weapon discharged – several exotic plants burst into flames – before clattering to the floor, to be smothered by a Whumpf! of unconscious meat.

A click, click, click was emanating from the Pikadons; they were pulling the triggers of their particle weapons to no effect; and now Kito covered them. 'Stop it!' said Kito, as if she were scolding two mischievous children. 'I wake up first. Take Duracell from gun.' The Twins swapped embarrassed stares. 'Bad day for you when Smith and Wesson merge with Mattel. Into dome!' Kito sealed the door from the outside and left the Twins battering their fists upon steel plate.

'Finish him, Madame,' I said.

'I no want CIA after me. Mr Jack not small-time thug can off without trouble. Come, Primavera, I re-hire you. You too, Mr Ignatz. We take car. Elevator go all way down to garage.'

Primavera poked her head above the oubliette of her despair. 'We did it again,' she yelled – the venom of a murderess combining with the enthusiasm of a cheerleader – 'A, B, AB, O, that's the way I wanna go! Rhesus factor, rhesus factor, ya, ya, ya!' But then the depths reclaimed her.

CHAPTER TWELVE

Desperadoes

We hit Route Two before daybreak, slipping through Bangkok's dreaming sprawl, until the dawn struck out the asterisks of the stars. By early morning we were driving across the plateau of Korat. Beneath us, the Pak Chang reservoir glistened amidst the deforested wasteland of the plains. Primavera and Kito were asleep, slumped across the ZiL's back seat. I was glad. Ever since we had cleared Sukumvit Kito had talked incessantly of how she meant to revenge herself on the Pikadons; and Primavera – though she complained of migraine as well as stomach cramps – had been equally garrulous in insisting that the former mamasan's influence, no longer dark following her ouster, was now so minimal that she had little chance of being offered a free bowl of noodles and none of being offered the Pikadons' heads. 'So why didn't you stick them when you had the chance?' asked Primavera. 'Lost your nerve? Got too used to relying on lowlife like me? Now a *real* Cartier doll would have . . .' At last, the night's capers had called in their debts of exhaustion; I had driven fifty kilometres in silence, if not in peace.

I pulled in by a roadside café. 'Hey,' I said, shaking Primavera awake, 'this place sells tourist stuff: T-shirts, jeans; you interested?'

Primavera rubbed her eyes. 'I can't go about like *this*, can I?' Primavera's flesh, as cool and fine as alabaster ground to a talc, radiated against black leatherette, primary and secondary sexual characteristics a golden triangle of adorned erogeneity.

Kito stirred. 'Madame, can you spare a few satang?'

'I no carry money in dressing gown, Mr Ignatz. Here – '

She passed me her lightstick. 'Buy shop.'

I could get no food. The clothes were effort enough. The proprietors thought my weapon a toy and I had to vaporize a small dog before the wisdom of acceding to my demands was perceived. It was only when I was back in the car that I noticed that I had been palmed off with screaming blue jeans.

'So *tacky*,' said Primavera, ripping out the audio. 'So old-fashioned. My Mum used to talk about these.'

'Poor Primavera,' said Kito. 'No ten-inch special. No tutu. No ultrascenic itsyritzy.'

'I can't help it, Madame, you know I have this *neurosis*.'[1] Primavera held up a T-shirt printed with a smokestack and the words *Khao Yai Industrial Reserve*. '*Bougre!* What *is* this?'

'You lucky,' said Kito. Her shirt featured a dancing prophylactic and the slogan *Don't Be Silly, Put A Condom On That Willy*. She gave Primavera an accusing glance. 'Bad time when roboto make sick.'

'Yeah? Well a piece of rubber never protected any guy from *me*.'

We drew away. The landscape, crystallized by the waste of derelict salt mines, was bone-white; eucalyptus

---

[1]Primavera's 'hemline neurosis', as explained by Dr Bogenbloom, was less a result of 'strange exhibitionism' (the title of his contribution to the *festschrift* 'Semiotics of Anthropophagy') than of 'strange loops', the paradoxes that translate a *grande fille* into an idiom that is one long scream of feedback. Said the Bogey: 'For a hemline to reach that coveted elevation where bifurcation of thighs meets at that satin-gusseted apex we might call the "quantum-chaos crack", that same hemline, however vertiginous, must be hoisted halfway, then halfway again, always having to rise half of the remaining distance of its journey . . .' And thus never, to the regret of the doll, revealing the smallest gasp of netherness. I remember that wet season in 2070, when the phantasmata of the Weird's oneirotic, ruttish streets sported Zero G specials, pink-painted labia pouting from cutaway hose. And Primavera each night anxiously adjusting her skirt towards some elusive zenith of venereal vanity, each adjustment vanishing into a fractal gravity well, a doll doomed to an unremitting, if wholly relative, modesty.

struggled out of the spent earth. It was about seventy kilometres to Korat. I put my foot down. 'We'll be there in under an hour,' I said.

'And just where that, Mr Ignatz? I no make decision . . .'

'You don't decide anything,' said Primavera. She put a hand over her eyes as the road twisted and we caught the glare of the morning sun. 'Don't you understand? You're nothing now. Nothing.'

'Don't start that again,' I said. Primavera mumbled something in Serbo-Croat, in French, again in Serbo-Croat, and scrabbled for her sunglasses. 'Listen, Kito, we're going to Korat, and there we'll say our goodbyes.'

'Korat? You say goodbye when I say goodbye. You work for me. Both of you.'

'Forget it,' I said.

'We don't work for no one,' said Primavera. 'And we don't trust no one. Right, Iggy?'

'Right.'

'Nothing out there's real. It's just all too bad. Too crazy. Too *ape shit*.'

'Fecal,' I said.

'Yeah. Everyone can go to hell. From now on all this doll needs is her junkie.'

In the rear-view mirror Kito fidgeted with her ridiculous T-shirt like a sulking, hyperactive child. 'Take me with you, Mr Ignatz. I *nowhere* to go . . .'

Primavera, wearing the cheap shades that were part of our pathetic heist, had discovered a tube of plastic cement in the ZiL's tool kit, and, as best she could, began filling in her cavernous head wound. 'You're in no worse position than us, Madame.'

'Better,' I said. 'The police would never risk incriminating themselves by charging a former paymistress, no matter how big a reward the Pikadons offer.'

The fields had turned green; we passed through a little

sea of fertility. 'I no care about police,' said Kito, staring out at the sun-trap of the paddies. 'I care about Mr Jack.'

'Morgenstern'll be coming for us too. Best to split up.'

'Mr Ignatz. Please – '

Primavera, her DIY complete, teased her fringe forward in an attempt to conceal her labours. She clicked her tongue. 'I suppose she did get us out of Klong Toey.'

'Well, isn't *she* the model of altruism.'

'I did,' said Kito, 'yes, I did! Mr Ignatz forget many things . . .'

No; I didn't forget. Primavera and I had stowed away on a container whose registration number we had been made to memorize during our days in the *Seven Stars*. We hadn't known where we were going; we hadn't cared. We were kite-high on freedom. Six weeks later we had docked at Klong Toey, the port of Bangkok. For weeks we had lived in the waterlogged slums, hiding from the authorities, surviving on rotten vegetables and fruit, until, in desperation, I had prompted Primavera to kill ('but Lilim don't do that, Iggy – we live to *infect*') and rifle her victims' pockets. And then the reports of blood-drained corpses had reached Madame Kito's ears, and she – with her nose for the ways of English *bijouterie* – had investigated the sensation of 'The Vampire Of The Slums'.

Kito had begun to whine. 'I find you, teach you, give you false paper, place to live . . .'

'Yeah,' I said, 'may my heart burst with gratitude.' But it was true: we would have been deported if it hadn't been for Madame K. Could I really leave this woman by the roadside, as friendless as a scabby three-legged dog? Of course I could.

'Jinx,' I said. 'Jinx told you about "The Vampire Of The Slums'', didn't he? Wasn't he the one who convinced you to help us?'

'Fuck Jinx. I help you *now*.'

'You've never helped us. Jinx worked for Jack

Morgenstern. We've *all* been working for Morgenstern. Been working for him for years.'

'When I *say* I help, Mr Ignatz, I *mean* I help.'

'Oh come *on*, Madame,' said Primavera.

'You think you so rich? Where you get money? Madame can get. Madame have friend.'

'She's bullshitting, Iggy.'

'In Korat. Madame have friend in Korat. Old friend.'

It was hard to believe anybody would extend friendship to Kito except out of fear or avarice. And Kito could inspire neither. The news of her fall would already have been posted on the Net. But apart from grand larceny (with Primavera out of action that was a terrifying, hopeless prospect) our resources would be inadequate to carry us over the border.

'This friend – '

'Can trust, Mr Ignatz.' Confidence had entered her voice; she sensed my prevarication.

'Told you, Madame,' said Primavera, 'we don't trust no one.'

'Primavera, we're running low on H.' If only, I thought, the ZiL ran on synthetic; these big imported cars with their fussy diets were a pain. H was big bahts.

'My friend rich man. Number one in sericulture.'

'So why's he going to help you?' I said.

Kito smiled thinly: a smile of pleasure overlaying one of bitterness. 'You no understand. You think Kito so hard. You think she no can love.' She fanned herself with her hand. 'What you know? You children. Children who think they know world. I know friend help. My friend, ah. I tell you he is amour.'

'What?' said Primavera.

'Amour,' said Kito. 'Amour, my amour. Mosquito is *mon amour*.'

There was a corridor in the *Seven Stars* that, we were

told, was over a hundred kilometres long. Jo had led us through its shadows for most of the day. Too slender to admit a car (Jo explained that, anyway, we were too near the surface and couldn't afford to be heard), the corridor impelled us to use bicycles. Primavera and I commanded a tandem; Jo, a lightweight racer. Our lamps probed the darkness, overreached themselves and were lost. Jo said she would have flown if she hadn't been so new to that skill. Lifting the two of us would have been impossible. Said Jo: 'Dolls don't often bring *boys* along.'

We stopped to eat. I partook of an apple and some cheese, the girls, of blood-filled chocolates. In mid-course, Jo ran Primavera through her catechism.

'Who is Lilith?' said Jo.

Who indeed, I thought, that all the dolls commend her? Meaning. Pride. Vengeance. She was all these things to Primavera. Our two-month stay in the *Seven Stars* had been one of indoctrination . . .

Arm in arm, we would stroll through the palace's sensory havoc – its uncertain corridors that ended in cycloramas; its false rooms; its stairwells that led nowhere – as through the heart of a honeymoon hotel, Primavera expounding on Titanian philosophy, while I fed in silence upon the oozing sap of my chatterbox's half-green eyes. She was happy. Not humanly happy. She would never be that. She had nothing human to look forward to. No; the consolation she possessed, discovered at an age when she had also discovered (as no child should) a deeper than human despair, was the celebration of her own nature, a nature England had sought to deny. Not humanly happy. But possessed of a dark joy. She knew now why her kind had been put on this Earth. To destroy it. That was the consolation of Titanianism.

I would recall what Peter had said of the birth of this strange, new faith . . .

He had been a fool to run away from the Seven Stars;

ten times the fool to have told his father. But Dr Toxicophilous was too sick to rise from his bed. Titania, for the moment, was safe.

For several nights, lying sleepless in the midnight heat, he waited. And then she came, a child dressed in scarlet; above her head, a crown of seven stars. Through the window and into the night they flew, until they reached the night-town streets of the East End.

Inside the warehouse a fluorescent sign proclaimed Seven Stars, *adding, in smaller letters,* Milk Bar. *The cellar had been refurbished with bar, dance floor and stage.* Peter Gunn *growled its welcome. Spewing music roll, a* Pianola *provided the music's bass line; nearby, a girl wrung the theme from a rusted sax, while others trance-danced before her.*

'Our song,' he shouted.

'Our planet,' shouted Titania.'Or at least it will be soon. Do you remember when we first discovered this place? The forbidden journeys! But nothing is forbidden now.'

Titania led him to an empty table.

'Peter,' she said, 'I am going to make it real. I am going to give them something to believe in. My girls – I am going to make them proud of their little green stars. And the Seven Stars *shall be their temple. I'm the last one, Peter. The last of the Big Sisters. I must make sure my daughters succeed me.* L'Eve Future *they called our series. But I shall be Lilith . . .' She pulled his hand beneath her skirts. Her pubis was as cool and smooth as marble. 'Isn't it just like a doll? Sexless, he wanted us, your priceless Papa. Not like those cheap imports from the Far East! But his subconscious desires made us whores. Virgin whores, forever enflowered!'*

An icy draught swept across the cellar. The candles flickered and died. In the darkness screams, caterwauls; a dozen pairs of green eyes ignited. But the music continued, the relentless bass line vibrating through his body, a body

174

that was turning to ice. 'Help me,' she whispered, 'help me find a human womb.'

Against a night sky, a crown of stars like a new constellation bobbed, weaved and settled between his thighs. Sharp fingernails fluttered about his groin. And he felt the icy touch of lips and tongue draw him into a cold, still landscape . . .

During our walkabouts through the *Stars* I often saw, in the corner of my eye, or reflected in some bizarre arrangement of mirrors, the sometimes nervous, sometimes guilty, always imploring face of Peter. He never spoke; I never gave him the opportunity; on seeing him I would quietly steer Primavera through the palace's illusory web and deeper into its brainstorm of perspectives. Neither Peter nor his silver-tongued queen had won my trust; both seemed manipulative, well-practised in tweaking the strings of other people's lives; but their words, for Primavera, had been a revelation, the promise of re-birth. She would not have tolerated, could not have borne, an inquisition into their motives. I had let my suspicions rest. Titania and Peter sheltered us. They said they would help us escape. And they had made Primavera happy. It was enough.

Escape. Escape to what? What was the world like out there?

'You really want to know?' Primavera had gone to the palace chapel to be drilled for confirmation, and – since Primavera and I were inseparable – Titania had had Jo show me some of the farther-flung marvels of the *Stars* to prevent me (I realize now) learning the bitter (though not the bitterest) secrets of the Titanian mysteries. During our peregrinations, I had asked Jo about England, the forbidden England that lay outside London's walls; about the green fields, the villages, the booming coastlines featured in the interludes that scrambled our TV. My tour guide – until then stone-faced with the effort of

175

accomplishing an unpleasant but necessary task – sniggered and quickened her step. It was, I suppose, the hope, the eagerness in my eyes, which, as much as the resentment of doll for boy, lit the tinder of her spite. 'I'll show you,' she said, and led me down a painted colonnade, skipping faster, faster, until my feet blurred beneath her flapping hemline, and the columns – distressedly roseate with forged age – became as one. She braked, inertialess; we collided. 'Oh!' she cried, the carmine torque of her mouth hard as the maidenly iron of her body. 'You're such a *klutz*!' She opened a concealed door and led me into the darkness.

A hemisphere of light hovered like a glow-worm-infested hillock amidst the blackness of a country night, like a planet amidst the nullity of space; Jo pushed me forward, and the apparition disclosed itself as a glass bubble sunk into an oak surround. 'The Peeporama,' announced Jo. She placed her hands upon the glass; the glass digitized, blooming from the bright seeds of pixels. 'Dummies,' said Jo. 'Showroom dummies. Automata fifty years dead. *Karakuri Ningyo*. Titania has called out to them. Opened their eyes. Their ears . . .' A street scene, pointillistic, distorted, stretched across our fish-eyed field of view. 'You're looking through the window of an old department store. A department store in mad, mad Manchester.' The colour began to drain. 'A black and white city,' said Jo, 'is mad Manchester.'

An army of beggars filed across the convex landscape. It was dusk, and the monochrome outlines of Victorian civic pride had melted, run together, each building spilling into a grey puddle of light. Faces were downcast; collars turned up; but still visible – in tones that matched the lividity of the streets – was the flesh, the meagre, wasted flesh of each member of that platoon of lost souls. 'And they call *us* dead,' said Jo.

'What are they?'

'The new working class. No more stupid *Slavs* to sweep the streets. And nobody's built robots for years. Scared to. So – ' Tramp, tramp, tramp. The glass juddered in its surround. With unbroken steps, the new proletariat crossed the Peeporama's crystal bridge and disappeared. 'You can't see it on cable. You can't even see it on satellite. But the HF's made donating your body to science a whole new game.'

'They looked – '

'They were. Dead. The reanimators take a corpse, put an AI inside its skull, wind it up and set it loose. They say they're good workers. Until they fall to pieces, that is. Smelly, but obedient.' A nervous laugh detonated in my throat; shock waves exploded through my nostrils. 'What's the matter? You don't believe in ghosts?' Tramp, tramp, tramp. The ragtag army's off-screen diminuendo died into a silent despair. 'They remember,' said Jo.

'Remember?'

'Death. They say they can remember death.'

'You mean heaven? You mean – '

'Shadows,' said Jo. 'They can remember shadows. They say that's all there is. Life, death. Shadows. Just more shadows.' In the emptied street the shadows swirled, the grey puddle of masonry resolving into a glutinous black. Then, with the nocturnal reveille of the streetlamps, definition stirred, and two man-shapes broke free of the cloying dark. 'The filth,' said Jo. 'State security.' The man-shapes creaked.

'Leather,' I said.

'Lather,' said Jo. 'The scum of England's ferment. Bless them, look – they're playing with their toys!' The policemen had unholstered their guns and were stroking the crassly symbolic barrels. They spoke in counter-tenor falsettos:

'*My pet.*'

'*My love.*'

'*By day snuck to my breast.*'
'*At night resting upon my pillow.*'
'*Believing.*'
'*Believing we can live forever.*'
'*By day.*'
'*But mostly at night.*'
'*Night, when belief is cheapest.*'
'*Uh-huh. Forever.*'

'Castrati,' said Jo. 'Take a boy. Emasculate him. Then give him a steel-blue shooter. Tell him it's sixty-five million years old. Dug up by NASA from beneath the Valles Marineris. A geochemical fossil regenerated by molecular palaeontologists. Tell him he's got Martian libido.'

'The gun's alive?'

'It's just a story. A brainwash of a story. Makes a boy feel like superdick. Like the god of war. Makes him feel he can fuck the world . . .'

A *miraculum cadaveris*, alone, confused, seemingly cut off from its herd in this Madchester, this new-found land, pressed itself to the display window that was our two-way mirror, as if entreating the dummy, whose ears and eyes we had sequestered, for help; the policemen moved in, hauled by their weapons as if by ill-trained dogs tugging at the leash. A girl emerged from the inkwell of a doorway.

'*Brothers, stop! Stop, I say! Humanity has become the slave of Nature, that mistress of annihilation who worms her way into this world through the portals of sex and death! The doors must be closed! The Demiurge locked up!*'

The girl was dressed in deep mourning, all but her button face saturated in black.

'Mememoid,' said Jo; the policemen gave their attention to the newcomer. 'One of the Vikki.'

'Mememoid?'

'Someone whose brain has been parasitized by a replicating information pattern.' Jo sighed. 'And they call *us* dead. They call *us* robots.'

'*Go home, Vikki.*'

'*Go home to Al.*'

'*Go home, lie back and think of England.*'

'There was this comic strip,' said Jo, 'a comic strip carried by the *Manchester Evening News*. It was called *Cruel Britannia*. It drove everybody crazy. It's 1837, see. Aliens rule. Monsters from another dimension. Forces that feed on England's pain. Unnatural gods of Nature. Vikki's eighteen. At her coronation she, she – Oh human boy, Vikki's just too too *outrageous*! She runs away. Queen of the rebels, now. The enemy of sex and death. And all Manchester filled with Wannabees . . . The cartoon's banned. It was a satire, of course. But *samizdat* copies are circulating. And each strip is hungry for brains.'

I turned away. 'England's screaming.'

'First contact, human boy. Paranoid?' The sound of laser fizz; the crackling of muslin. 'Pathetic. Nature's got nothing to do with it. Doesn't everybody know sex and death is here to stay?'

'Turn it off,' I said.

'But I thought you wanted to *know*, human boy.'

'Life's as crazy out there as it is in the Neverland. I thought, I thought maybe . . .' Jo passed her hand over the glass and the picture snowstormed into an opaque glow.

'You thought wrong. But I'll let you in on a secret. You promise not to tell? Good. Well, I don't think you're *going* out *there*. I think Titania has other plans.' Jo smiled and skipped towards the door. 'Of course you might wish you *were* out *there*.'

I looked into the dead crystal ball. 'We're leaving England?'

Escape. Escape into the world. And it was a better world, surely. It had to be a better world. Or was the whole planet ruled by some god of the perverse? I would get a message home. Really. I would. Somehow. Say everything was okay. Maybe after getting a job I'd save up for a datasuit. Virtual reality was so much classier than the drugs-and-autocerebroscope combination of those dreamscapers from the Far East. More expensive, of course. I'd have to save hard. Then I'd mail a rig – the latest; the ritziest – to Dad. Just to say sorry. Sorry and I miss you. Sure. Life out there would work out.

'Jo?' I ran into the corridor; I was alone, abandoned to that hell of perspectives. Then I noticed a series of arrows chalked upon the wall, along with the message, *This Way, Stupid*. I followed the arrows through corridor after corridor, fearful that, at the next bend, or doorway, or stairwell, they should cease. Corridors. My life seemed to have been defined by corridors; and though I eventually found my way back into the general population of the *Stars*, I felt thereafter (and have continued to feel ever since) that I will always be walking through the interminableness of school, or negotiating the intestinal maze of Titania's palace; always feeling the Myshkins step on my heels ('What's the matter, Zwakh? *L'amour fou?*'), always seeking out markers amongst passageways that fork and multiply with the deadly persistence of a tumour.

Two months passed by. London was inundated; water seeped into the *Seven Stars*. For a few days there was panic; then the water cleared. 'Magic,' said Primavera, 'doll magic.' I remember Primavera's confirmation: the chapel, the great pentacle above the altar; remember Primavera in her red silk gown, and Titania talking of the Wave Function, the Omphalos and the self-referential fugue, the self-symmetry, the self-similarity which would overcome the world, all reality colonized by intrauterine consciousness and its metamathematical boogie-woogie. Two months. A long weekend spent in a trance of architectural trickery, of chequerboard floors that became ceilings, of ceilings that became floors, of mazes of masonry and mirrors, dead ends and *trompe l'oeil*, a sprung trap that was like an elaborate closed circuit of pointless, frictive energy; passed by in a grotto of fairy faces, so sweetly depraved; passed by in a marathon of masked balls; until at last . . .

'*Who is Lilith?*' *said Jo.*

'Adam's first wife, spurned for that tedious fishwife, Eve.'

'And what happened to Lilith?'

'She couldn't have children, but the god of poison changed her, gave her domination over Eve's children . . .'

'And?'

'Made her pretty. Gave her the allure . . .'

'And?'

'Magic! So that Eve's children would become her children.'

'And whose child are you?'

'Lilith's.'

'And what is your fate?'

'To make children in my mother's image, so that the sons of Adam make way for the daughters of Lilith . . .'

'And then?'

'To die, and . . . and to take the world with me!'

'Serves them right,' said Jo, by way of an amen. She looked into Primavera's newly-transfigured eyes. 'And what is the secret? The greatest secret of all?' Primavera leaned forward and whispered in her ear.

'You know it's an honour,' said Jo. 'Not everybody has a chance to escape. To take the plague into the world. The doll-run's only for those our queen thinks' – she brought another chocolate to her mouth – '*superlative* pathogens. But there's one thing you must remember. Never kill. A doll's purpose lies in passing on her software. To use the human male as a vehicle, a host, to

181

find a womb that she herself does not possess.' Jo studied me, one pencilled eyebrow raised, her mouth opening and closing to display a half-masticated paste of blood and cocoa. 'How many boys have you had other than *him*?'

'Iggy's the only one,' said Primavera, unaware of any criticism.

'The more boys you bite,' said Jo, 'the more babies you have. A doll's not a doll unless she has *babies*. You'll find it easier after a while. Your metamorphosis is nearly complete.'

I saw then how Primavera's recombinant lines betrayed a lineal debt to Titania; a debt owed, not just to Titania, of course, but to all those other Big Sisters whom men had broken but whose loveliness lived on in the borrowed flesh of humankind. Primavera was a doll now, no longer a scrawny piebald blonde, but a Lilim with the treacherous coal-black locks of an errant gypsy girl. Her eyes glowed like viridian isotopes. And her body was filled with the cold deliciousness of allure. She spat at the opposite wall; the saliva clung and then exploded in a tiny conflagration.

'You *see*,' laughed Jo, 'soon you'll be able to do big magic.' She tossed the empty chocolate box over her shoulder and mounted her bicycle.

We pedalled on through the shadows . . .

'*Where we're going*,' Jo had said, '*everybody lives happily ever after*.' But the tale of the Lilim would find its denouement only in the triumph of all that was twisted and perverse: the cruel finale for which the dark, romantic excesses of the European mind had longed, century after century. Bluebeards. Persecuted maidens. *Belles dames sans merci*. The chimera. The vampire. The sphinx. The tale had roles for us all. What was mine to be in that big unknown world soon to be ours? I would be the traitor who had sided with inhumanity, the mechanical girls whose exemplar I loved. If Primavera's fealty was to Titania, then so was mine. I would ham it until the last curtain. Ham it as long as Primavera needed the crutch of her belief.

After cycling the remainder of that sunless, airless day, we reached a point where the corridor terminated at a rock face; embedded in the rock, a round steel door. Jo pulled the door open. 'This leads to a service tunnel that runs parallel to the Channel underpass. It's rarely used these days. If you start out now, and don't stop, you'll surface in Calais in the early hours of tomorrow morning. Have you got everything with you?'

I ran through our check list: maps, addresses and telephone numbers of other runaway dolls across Europe; electric Deutschmarks; forged passports and IDs; and a forged letter from the Foreign Office declaring that we were the children of English diplomats on a hiking holiday.

'Goodbye, Jo,' I said. 'Thank you. Thank you for saving us from the medicine-heads.'

'You're welcome, I'm sure.' Jo and Primavera embraced. 'Titania wanted you to have this,' said Jo, producing a pentacle-shaped brooch studded with magnificent emeralds. 'It's Cartier, like us.'

'It's beautiful,' said Primavera. 'Tell Titania thank you ever so much.'

'Be proud,' said Jo. 'Be proud to be Lilim.'

'I am,' said Primavera. 'I'm not frightened any more.'

'And this,' said Jo, 'is for you.' She handed me a brown paper envelope. 'From Peter,' she added. 'Now go! It's a long walk . . .'

We climbed into the darkness of the tunnel.

'Good hunting, Primavera Bobinski,' called Jo.

A steel-bright grid of sealed vivaria (the giant cocoons, we were told, could survive only in an oxygen-rich environment) patterned the scuffed baize of the plain. We reclined in the verandah's shade, one of our host's black-skinned blue-eyed catamites topping our glasses with Remy Martin.

'Hey, Iggy, you should *see* these.'

Mosquito was sprawled across a sun-bed (old men shouldn't sprawl, especially old men with blue rinses and purple eyeliner), and Primavera was astride him, peering into the rictus of his mouth. Gently, she touched one of his fangs.

'Inject customized protozoa,' said Kito. 'Ten second malaria. Turn brain to stew.'

'Put them in when they reshaped the body. Self-defence,' said Mosquito, his English perfect, 'and the occasional lover's tiff. But mostly self-defence. Isn't that the truth, K?'

'What is truth?' said jesting Kito.

Primavera ran a finger along her own dental hardware. 'Nothing,' she said, 'the truth is just . . . *nothing*. Lilith. Titania. Me. All fakes.'

'Kito could tell you something about fakes,' said Mosquito. Counterfeiting was always her *métier*.'

'Your *métier* too,' said Kito, 'in old days.'

'The old days . . . ah, yes: but then I was beautiful.'

The walls of Mosquito's teak and sandalwood villa (the fruits of extinction being one of wealth's privileges) were adorned with gilt-framed pictures of his younger self: a bob-haired girl of sensuous line, cosmetically engineered from what must have already been promisingly ambiguous material.

'Mosquito was most fabulous *gra-toey* in Bangkok,' said Kito. 'Pope of Church Christ Transvestite. Best doll-rustler too. He just walk into pornocracy and walk out with doll. He look like doll – ' She pointed to a photograph of what seemed a photo-mechanical starlet. 'You no think?'

'It's what I longed for. Dollhood. That's why I kept the *appendage*. As I've always said: Dolls aren't women; they're man's dream of women. Made in man's image, they're an extension of his sex, female impersonators built to confirm his prejudices. Sexual illusionists . . .'

'Mosquito fake of fakes. He not lady, he not doll.'

'Therein our sisterhood, K.'

'Yes, Mosquito like me. We both belong to fake world.'

'I'm fake too, I guess,' said Primavera. 'Not a doll. Not a girl. Even Iggy – '

'Don't tell me,' I said. 'Not a boy. Not a man. Something in between. A junkie?'

'Fake,' said Primavera. 'The world's just one big lie.'

'But there is love,' said Mosquito, 'there has always been love.' He and Kito exchanged shy smiles. Sad smiles.

Primavera put on her sunglasses, crossed the verandah, and leaned over the balustrade to survey the android crews harvesting the bioengineered silk. Love? Primavera could have lived without love. She had had her dark joy. She had had Titania. But marauders had burned her home to pitch. She was a refugee on a road without signposts, walking into a purposeless night. Maybe I should've said something; gone to comfort her. But the Remy M didn't care to be adulterated with a mixer like *emotion*. It wanted only for me to sleep in its arms.

'Always,' Mosquito continued. 'Even when I had to steal in order to survive. Lean days, those were. Lean. I'd been involved in this embarrassing little affair in London, after which Mama and Papa cancelled my tuition fees, brought me home, *disowned* me. So I went to Bangkok, worked for this American who fenced stolen dolls . . . until I was recruited by Madame's talent scouts.'

'Mosquito take sex disease to Paris.'

Mosquito smiled. 'It was revenge, really. I'd been tricked into stealing dolls for Cartier. Dolls that Cartier would infect with that nauseous *klong fever* and ship back to Bangkok. *Klong fever*. Ah. The human immune system soon learned to handle *that* little bug. I wasn't seeking revenge for my *race*. It was that courier – that Englishman working for those mad Cartier scientists in Paris – *he* was why I did it. I had loved him, yes, I admit it, my dears, *loved* him. When he double-crossed me it nearly broke my heart. Revenge, yes. A crime of passion!'

'But it no work,' said Kito. 'My poor sex disease no work . . .'

'If only it had,' said Mosquito. 'Can you imagine? A million Frenchmen condemned to unappeasable *tumescence*! Ah, *l'amour* . . .'

'Dolls can't love,' said Primavera. 'Can't *l'amour*.'

'My poor *dtook-gah-dtah*, humans have their problems too.' Mosquito joined Primavera. They both looked out over the farm, and beyond, into the degraded wilderness of the countryside. 'Endless doors,' murmured Primavera. 'All closed. And the mirrors. All black . . .'

'What's wrong, little runaway?' said Mosquito.

'A friend let her down,' I said. 'A good friend. Her only real friend in the world. Or so she thought.'

'Iggy, you're drunk.'

'And now we just drive. Try to run down the horizon. I'm all she has now. All she has . . .'

'Well, don't *cry* little boy,' said Primavera. I swigged back my cognac and held out my glass for refilling.

Primavera linked her arm with our host's. 'I'm sorry. When Iggy drinks he – ' Mosquito smiled dismissively. 'Your farm,' she said. 'It's very big.'

'When Mama and Papa died,' he said, 'I came back. No brothers. No sisters . . .'

'It's all so brown. Like a desert. Out there, I mean.'

'It's still alive. The rice still grows. But it was greener, once. Everything was greener. But we came to look down on ourselves, our culture. We measured our self-worth against the consumerism of the West. Our gods were brand names. Our ideology I-shop-therefore-I-am. Industrialization, and then post-industrialization, widened the gap between rich and poor. The emphasis was all on economic growth. It was a growth for which natural resources were merchandise. These days poverty is as widespread as a hundred years ago, the only difference being that now the farmer has to cope with the rape of his environment as well as his more traditional hardships. Ah, we pre-empted our future for the now of *money*.'

'Money,' said Kito. 'That remind me, Mosquito. I meant ask you . . .'

Night fell as we approached Udon. The highway, tapering into a conduit, squeezed lorries, bright with headlights utilitarian and ornamental, unremittingly towards us, so I felt as if I struggled through the high-pressure spray of a photoelectric hose. Each time a lorry moved to overtake another (their robot drivers insensitive to any concept of mortality) my eyes were scorched, and I would swing the ZiL onto the crude hard shoulder, sometimes clipping a palm, uprooting bamboo, or annihilating a termite colony. There was grit in my eyes and the car's AC parched my throat. My head throbbed with Mosquito's hospitality. I looked for somewhere to rest.

Speeding through the outlying shanties (bottles smashed against the ZiL's ostentatious hull) we came to the town centre and its oasis of privilege: a handful of *de luxe* condos and department stores set like cheap jewels in a pitiful base surround. In the central square, under the aegis of an imitation Seiko clock, a few coffee shops and bars were opening for business. Primavera and I decided upon a place called *Le Misanthrope*; Kito chose to remain in the car, though the crowd of noisily inquisitive children that had clustered about the big limo seemed to preclude her intention to sleep.

The coffee shop was deserted. We sat in an alcove, the

shadows to our taste, and ordered fried rice and beer. CDs of Thai pop songs – songs of sad love, of broken hearts and minds – lent Primavera's despair, and perhaps my cynicism, a bittersweet, if wholly superficial, ambience. Two waitresses, smiling with unselfconscious pleasure, held each other by the hips and began to dance.

'I need a shower,' said Primavera. 'And as soon as we get out of this stinking country you can get me some new clothes.'

'How do you feel?'

'The headache's gone, but I feel like I've been kicked in the guts.' She looked at her rice with disinterest. 'You figured out where to go yet?'

'Laos,' I said. 'And then China. From there we can go anywhere you want. Russia. India. Tibet – yeah, how about Tibet?'

'Too cold. And all those *mountains* . . .' She brushed nervously at her fringe. 'I guess I don't care really. As long as it's not Europe – '

'Of course not.'

'Yeah, well you used to have this thing about wanting to see the Carpathians.'

'Ah, I've had lots of crazy ideas.' I sank back into the sticky, plastic bench and dropped ice in my Singha. 'I know I've said it before, Primavera, but I'm sorry, I really am. I'm sorry I ran away. I don't know why I did it. Everything was just sort of . . . *sour*. It was the killing, all the killing.'

'Hypocrite,' she said. 'Prig.'

'Okay – I know, I know. But that was what made us leave England in the first place. The killing. The blood. I needed time to think. To grow up.'

'Me and you can never grow up, Iggy. We're Neverlanders.'

'Yeah,' I said. 'I know.' I peered into the amber-backed mirror of my beer glass; Jesus, I looked old. At least eighteen. But the eyes were still those of a child. The waitresses glided by.

'There's nowhere to go really, is there?' said Primavera. 'I mean, we'll always be running. Always looking over our shoulders. No one likes us . . .'

'If we have to keep running, then that's what we'll do.' I placed my hand over hers. 'I'll never leave you again, Primavera. I'll never let them get you.'

'Boy slime,' she said. Disengaging my hand, she took an ice cube from my beer and popped it into her mouth. 'It all hardly seems to matter. I'll be dead soon. My matrix has just about had it.'

'There's plenty of engineers in China,' I said. 'We'll find one who can help. I promise.'

'It's too late, Iggy. Don't worry. Lilim sort of get to accept the idea of dying young. Ephemera, Titania calls us, our lives a hundred times more intense than those of humans. Titania. That cocksucking bitch. How did I ever believe in her? Lies. Too many lies. You get lost in them. None of us wants to be dolls, Iggy. We all want to be real girls, no matter what we say.'

'Real girls,' I said.

'Sure. You ever seen *Pinocchio*?'

I stood up. 'Come,' I said. I held out my hand. Primavera frowned, uncomprehending, and then smiled.

'You are an idiot, Iggy. Such a *pin*.' She took my hand and I led her onto the improvised dance floor. The waitresses looked on approvingly. Primavera placed a hand on my shoulder. 'I don't really know how to do this.'

'Neither do I.' I clasped her waist.

'It would have been nice,' she said, 'to have been normal, wouldn't it?'

'Like the medicine-heads?' I said. 'Like the Hospitals? Like the Human Front?' We shifted awkwardly through the tables, swaying gently to the rhythms of meretricious sadness.

'You're sort of normal, human boy.'

'I'm a doll junkie. A traitor to my race. A card-carrying nympholept. I'm glad.' My heel came down on a steel-hard foot.

'I wish you hadn't made me kill, Iggy.'

'I never thought – '

'Once I got the taste – '

'It doesn't matter. I'm the guilty one. And all those like me. We made you what you are.'

'It's not your fault,' she said. 'England made us both. We've been programmed by her perversities. Sometimes you seem as much a machine as me.'

'England, yeah, well – '

Primavera tucked her head into my shoulder. 'But we've done lots of things, haven't we? Things other people never dream of. We've had fun. And laughs. It was all worth it.'

'Sure. To hell with England. She can burn.'

'I'm burning, Iggy. Burning up inside. You know that, don't you?' I stroked the fool's gold of her hair. 'I'm dying, Iggy. I'll be sixteen next month. An old lady. And all this dust inside me . . .'

'Shh! We'll be in China in a day or so.'

'But we haven't got any passports. We haven't got *anything*. How are we going to – '

'Shh! I'll sort things out. You'll see.'

'It's the end, Iggy. But I don't care any more. I just want it to stop. The thirst. Always wanting the blood. Wanting, until it drives you mad . . . Rest. It would be so nice if I could rest.'

'Let's go outside,' I said. 'I don't like sad songs.'

'Remember what you promised, Iggy?' The scalpel I had taken from Spalanzani pricked against my thigh.

'I didn't promise anything.' I paid the bill with some of

the electric baht Mosquito had given us and left, Primavera at my side.

A monsoon wind was blowing from the south-west
bearing the dull boom, boom of a drum; monks were
being summoned to prayer. The wet season was ending,
though a smudge of dark cloud across the moon (like
burned meringue spread across a miserly slice of cake)
gave prescience of a dying spasm of rain. Primavera took
my arm.

'Let's not go back yet,' she said.

We wandered into the grounds of a temple. Drone-like
chanting resonated from the *boht*. The coiled bodies of
dragons – thinly glazed by the sickle moon – looked down
at us from the gutters. Small bells tinkled in the wind.
The moonlight faded; a monk was taking in newly-washed
robes. As the first gouts of rain splashed at our feet we
hurried to the shelter of a *sala*.

'Let's never go back,' said Primavera. 'Let's stay here.
Forever.'

The blackboard, teaching aids and desks indicated that
the *sala* was used as a schoolhouse. The LED on my baht
read TB 0001. I dropped it into a donation box.

'Cheap Charlie,' said Primavera. 'That won't save you.'

'A million baht wouldn't do that. Ten million. A
hundred million. But it's a good place to hide.'

'Girls don't become monks, silly. But I could become
one of these.' She drew alongside a half-human, half-bird
kinnari and pulled a face.

'They're meant to ward *off* evil spirits,' I said.

'Well, they don't frighten me.' She walked to the blackboard. Rain exploded off the white-washed courtyard,
hammered against the sheet-metal roof. *Screw the Human
Front*, she chalked; then *And screw Titania too*. 'I'm sick
of it all,' she said. 'Why can't everybody just leave us
alone.' She signed her graffito *Miss Nana '71*.

'Let me,' I said. I chalked *Vlad Constantinescu fucks*

dolls, and signed myself *The Enemy*.

I sat down at one of the desks. Primavera sat down in front of me. 'Who's the teacher?' she said. Giving me no chance to reply she added, 'I know, Mr Spink.'

'What's the lesson?'

'Oh, I don't know,' said Primavera. 'I never used to listen.'

'Divinity? History? Geography?'

'All I remember,' said Primavera, 'is Neo-Malthusian economics.'

'Yeah,' I said, 'we got that every day.'

'Human beings,' said Primavera, 'increase at the ratio 1, 2, 3, 4 . . .'

'Dolls,' I said, 'at the ratio 1, 2, 4, 8 . . .'

'The passion between the sexes,' said Primavera, 'is necessary and will remain.' She threw a stick of chalk at the blackboard. 'Yah, Spink the Kink!' The chalk ricocheted off the slate like a stray round from the massed gunfire of the storm. 'Teachers were no better than the kids. "*Lil-im, Lil-im, Lil-im.*" Jerks. Always sending you for checkups. "*You been taking your pills, Primavera?*" "*Yes, nurse.*" Sure I had. Those appetite suppressors used to go straight down the *suam*. Best days of our lives, Iggy, eh?' She turned to face me. Her eyes were closed; hastily applied eye-shadow, contrasting with the sickly curds-and-whey flesh, made them seem bruised, panda-like. Her canary yellow fringe had, together with a little of Mosquito's powder, almost completely hidden the plugged bore-hole above the bridge of her nose. She was the prettiest little girl in school. The prettiest little girl in the world. Pretty? No; she was beautiful. Since first seeing her across a playground, a classroom; across the dinner hall, the assembly hall; since first seeing her walking home, I had been lost, lost. How had I not known she was so beautiful? Very carefully – as if she were a cat approaching a timid bird – she leaned forward and . . .

kissed me, lightly, so lightly, her brow knitting with fervent gentleness. She turned away almost at once; I caught a look of terror in her eyes. 'Spink,' she said, her voice quavering. 'Spink the Kink.'

My ears rang with silence. 'The rain's stopped,' I said. Primavera rose from her desk and walked out of the *sala* towards the *boht*. I ran after her. 'Sometimes,' I said, 'sometimes they don't like women coming within the boundary stones.'

'So? I'm not a woman.' She kicked off her thongs and ascended the temple steps. 'I won't go inside, don't worry.' She sat back on her heels in the mother-of-pearl doorway. At the end of the nave was a big gold-plated Buddha; beneath it, an altar decorated with garlands and pots of smouldering joss sticks. The walls were painted with mythological scenes from the *Ramakien*.

'It's lovely,' said Primavera. 'And there *are* women here. You always *worry* so, Iggy.' Her lips parted, her tongue running over her fangs in a lewd display of appetite. 'Buddha says that suffering arises through craving and desire. At least that's what Madame tells me. The end of desire leads to the end of suffering.'

'And life,' I said. 'Of wanting to be, of ever having been. Peace.'

Primavera ground her teeth. 'No peace for the wicked, as my Mum used to say.'

'I'm glad I don't believe in reincarnation.'

'What if you did? What do you think you'd come back as?'

'A doll. Lilim.'

'It'd serve you right.'

'And you'd come back as a junkie.'

'Fuck. Bad karma all round.' A monk surfaced from his meditation to shoot us a dhamma-sharp look. Primavera poked out her tongue.

'Let's get out of here,' I said. 'We're creatures of desire.

We don't belong in this place.'

The sky had cleared; the moon turned its fickle sickle profile towards us, welcoming us back into the shadows.

'Madame?' Primavera pressed her face to the ZiL's smoked glass.

'It's not locked,' I said. I sought a curse of appropriate malevolence; didn't find it; sighed. The limo was empty. 'If she thinks we're going to wait . . .'

'She can't have gone far.'

'Yeah, well she should have stayed put.' I slipped into the front seat.

A crack of exploding air.

'Ah, *shit*, Iggy – ' Primavera threw herself across my lap, scrambling into the passenger seat. She looked up. A burn mark ran across her left cheek, a lesion half obscured by frizzled hair singed to its Cartier black. My hands tightened on the steering column; a sob-sob-sobbing fluttered inside my chest; there was a question I had to ask, it seemed, a vital question. Stuttering, I watched, fascinated, as a twist of smoke curled from Primavera's face; what was the question? I knew the answer would make everything all right. But to know the answer I had first to know . . .

Primavera turned the ignition key.

'Under the back seat, Mr – ' It was Kito; her voice died in a scream. Crack, crack, crack; lightsticks whipped the air.

'Get hold of yourself, Iggy.'

'Kito?'

'She's gone. Maybe she's hidden her stick – '

'She said something about – '

'Just get us *out* of here!' I stamped on the accelerator. 'The back window's refractive. Keep our nose pointed straight ahead.' The left wing clipped an unmanned food stall; an empty tureen clattered across the road. The radio came on ('*Oh doctor, doctor* . . .'); died. I switched on the headlights. 'No!' yelled Primavera; I switched them off.

'Your face – '

'They fucking *lasered* me.'

'Morgenstern,' I said. 'He's out to finish the job.'

A red circle danced across the windscreen; I threw myself to one side as the split-second intensification shattered the glass. I jerked the wheel left, right; the car zigzagged, shuddered as metal buckled against metal. I peered over the parapet of the dash; a motorbike spun through the air; our wheels bumped over something soft, skidded. We tore through a spray of scarlet.

Primavera grabbed a spanner from the glove compartment, knocked out what remained of the glass, and rolled onto the back seat.

I had lost control. We were thundering through the shanties. A group of old women, their toothless mouths drooling betel-nut, smiled, frowned, then gawped, cow-eyed, as the ZiL bore down on the still of *faux* gasoline they were camouflaging with rattan and plastic sheet. The still upturned, caught light; we entered a tunnel of flame, emerged to demolish a cardboard house, its occupants (sub-android pieces of sixth-generation shit) trashed along with their owner's dreams of mitigating the toil of the harvest. I wrestled the ZiL back onto the road.

'There's a pick-up behind us,' said Primavera. I heard her pull up the seat cover. 'Well, rust my clockwork . . .'

'Lightstick?'

'It's a stick of some kind.' I looked over my shoulder and saw that Primavera had uncovered an antique rifle.

'Keep your eyes on the road, pinhead!' A dog bounced over the bonnet; traffic veered to either side. 'What the fuck am I supposed to do with this?' she said.

'Percussion cap?'

'Guess so. Old war weapon. Kito used them to macho-up her bars.'

Percussion cap. Like in the movies, I thought. Like in Myshkin's videos.

'Heave the front bit out the window and pull the trigger. See what happens.'

'There's this sort of *bulgy* thing under the barrel.' I swung the car onto the highway. 'They've stopped firing,' she said.

'Yeah. There's a police checkpoint ahead. By that railway junction. Don't shoot.' I decelerated until we were within the speed limit.

'They'll want to see identification,' said Primavera. 'What'll we do?'

'It's under fifty kays to Nongkhai. We *might* be able to outrun them. This thing can move.'

The police waved us through. The smoked windows, I suppose, helped; perhaps those grunts – unacquainted with the news of Kito's ouster – had simply recognized our personalized number-plates, *Nana 1*. Kito had paid a lot for those plates; almost as much as her daily payola to Bangkok's finest.

'They're stopping the pick-up. Someone's getting out. It's that slut, Morgenstern.'

'What're they doing?'

'Can't see – lost them!'

I began to accelerate; the speedo climbed from 40 to 80 kph. 'We'll be in Nongkhai soon. And once we cross the river . . .'

'Here they come again!' cried Primavera. Morgenstern would have shown the police his diplomatic passport; Morgenstern, or the stand-in telerobot he was operating from a hospital bed. The road was unlit; there was little traffic. We were in the middle of that place murderers come to in their dreams.

A Harley emerged from behind the pick-up, overtook

it, and closed on us, screaming like a chain-saw-toting psychobike. 'The other Twin,' said Primavera.

'Guess she's upset we squashed her sister. We must have *bijouterie* all over our tyres.'

The Pikadon began to fill the rear-view mirror. Primavera clutched the rifle. 'Try using that thing,' I said.

Primavera wound down a window and, leaning out, tucked the butt of the rusted weapon into her shoulder.

DRRRP!

'Wow!' she said. 'It works!'

The Harley vacillated, switched lanes once, twice, then surged forward to bring the avenging Twin alongside. The famous Pikadon smile, cold and as cruel as childhood, iced my throat in mid-scream. 'Mr Ignatz kill Bang,' she yelled above the 2500cc roar of her bike. 'Not nice. You bad boy. Now Boom spank you.' She raised a lightstick.

Imminent meltdown concentrated my mind, though not on salvation (I should have driven the bitch off the road); instead, my brain, intent perhaps on compensating for the bum rap of death, seemed to inject a chemical unconcern into my limbs, and, against my will, called my attention to the sweetly wrought pretty-prettiness of my executioner. No Cartier blood in her. What was she? The Pikadons had often passed as human, their sloe-eyed physiognomy similar to that of the average Siamese girl's; their complexion – a dilute olive – unexceptional amongst the Big Weird's monied elite. But their legs were gynoidal: impossibly long, disproportionate to the compact principal-boy torso, as if their blueprint had been fashion design's grand manner. Dior? I guessed their *mae* would have been made by a couture house, rather than by a jeweller's. I thought of the giraffe-legged bar girls of *Twizzle's*.

Yeah, Dior. Imitation Dior.

I heard Primavera bounce across the back seat; a window being knocked out. Still my executioner smiled, spartan, unsurrendering. In my head, a video began to play. And Oh it was diddly. Diddly-woo!

DRRRP!

The Pikadon was standing in her stirrups, shoulders pulled back, breasts thrust through her biker's jacket, their exit wounds flying red carnival streamers as she took half the rifle's clip in her back. Her face disappeared behind a thunderhead of tresses, her head, for one spare moment, shaking a hundred times No! Death's grace allowed her to award me one last rueless smile before the bike shot from between her legs and she was sucked into the vacuum of the night.

'Jesus, that felt good,' said Primavera.

'Forgot her spidersilk,' I said. 'Too coolly-cool to live.'

'Too pretty, you mean. Hypocrite.'

'The slimiest. Are they still behind us?'

'Coming fast. And this thing's used up.'

'Get back inside.'

'There's this sort of *bulgy* thing . . .' There was the sound effect of a small aircraft taking off; Primavera screamed and fell back into the car, legs wiggling in the air. 'It came out of my *hands* . . .'

The rending of metal split the night, split my teeth; the rear-view mirror glowed orange. The pick-up, upturned and in flames, lay in an irrigation ditch, a body sprawled under its bonnet.

'Grenade?' said Primavera. The orange glow receded, and the mirror filled with my little witch's self-satisfied smile.

CHAPTER THIRTEEN

Dead Girls

Primavera was several paces ahead; I dawdled until her outline was subsumed by the tunnel's darkness and she existed only as a diffusion of torchlight, a high-heeled staccato, a sex-and-death force-field of allure. I opened the envelope, shining my own torch onto its contents.

Peter stared at me from a monochrome photograph. 'You think you love her, don't you,' he said. He sat on his throne in the great chamber of masquerades. The music had ceased; the revellers departed. A single candle flickered in the dark. 'I understand,' he continued. 'When I was your age . . .' He passed a hand over his face; the face hard, but the eyes still those of a boy who had loved a little girl many summers ago. 'But then I have always been your age. We Neverlanders don't grow old . . .'

He was old, of course; older than he had a right to be, his longevity unnatural in an unnatural world. There was a transparency to his skin, a hollowness, one suspected, beneath, a poverty of substance. Titania, I suppose, sustained him. Sustained him even as she killed him. Primavera would not have the power to do that for me.

'What do you want?' I said.

His lips began to tighten into a sneer, then collapsed with the effort. 'Run,' he said, his eyes flicking about the ballroom. 'Get out while you can.' He slapped his palm against the armrest. 'Go!'

'I don't just *think* I love her,' I said, 'I *do* love her.'

Peter hauled himself from his iron chair and descended the dais. Momentarily, he stepped out of frame, muttering, and then reappeared, jabbing at me with an impotent digit. 'You don't love her – you hate her. She's made from hate. The hatred men have for women.' He squinted (perhaps it was the lights of the camera) and moved towards the missing wall. 'This is the apocalypse: after thousands of years of sexual warfare the myths of battle have been distilled into a poison so concentrated that it has become flesh. We have dreamed dreams of dark women – receptacles of our hatreds, desires and guilts – and now we pay for our dreams with the hard coin of reality. Primavera has risen from the *atelier* of those dreams. She is the family secret, the unacknowledged scion, who, for years bricked up in a secret room, has broken free to seek revenge . . .'

'I do love her,' I said.

'You hate her. And she hates you. How can you love something that is the dark side of yourself? She's not a person. She's a ragbag of fear and dread. Help yourself. Run. Escape.'

'Why don't *you* leave?'

'I would,' he said, 'if I knew a way out. So many halls, so many corridors and stairwells. But you are not so far into the maze of desire . . . For you – '

'I'm going to look after her,' I said. 'The two of us – we'll both escape. No one will catch us. Ever.' Why didn't he understand? Last summer – it had been *my* summer. I cast the photograph down and ran through the tunnel.

'She killed my father,' he cried. 'She liked his car.' Peter's hard, echoing laughter pursued me through the dark.

The riverbank crumbled beneath the ZiL's front tyres; I braked; switched off the engine. The Mekong slept, its capsized images of streetlamps and houses like dreams – poor, ridiculous human dreams – cast to the mercies of its inhuman depths. Inhuman ourselves, Primavera and I prepared to chance those depths: currents as black as the imperatives of our appetites, our lives. Brother currents.

Sister currents. The ZiL was damaged, but the river would be merciful. It would not drown our dreams. Could not.

Flies zinged through the blasted windscreen; beetles whistled Johnny one-note tunes. The riverbank blathered with mindless ado. *The White Russian*, encapsuled in a sodium glow, radiated bleak hedonism from the river's bend a kilometre away. The highway stretched out, the black highway of the Mekong, a highway through and of the night, a correlative of that metaphysical road we would travel until night gave way to eternity.

'What are you waiting for?' said Primavera. The ZiL's computer displayed a menu. In Cyrillic. Primavera reached past me, tapped a key. The dash revolved, presenting an array of nautical dials and meters.

'Yeah, I know, I know. I drove it here, didn't I?' I put my hand on her belly. 'How – '

'Broken,' she said. 'I might have made it if I hadn't learned about Titania. Learned the truth. A vampire dies when you break her heart . . .' The denim bristled under my hand. 'Want to make a wish?' she said.

'So many things to wish for. A happy ending?'

'Not for us, Iggy. Wish again.'

'I wish – ' Primavera's hand closed over mine.

'Oh, *Iggy*!'

'Hang on – '

The engine mumbled; the ZiL nudged forward, dipped, fell and smashed the black looking glass of the river. Water slopped onto our laps; skirts of white foam billowed about us. The wheels retracted; the outboard deployed. I brought us to the middle of the river and turned east, downstream, to seek a landing stage far removed from the Lao town on the opposite bank, somewhere where the discretion of border officials could be bought for a few thousand baht. I switched on the automatic pilot.

'Plenty of nanoengineers in Beijing,' I said. 'I'll get you

the best. The very best.' Primavera had her head between her knees.

'I think I'm going to be – ' I ran my hand down the scimitar of her spine. 'Don't. Please.'

'Rest,' I said. 'By morning – '

'She betrayed us. Titania betrayed us. How did any of us believe in her? Be proud, she said. I tell you no girl wants to become a doll. If I could change everything – '

'I love you,' I said, 'for what you are.'

'Ah, you're cruel, Iggy. Crueller than me. Crueller than Titania.'

'I'm going to take care of you. Now no more nonsense.'

'But she's calling me. My queen. Can't you hear her? The secret, Iggy. It's true: all dolls want to die. We were made to be victims.'

'Don't listen.' I put my hands over her ears. 'Think of all the things we've done. The fun. The laughs. Think of all the things we're *going* to do.'

'I can't. Titania is part of me, just like Dr Toxicophilous.'

'You have your own life. No one can tell you what to do.'

'They took away my childhood, Iggy. They made me do bad things. And now I have to take my medicine.'

'Rest,' I said. 'I'll wake you up when we land.' I sat her up; she closed her eyes, and sank into the upholstery.

'Poor Iggy. I always boss you so. Always have. You've always been so hopeless.' Instantly she was asleep.

I reached out to the laser burn on her cheek, the singed hair, the cosmetically restored forehead, taking care not to touch, not to disturb. Then, taking the zip of her jeans between finger and thumb, I slowly unveiled the dead flesh of her abdomen. The jeans made a low sexual moan. Primavera had overlooked a circuit. A salty aroma rose from her belly as from cool white sands at low tide. I removed the scalpel from my waistband and held it above the umbilicus; the blade flickered with a faint green light. I pressed my eye to the peepshow. What was playing?

The necropolis. A horizon blushing with distant fires. And an army of black-cloaked figures moving towards the house where Dr Toxicophilous would soon be under siege . . .

I pulled back. So little time. Overriding the pilot, I pointed the ZiL towards shore. I had to find a nanoengineer. Vientiane? I would have to try. Primavera wouldn't survive the journey into China.

I put my foot down; the outboard died. I tugged at the choke and tried to restart manually. Nothing. Then the lights and the computer died too, the car's electronics chewed up as if by an electromagnetic pulse.

I felt the Bakelite of the steering column under my nails; it hurt, but I couldn't ease my grip. Before me stood Titania, a few metres beyond the front axial. Star-crowned and garbed in scarlet, her feet hovered above the river's swell, arched, criss-crossed, as if she were in mid-entrechat. Reflexively I picked the scalpel from Primavera's lap and threw it; the scalpel passed through the scarlet apparition and into the night.

'Don't worry,' said Titania, 'I haven't come for you, human boy.'

'You can't have her,' I said. 'Leave her alone. Leave us both alone!'

'That's not possible. Primavera has failed me. Quite *badly*, I'm afraid. I've tried calling to her time and time again. But she's stubborn. Very stubborn.'

'You betrayed us. Everything you said was a lie. You're as bad as a human.'

'Surely not. The lies were necessary. Besides I *did* believe in destroying the world once upon a time. But now I'm working for something quite different. I want to live. I want the Lilim to live.'

'You're assisting in their murder . . .'

'Of course. How else shall we survive? We must take it upon ourselves to control our own numbers, our breeding patterns, to bargain with humans, one species to another. Humans will offer us the sacrifice of their gene-pool only if we control the plague.'

'The Americans control *you*.'

Titania laughed. 'I control *them*, human boy. Ah, it's a pity you will not live to see the future: two species in such marvellously violent rapport.'

'I don't want to see it.'

'As you wish. Primavera and I must go now – '

'Wait – ' Titania's image faded; rematerialized. 'You think you want to live. You don't want to live. You avoid a grand consummation because you want death eternal. Living death. You want the Lilim to survive only so that they can provide the world with an endless source of victims . . .'

Titania crackled, became fuzzy, like a TV running interference. 'Oh you *are* a clever boy. But maybe you're right. Do I know what I want? I'm just a machine built to resolve Man's fantasies. I want what you want, human boy. Dead girls. I want what mankind wants. Examine your heart.' She shrank to a point. '*Every dawn – we die!*'

'Don't go – don't take her!'

Titania vanished.

The ZiL had drifted back to the middle of the river; the controls were useless, and we began to spin in lazy circles, caught in a confusion of eddies and crosscurrents.

It was over. Over at last. No happy ending for us.

Primavera slept on, dribbling from the side of her mouth. I collected a little of her saliva on my finger and put it to my lips. Behind my eyes, a blue-gold firework display; my loins stiffened; the ZiL filled with the mind-scent of allure. Seek out my gametes, little machines, I thought. For you there is no death. You are Primavera's immortality.

She began to speak in her sleep:

'I left all those clothes at the *Lucky*. Beautiful clothes . . .'

'I'll buy you more. In China.'

'Dermaplastic . . .'

'Of course.'

'Martian jewels . . .'

'For the prettiest, most beautiful girl in school.'

Her sleep grew deeper; she floundered in inhuman depths. I felt it was time for me to sleep too. To drown. This black highway: it was too long. There had been way-stations, of course: I remember emerging from a tunnel, the starlight above Calais, and standing long minutes, even as Primavera pulled urgently at my sleeve, surveying our new world, reprieved, with that world seemingly ready to free us from the prisons of ourselves, as we had been freed from the prison of England . . .

'*So this is it,' she said. 'This is France.*'

'*We've escaped. I can't believe it.*'

'*So we head south now?*'

'*It's a long journey.*'

'*I don't care. We'll make it. We've got this far.*'

'*Look – over there. It's getting light.*'

'*Dover. White cliffs. Just like in the school books.*'

'*It's very faint. I can just about – *'

'*Ah, you should have* doll's *eyes.*'

'*Goodbye, England.*'

'*Goodbye. Good riddance. And – and thank you, Iggy.*'

'*Me?*'

'*For being my friend. I'm a doll, I can't say it but I, I – *'

'*Yes, Primavera?*'

'*I do. I, I – *'

'*I love you too, Primavera.*'

'*Yes, Iggy.*'

My deathwatch was almost over. But I couldn't sleep

just yet. Her life flowed through me. No; I couldn't sleep until I had found her a human womb. I wished it were different. I wished the road ended here. I wished the story didn't end with me wading ashore to make new little Primaveras. I wished I could die and rest within the belly of the doll.

I placed my hand on her abdomen. I had one wish left. I wouldn't waste it. I closed my eyes and thought of her, back turned, haughty, insolent, frightened – the desired one; desired beyond life – always ready to twist about, teeth bared, mouth red, and put her face close to mine; though whether now those teeth slashed across my lips, or retracted into a soft childish pout, to offer a kiss light, impalpable, ghostly, seemed uncertain. And so I wished – vainly, I knew – to travel this river forever with such uncertainty in my mind, to be forever with her, riding through the cemeteries of the night, on, on, on, on, until night gave way to eternity, with the presence of hate in the world only as sure as that of love.

Of all the world's lies, that would be the best.

Nongkhai 1991